THE
LONG
DECEPTION

ALSO BY MARY MCCLUSKEY

Intrusion

THE
LONG
DECEPTION

a novel

MARY McCLUSKEY

Little

Published by Little A, New York

www.apub.com

Amazon, the Amazon logo, and Little A are trademarks of Amazon.com, Inc., or its affiliates.

ISBN-13: 9781542046329 (hardcover)
ISBN-10: 1542046327 (hardcover)
ISBN-13: 9781542046312 (paperback)
ISBN-10: 1542046319 (paperback)

Cover design by Kimberly Glyder

Printed in the United States of America

First edition

For Nick, always
And for Mark and Robbie, in absentia

SOPHIE

That dark day, the last day of Sophie's life, began with a storm coming in from the west. By late afternoon, the sky was still low and leaden, the light strangely metallic. Sophie had been driving for half an hour and felt as if the entire world had shrunk to reflected brake lights and a gray and relentless drizzle. She was late. The package, now hidden under a tartan blanket on the back seat of the car, was not, at first, where she had been told it would be. She had waited near the ticket office at Birmingham New Street station—waited, rigid with anxiety, for thirty minutes, then looked away for just a moment, and when she turned back, there it was: a foot-long envelope, leaning up against her travel bag. In one swift movement, she tucked it into her bag and pulled out her cell phone.

Linda, tired of babysitting, answered in a voice edged with irritation.

"Sophie, you said—"

"I know. One more stop and I'll be back. Two hours. Tops."

"Two hours!"

"Maybe less. The girls?"

"They're fine."

Sometimes Linda called the three-year-old twins to the phone so that Sophie could talk to them. Not this time.

In the black Ford Fiesta, Sophie darted through traffic at speed. She was only five miles from the hotel. An hour, that was all they would have together. It wasn't enough. The Birmingham collection had cut into their time together. That would be the last pickup, she vowed. No matter what kind of money Zak promised her, no matter how many dope samples he allowed as partial payment. If she were caught, she could lose the girls. Social Services would say she was unfit, they would say there was evidence to prove it. They could take them into care. The thought chilled her blood. Her mother's dire predictions would finally prove correct.

And what would Matt say if she were arrested? How would he explain her incarceration to his beautiful, incomprehensible bitch of a wife, safe in their country home in rural France? They had visited her in rehab. She doubted they would visit her in prison.

A few seconds too late, Sophie realized that she was in the wrong lane: the Regent Hotel was at the next ramp. In a reckless sprint, hitting seventy, she crossed two lanes of traffic, struggling to see. Tires squealed behind her, a horn blared.

She slammed into the hotel parking lot and let out her breath. Here, at last. A hard tremor had begun at her fingertips; soon her entire body would shake badly.

She must not tremble like this. It would ruin their time together.

She lifted the package from the back seat, placed it in her bag, along with the bottle of Stoli. She would carry them up to the hotel room. Just one hit, one small drink, to calm her nerves. To take the edge off.

ONE

The news of Sophie's death reached Alison by text message. In the darkened screening room, waiting for her newest commercial to start, she gripped the cell phone with both hands and stared at two impossible sentences, so cold in their brevity that the chill transmitted to her, creating a hard shiver, her limbs weak.

She read the text twice. Even the *Sorry, so sorry* of Liz's sign-off couldn't soften it. "No," she said aloud. No. And thought, a moment later, people used to get bad news like this by telegram. The words truncated, bare. The harshest abbreviations in the language.

The morning viewing was for one of her recent accounts, a fledgling cosmetics company, and her own phrase, *Softer skin that seduces*, echoed back to her as she headed for the door. Her art director, Marcus, caught up with her before she reached it.

"Alison. Hey, where—"

"Sorry, Marcus. Have to leave. Emergency."

He frowned. His small, sharp face showed more annoyance than concern.

"A friend just died," she said.

"Sorry to hear that," he called as she walked away. "You coming back?"

Alison ignored him and kept walking, moving fast through the wide corridors of the contemporary Century City advertising agency, newly decorated in minimalist shades of gray and taupe. Navigating the building reminded Alison of walking through fog. Then, a blast of acrid Los Angeles air as she exited the revolving doors into the company parking lot. It was hot that day, smoggy; the air tasted like copper. She called Liz from the air-conditioned sanctuary of her car.

As the phone rang in England, Alison had a sudden clear memory of Sophie's face the year they began high school. She had tried to draw that face so many times, in charcoal and in chalks: cheeks that curved roundly, as a baby's cheeks in a cartoon might curve; eyes the soft blue of a washed sky, shot with light. Sophie's fair hair was long then and often wild or tangled. She was blooming in those days, full of good health. Full of *life*.

"Please tell me it's not true," Alison said when Liz answered.

"I'm so sorry, Ali. And sorry to text. Your phone—"

"I was in the screening room. Was it an overdose?"

"Looks like it. Or suicide. Dope and booze in a hotel room."

"Not suicide. No way. Why? And what was she doing in a hotel room?"

"Nobody knows. She must have been meeting somebody, but she was alone when they found her."

"You don't know who she was meeting?"

"Haven't a clue. She'd left the twins with a friend. Said she'd be back in a couple of hours."

"Those poor little girls," Alison said. Three years old now. They had been toddlers, cherubs with angel faces and just beginning to run around when she saw them last. "Who's taking care of them?"

"The old witch. Mrs. Stuart. And Matt and his wife are over from France."

"Matt?" Alison repeated, aware of a small seismic shock at hearing his name. "Matt's come home?"

"With his posh French wife, apparently. God, he must be dev-astated." Liz paused, began again. "I really want to go to the funeral, but Mrs. Stuart says family only and I haven't exactly been supportive recently and—"

"You should go. Matt will need Sophie's old friends there."

"Maybe. If you were here, I'd go. It's just . . ."

For Alison, a moment of indecision and then a series of tum-bling fragmented images of Sophie, her best friend once. Sophie had remained, despite the miles between them, the most rewarding and infuriating person Alison had ever known. And Matt, Sophie's brother, the boy who had invaded all of her teenage dreams? He would be there. Her old neighborhood friends, the teenagers who once gathered in the Stuart basement and called themselves the Savages would likely turn up, too. They had all loved Sophie.

She could go. Why not? She could book online, be packed in a heartbeat. All she had to do was get on the plane.

"I'll come," Alison said. "I'll fly out tomorrow."

"What?"

"I'll come. I'll text you details."

~

The light was fading, the muted shades of rose and gold seeping from the Hollywood Hills when, hours later, Alison stood at her bedroom window, waiting for her husband. The high towers of Los Angeles, an eerie vision in the distance, had almost disappeared into a misty twilight.

She could see the automatic gates of their home, and they opened slowly when, at last, Jake's silver Lexus purred through. Alison watched him as he hurried from the car, listened to his footsteps on the stairs, and then turned to greet him. He hugged her hard.

"You okay?" he asked. "Sorry I was short on the phone. Middle of a meeting."

"It's fine."

"Sophie. So young. Jesus." Jake pulled away, loosening his tie as he studied her face. "It was drugs? An overdose?"

"Not sure yet. She was meeting somebody in a hotel room. Maybe a dealer."

"If she overdosed, she'd met the dealer already," Jake said. "Sounds like she planned to party." He paused, thinking. "She was clean, wasn't she, when we met up in that pub with the garden? When she had the twins with her."

"Think so. She seemed fine then. Healthy. Chasing after them."

"She did hit me up for money," Jake admitted. "When you went off to find the bathroom."

"She did? Me too."

Sophie had waited until Jake had gone inside to the bar before she made her request. As Alison pressed notes into her hand, Sophie leaned forward, kissed her friend's cheek, and then, surprising Alison with the sweet remembered softness of it, kissed her mouth. Alison recalled the shock of that. The awareness that it was a public place, full of families and groups of friends. She remembered that her cheeks were still hot when Jake returned, carrying their drinks on a slippery tin tray.

"Did you give her anything?" Alison asked now.

"Yep. Of course."

As Jake moved away, Alison said quickly, "I'd like to go to the funeral."

He turned.

"Honey, I can't go anywhere right now. You know that. This new drug trial and—"

"No. I can go alone. Just for a week or two."

"Or *two*? Why so long?"

"Visit my dad. Catch up with old friends."

"That include the handsome brother?" he asked. "The boy next door?"

Alison had told Jake, during the first months of their marriage when they laughed about youthful secrets and shared details of their young lives, about her teenage crush on Matt. Her husband became wary at any mention of her old life. She could detect that wariness in his voice now.

"He'll be at the funeral," she said levelly. "With his French wife."

"Ah. So when will you leave?"

"I'll book a flight for tomorrow."

"And work?"

"I'm owed weeks of vacation. We canceled Maui, remember. And canceled the long weekend in Big Bear. That time's due to me."

He nodded slowly, not entirely convinced, eyes worried.

"Okay," he said. "If you're sure." He turned away, talking over his shoulder. "We better move, sweetheart. We don't have much time."

Alison indicated the jade-green garment on the bed.

"Won't take me long."

In the shower, she leaned back against the cool tile, sighing. Tonight's formal dinner, to be held at the Biltmore Hotel, was a retirement party for one of Jake's directors. Alison hated these functions, even on a good day, hated the bland smiles; the brittle, thin conversations; the shoptalk about drug trials; and the successes and failures of rival pharmaceutical companies. Jake had said weeks ago that attendance was mandatory. He was aiming for a promotion to head of the division, and he wouldn't risk jeopardizing that. There was no way out of this function, no matter what she said.

She was wearing the jade dress, tweaking the ends of her hair, when Jake, clearly uncomfortable in black tie, tugging irritably at his cuffs, came into the room.

"Feel like a stuffed toy penguin," he said. He stopped, stared at her.

"Wow. Look at you . . ." he said.

Alison scrutinized her reflection. Her auburn hair had been cut and styled in a Beverly Hills salon and hung in a smooth, symmetrical fall; the silk gown she wore was the most expensive item of clothing she had ever purchased. The image in the mirror looked unreal. Her head, right then, held vivid pictures of her teenage years. She could visualize her young self: the crazy spiked haircut, the purple streak, the junk-shop tops and torn jeans she had believed looked artistic and creative. The adult woman staring back at her, with the handsome male, shadowy in the background, could be a player in one of her own commercials for celebrity scent. A total stranger. Alison, moving across the bedroom, felt an odd dizziness, as if the floor were not quite steady beneath her feet.

She turned.

"I don't want to go to this thing, Jake," she said.

"What?"

"I can't. The shoptalk and chatter and all that fake laughter. No. It feels wrong. Disrespectful."

"Because of Sophie? Please. Come on, Alison."

He pulled her close, told her it would do no good to sit home and mope, and then he released her, reaching for his wallet and car keys.

"You'll be okay," he said. "It'll be fine. We'll leave early."

"Promise? You won't get involved in some long discussion about abandoned drug trials?"

"I won't."

She picked up her bag. It was not worth arguing over this one evening. A confusing mix of emotions assailed her as she followed Jake to the car: the shock and pain for Sophie still lay heavy on her chest, but she felt, too, a small, snaking excitement at the prospect of seeing those old friends again, of time out from her job, time out from the demands and repetitions of her daily life.

~

Jake drove her to the airport. She walked fast toward the security line and turned to see him watching her. She paused then. Seeing her hesitation, he came forward.

"I'll miss you."

She hugged him.

"Miss you, too."

"Safe journey," he said.

Once through security, she turned again, intending to wave to him. Jake was already walking away. He looked at his watch, lengthened his stride: a busy man in a hurry, heading to the exit doors.

~

The first time Alison saw Jake Eastlake, she wasn't impressed. She thought the stranger appearing at the door of her motel room looked dark and rather dangerous. Eyes of a murky shade, neither blue nor green, tanned skin with the pitted appearance left by long-ago acne scars, and a gaze that appraised her carefully. He was tall, slender, did not have the buffed body of the typical Californian male. Andy, a mutual friend in London, had set up their date.

"You can't explore LA by yourself," Andy had said, upon learning that Alison's college roommate had backed out of the trip because of a family crisis. "Jake can show you around. You'll like him. He's fun. And he's smart, too."

He didn't look like fun. He looked like he didn't want to be there in her motel room at all. Later, she learned that Andy had told Jake his date was an artist, but she was English so might seem reserved by LA standards.

"Not my type," Jake had said. "Sorry."

But he had been persuaded, and so he arrived at her door wearing jeans and a black T-shirt, holding his car keys as if ready for a fast getaway.

"Jake Eastlake," he said.

"Alison McDonald."

"Pretty name."

He studied her, taking in the purple streak of her hair, the all-black clothing.

"You don't look reserved and English," he said.

"I'm English," she said. "But not the least bit reserved."

He grinned.

"Okay. What would you like to do? I'm guessing you want to hit the clubs?"

"No. I'd like to hit the ocean," she said. "And walk along the beach."

She thought he looked pleased at this, relieved, but he glanced dubiously at her leather ankle boots and their perilously high heels.

"Oh, I can change these," she said, leaning back against the wall for support, balancing on one leg as she bent her knee, unzipped one boot, and kicked it off. "I brought flip-flops. Just give me a minute."

He laughed then, delighted, and she realized he was not dangerous at all.

That was the beginning. After three days, Alison found she did not want to return to her art classes at Bristol University and the master's in fine arts she had planned. She did not want to return to the closed-in days of wintry England; the parties in dark, crowded rooms; and the intense student talk of authenticity, of never selling out.

Jake's studio apartment, perched on the edge of Topanga Canyon, had a wall of windows and endless views and seemed to offer a new way of looking at the world. Alison was intrigued by this science major and entertained by his all-encompassing interest in the natural world. He took her hiking in the canyons, describing the structure of rocks, the history of the fauna and flora, wanting her to be as amazed as he was.

Sometimes she took her sketch pad on these hikes, and Jake, as indiscriminate as a parent, admired her drawings, even those with awkward perspectives and clumsy execution, so that she shook her head and smiled. But after the focused criticism of her student friends at Bristol, where she knew, artistically, she was well outclassed, it was nice to feel so *approved*.

Jake devoured scientific journals with the enthusiasm of a child with a comic book, reading sections out loud to her, his voice rising with excitement. Alison, listening, bemused, wondered if he was actually speaking in a foreign language.

In exchange, she took him to galleries, to both the new Getty and the old, and also to the Los Angeles MOCA, where she could show him examples of paintings she loved—Rothko, Diebenkorn, Motherwell, and Hockney. She was happy that he found favorites of his own, though they were never the same as hers.

Alison found that Jake's enthusiasm for the wonders of nature extended to her, too. The most persuasive thing, the most surprising, was his frank delight in her body—*How delicious you are, let me taste you,* he said, shocking her, his tongue licking and flicking until she cried out, her fingers tight in his hair, as he dove down between her legs. He took pleasure in watching her walk around his apartment naked, and, because of his close attention to every curve and texture of her body, Alison became aware of a sexuality previously undiscovered. Most of all, although he teased her about the black clothing, the purple-tipped hair, and the goth-style eye makeup, he made her feel beautiful. She had never felt beautiful before.

He was about to complete his doctorate when he was offered a position with a top pharmaceutical company on the north side of the city.

"They're involved in some pretty exciting research," he told Alison. "It's a great opportunity. You know what would make everything perfect?"

"Double the salary? A corner office? A sexy blonde secretary?"

"If you'd marry me."

They had been together seven weeks. They were married ten days later in Las Vegas.

～

Now, half an hour out of LAX, she sipped at a gin and tonic, watching the pink-edged clouds through the plane window. Jake would be back at work already. When she imagined him in his office, making decisions about drug trials, about new testing and releases, checking always the bottom line, she visualized lines of figures, red lines, black lines, a grid, order.

Their life had become so streamlined, she thought, as the color faded from the sky and dusk began to creep up from the earth. The untidy romance that began seven years ago with laughter, sexuality, hikes in the canyons, and talk—political arguments that livened breakfast, Sundays spent in bed, laughter-filled evenings with friends who came late, sat on the floor, drank wine, and listened to music—had slowly evolved into a luxury lifestyle of strict routine and predictability. A lifestyle that focused on careers and material success. *We all become what we most despise,* she thought. Who said that? Benchley? Maybe it was true of everyone.

Would her old friends, gathered together at Sophie's funeral, see her differently? Would Matt? *It will be interesting to see how much* he *has changed,* she told herself. *It will be interesting to meet his wife.*

TWO

A striking blonde as tall as most men, Liz was easily visible at the arrivals terminal at Heathrow. She wore a tailored coat, a bright, striped scarf and waved wildly as she called out to Alison.

"Didn't know whether you'd dress properly," she said, wrapping a cashmere shawl around her friend's shoulders. "They promised an Indian summer, but it's already bloody freezing here."

She inspected Alison, her face serious.

"Love the new hair, Ali," she said. "Elegant. But you look tired."

"Of course I do. I've been on a plane for a hundred years. How are you?"

"Still stunned. Can't seem to take it in. My mum called Thelma Stuart. The funeral's next Monday."

"And it's okay for us to go?"

"Don't know. Might be family only. Just Mrs. Stuart and Matt and his wife."

She took Alison's arm.

"We'll go anyway. Bugger that old bat. Anyway, let's get your stuff in the car."

As they pulled out of the parking lot, Liz asked, "Jake couldn't get away?"

"No. A big conference next week. And a new drug trial. So, tell me what you've heard about Soph. Does anybody know what happened?"

"Nope," said Liz. "Not so far. Officially, it's accidental death. I hadn't seen her for a couple of weeks. I don't know what was going on with her."

They had been a trio of girls, two tall blondes, one shorter redhead, always together in the elementary school years and right up until the last year of high school. Then Sophie lost focus, became involved with people Alison and Liz didn't know, didn't want to know. She became hard to find and, as she was so often stoned, even harder to help.

"We had a bit of a fight," Liz said now. "She turned up at our place really, really late. I told her off. I could see she was high. She needed money."

She glanced sideways at Alison.

"And yes, I feel guilty. And yes, we did give her some dosh. Simon actually took her to the cash machine, followed her in his car to get it. He said she was upset. But honestly, what else could I do? Force her into rehab against her will and take care of her twins? I had Jamie to think about. She texted a couple of days later, said she understood why I was angry, but I'm not sure if she really did. Did she tell you about that?"

"Briefly. Her e-mails weren't always very clear."

She didn't add that Sophie's communications were often crazy and incoherent, sometimes full of despair, sometimes written when Sophie was clearly high or joyful, babbling on about the mysterious people in her life, people who were never named. Alison wondered if Sophie had been involved with a married man. Or a married woman. There had been a number of doomed relationships in her past.

"How could she do it?" Liz asked. "Leave her two little girls like that?"

"It couldn't have been deliberate. Must have overdosed."

"An overdose?" Liz asked, disbelieving. "She'd never make a mistake like that. Sophie knew chemicals better than anyone."

Alison turned away to look out of the car window. They had argued about Sophie since their earliest school days, fought about her and fought over her.

"Well, you'd defend her no matter what," Liz said. "I know how you saw us, Ali. Remember what you said to me once? You said the difference between Sophie and me was simple: If the house caught fire, she'd knot sheets and swing to the ground like Tarzan's Jane. I'd burn to death, dithering, trying to decide which dressing gown didn't make me look fat."

"I only meant—" Alison began, smiling.

"I know what you meant. And it's probably true. But why couldn't she just grow up? Like the rest of us."

When they reached the Midlands, Liz pulled off the motorway, taking a shortcut through the villages that, years ago, they used to visit on their bikes. As they drove through the Worcestershire countryside, Alison gazed out of the car window at the square, green fields with their crumbling stone walls; the old farmhouses; and, in the pastures, the still horses, waiting. Even in the smallest village a church spire was visible. Always a church, always a pub. England's green and pleasant land. She had forgotten its colors, its dewy freshness.

"Be strange to see Matt again," Liz said after a while, her voice too casual, weighted with unspoken questions. Alison kept her face averted so that Liz could not see her expression.

"Yes."

"I'm dying to see that Frenchwoman. I bet she's beautiful. I bet she's got the clothes."

"Not necessarily. She might be a frump," Alison said.

"Yeah, right. Like Matt would go for a woman who wasn't perfect. Apparently, he's teaching in Montpellier. American literature."

"No surprise. He was reading Bellow and Roth in the fifth form."

"Our fearless leader. God, he used to piss me off the way he tried to rule us all. Like some bloody monarch."

"That's an alpha-male trick," Alison said. "Assume control and expect everyone to do as you say. Jake does the same thing."

"Jake?" Liz said. "No. Jake seems so mellow to me. Matt was different. I used to feel really stupid around him. Remember how he'd ask what you thought of some strange writer or artist and you'd feel like an idiot because you'd never heard of them? I think he made those names up."

"Of course he didn't! He was smarter; that's all. Anyway, I liked our friends. We had fun."

"At first," Liz admitted. "But really—the Savages! Can you believe we called ourselves that? Well, I suppose that was Matt's idea as well. He called the shots. Or Sophie did. So bizarre, the way he took off like that."

"Yep. Was a bit," Alison said, struggling to keep her voice level.

"One term at Oxford and he legs it! How crazy is that? And it wasn't because he couldn't keep up academically. He was doing well, apparently."

"Of course he was doing well. He was brilliant."

Alison noted that Liz had turned onto the bypass that crossed the countryside close to their old homes. At the sight of the signpost pointing to the small town, Alison felt again the hollow ache of loss. So much of Sophie's short time on earth had been lived there, just a mile away. They had all walked to school along those streets, had learned to ride bikes, to skateboard, to steer their way from childhood to teen years.

As exhaustion began to hit, coming at her in huge waves, Alison watched as the patchwork of green fields blurred. So familiar, the soft-focus landscape of home. Eventually, they pulled into a graveled driveway and Liz parked the car outside a large detached house.

Alison gave a low whistle. "Wow, is this the new place?"

"Yep. The mortgage is killing us."

The house was imitation Tudor, with half an acre of grounds. The garden looked impossibly green to Alison, after the ochre and burnt-sienna shades of California. The lawns stretched and undulated down a soft hill, the leaves were just beginning to change color, a shimmer of bronze, gold, and red. She stood in the driveway admiring the house and the gardens.

"You've come a long way, baby," she said to Liz.

~

Later, in the cool darkness of the bedroom, Alison moved restlessly in Liz's guest bed, a down quilt snuggled around her, disturbed by memories of Sophie. Sophie as a child swinging from the low branch of the oak tree as she yelled like a jungle creature or, later, the teenage Sophie dancing in the Stuart basement, singing along to the music.

Sophie had been six years old, Matt seven, when they moved into the house next door. Before the new tract homes were built, the area was a wild expanse of woods, ponds, barren fields. Alison remembered Matt dragging a box labeled *Treasures* into his new home. It appeared to contain mostly books and Lego bricks. Sophie, her blonde hair a halo, trailed behind him, carrying a doll and crying for no obvious reason.

"They're just babies," Liz had said, as they sat on the doorstep of Alison's house and watched the newcomers move in.

"The girl is the same age as you two," Alison's mother responded sharply, calling from the kitchen. "And the boy is only a little bit older. Go over and see if they want to play."

They did want to play. They would meet up nearly every day for all the years of their childhood. Later, they formed their gang, the Savages, and, throughout their elementary school years, recruited new kids, fresh from the city and hungry for adventure, who stumbled around the growing village looking for friends. Matt led them. Sophie was his second in command, a position she earned because she was fearless, stronger than some of the boys, braver. Sophie could always climb to the top branch of the tree, jump over the muddy brook, swing highest on the rope swing.

It was Sophie's idea to create a headquarters for the group by building a fort in the woods. They built it into a copse, a natural dip in the roots of an old elm tree, surrounded by fallen branches and far enough away from the path through the woods to make it invisible to hikers.

Inside it, with the gang members seated in a circle, Alison, in those preteen years, felt part of something special and secret, and she hated that, because of the curfew set by her parents, she was always one of the first to go home. The fort was where many of the rituals of growing up took place: Alison tried her first cigarette in that circle of friends, had her first sip of beer, and one damp day when she and Jonathon, two of the earliest members of the Savages, were the only ones who braved the rain to get there, experienced the awkwardness of her first, unwanted kiss. She had pushed Jonathon away in a panic. What if Matt should see them? If anyone were to kiss her, she wanted it to be Matt. And Jonathon, she knew, really wanted to kiss Sophie. Jonathon had mumbled apologies, then laughed, embarrassed. They remained friends.

In Liz's guest room, unable to sleep, Alison recalled the woods on a summer's evening; the filtered light through the trees and the shifting shadows; the darting bodies, hiding from each other, the voices calling out; the stream, so cold with hard pebbles, her feet turning blue and iced. In summer the fort had a musky smell of rich earth and undergrowth; in autumn the air was heavy with the scent of bracken and damp, disintegrating leaves. The Savages made solemn promises in their early teens. *We will always have each other,* they said. And Sophie, her voice so serious, calling on them to make vows that would bind them, bold them.

When the members were older, they hung out in the basement of the Stuart house. The gang was smaller then, some members had simply lost interest or moved away. Liz, Sophie, Alison, Jonathon, Ronnie, and Matt remained at the core.

The last time she saw Matt was on a warm evening in the garden of his house, the night before his sister's wedding, the night he ran away from home. They had talked then, though nobody knew about their conversation. He had kissed her, too, finally, and the memory of that kiss had haunted her for years. *We were just kids,* Alison thought, turning over in bed to look through the window at the bending trees and the night sky. *We won't be able to talk so honestly now.*

THREE

Still the girl whose cardigan never lost buttons, whose socks stayed up and hair remained neatly braided, ribbons intact, even after a wild race through the woods, Liz sat at the table in her glossy, coordinated kitchen wearing silver silk pajamas and a matching dressing gown, holding her coffee cup with both hands. She looked up as Alison came into the kitchen, and Alison saw that Liz's face was pale, her eyes shadowed.

"I heard Simon's car," Alison said. Liz's husband, a balding, soft-spoken man, was an executive at a large manufacturing company. "He's gone to work already?"

"Yep. He's dropping Jamie off at school on the way."

"I was hoping Jamie—"

"He wanted to run up and bounce on you, but I wouldn't let him. You'll see him later."

Alison studied her friend, concerned.

"You okay, sweetie?" she asked.

Liz gave a little shake of her head, and then smiled.

"I'm fine really. Just thinking. Look, help yourself to coffee, Ali. Some toast. Whatever you want. I'm dragging this morning. I should be starting a new project today, but, honestly, I just can't be arsed."

A web designer, Liz worked from home in an office at the top of the house.

"So start it tomorrow. Give yourself a break."

"I might. Didn't sleep much. My mum called last night, after you'd gone to bed. The Wicked Witch is laying down the law. She doesn't want any of Sophie's druggie friends at the funeral."

"That doesn't mean us. We're not Sophie's druggie friends. She can't dictate who attends a church."

"True. Evil old mare. No wonder Sophie hated her."

"She had good reason."

"Yes. You know what I was thinking about last night?" Liz asked. "When we all had nits at school. We got ours washed out with that awful shampoo treatment, remember?"

"Oh God, yes. The smell of that stuff."

"Okay. But it worked. Right? And it worked fine on Matt, too. But remember what that woman did to Sophie? She cut all her hair off!"

Alison had a clear recollection of Sophie's blonde curls in those elementary school years and recalled the day she walked into the class-room with her hair cropped, red abrasions on her neck, scrubbed skin. The defiant lift of her chin as she walked into the room and everyone, including the teacher, gasped.

"Why did she do that?" Liz said. "She didn't do it to Matt. It wasn't necessary. And she knew it. She bloody knew it."

"To humiliate her," Alison said. "Poor Sophie. I keep wondering if there's something we can do. I'd like to see the twins."

"No chance of that. Mum says Matt's wife has pretty much taken them over. And Ronnie called. Wanted to know about the funeral. I told him the details. Why shouldn't I? People should be able to go if they want to."

Ronnie, an early member of the Savages, had been openly crazy about Sophie when they were teenagers, even though she teased him unmercifully. Alison hadn't seen him in years.

"Ronnie? You still keep in touch? He stayed close to Soph?"

"He would have followed her anywhere," Liz said. "He was always in love with her. She was the first girl he ever had sex with. Probably the *only* girl he's ever had sex with. I mean, you should see him now. He's huge. He needs to lose some weight, he's way too—"

Alison stared, astounded.

"Sophie had sex with Ronnie?" she interrupted. "When?"

"When we were still at school. I think she felt sorry for him. All the other guys were talking about hand jobs and blow jobs, and he'd never even kissed anybody."

"Oh, my God," Alison said. "Sophie told you about it?"

"No. Ronnie told us. We bumped into him at Janine's wedding a few months ago. Remember her? Heavy girl, funny haircut, looked like a button mushroom? Anyway, Ronnie was there, wearing a tacky black T-shirt that said *Fat People Are Harder to Kidnap*. I mean, can you imagine? To a *wedding*? And the bride a bit chubby, to say the least. He was drunk out of his mind, doing dope in the bathrooms and looking for Sophie as usual. He was crazy about her."

"Always. But I didn't know she—"

"She never stopped teasing him. Remember when she did that reverse striptease? In the basement that time? Took her top off when we were talking about those topless women on beaches. Then she ran over and played that stripper tune."

Liz sang a few bars, tapping on the kitchen table.

"Funny she'd recorded that tune when you think about it. Wonder if she used to practice? Anyway, then she did a striptease in reverse. Put her clothes back *on*."

Alison smiled at the memory.

"She was good, too. Looked pretty authentic."

"Ronnie could hardly speak. And Jonathon. Remember?"

"Drooling. And his eyes out on stalks."

"And Matt was furious and told her to behave herself, and Ronnie said, *Matt, you sound just like my dad.* And we all laughed."

"She could be crazy," Alison said. "No question. But it didn't matter, did it? People always forgave her."

"I hope a whole bunch of people come to the funeral," Liz said. "That will really piss off Mrs. Stuart."

FOUR

The church of ancient gray stone, half-hidden by aging trees, stood at the edge of what had once been a village and was now a small town. Alison looked around, frowning. Only three years since her mother died and was buried here, and yet in that short time the area had changed. Where there had been woods and streams, the playing fields for the Savages in their elementary school years, she could see more tract homes. They hugged the hillsides in neat, white curves, like rows of dentures.

The churchyard, though, looked just as it did when they were children. Drooping silver birches shadowed the old graveyard, the same trees she remembered. They used to gather here at dusk when they were teenagers, sit on decaying graves and smoke and talk. Sophie would be restless, roaming among the gravestones, reading the inscribed epitaphs aloud; Matt lounged against the cold stone, a paperback book always sticking out of the pocket of his jeans, a cigarette burning his fingers.

Today, a long procession of cars crawled along the drive.

"So much for Mrs. Stuart's small and private," Liz said with some satisfaction. "We better park here. It's a bit of a walk."

"Don't mind a walk. Who are all these people?"

"God knows. Dopers? Dealers?"

"Liz!"

"They look a bit rough around the edges, though, don't they?" Liz said, eyeing a young woman in torn jeans and a combat jacket. "Oh, that looks like Mrs. Stuart just going into the church."

Alison caught sight of graying hair, severe black clothing. Thelma Stuart's back was, as always, ramrod straight. The people crowded on the steps of the church began to move inside.

"They're starting," Liz said. "Come on."

The organ music began just as they entered the building, as the congregation stood for the first hymn. Alison, edging along a pew at the back, saw Matt at once, and she paused, shaken, gripping the wooden rail with tight hands. He stood at the front of the church next to his mother; a slender brunette, wearing tailored black, stood on the other side of him. That must be the French wife.

Far back in the church, hidden, Alison was able to study them both. Matt's hair appeared darker than she remembered: as a child he had been as fair as his sister. Today, his hair looked recently cut, in a neat, traditional style so different from the long untidy mop of his youth. The stance was familiar: the way his jacket fell from his straight shoulders. Even during the clumsiest of the teen years he had not been hunched or slouched like so many of his self-conscious classmates. Even among taller boys he had seemed tall. *Taller far than a tall man.* Sappho's lovely line. Noting the immaculate dark suit, the fashionable wife, Alison wondered how the crumpled, chain-smoking teen with the blond curls had somehow morphed into this middle-class adult.

If I did not know him, she thought, *if he had not always caused my pulse to race and speed out of control, I would think he looks like a young politician.* His wife, fashionably thin in her tailored suit, had fine bones, good posture. The perfect wife for a certain kind of man. Not the kind of man Alison had imagined Matt would become. *Is he the same person underneath that veneer of respectability,* she wondered. *Am I?*

In the chill of the church, the air felt dank, damp with a mustiness centuries old. Alison, struggling with an odd disorientation, tried to pay attention to the service. She had attended weddings here: Sophie was married in this church, her young bridegroom's voice shaking during the vows. Her own mother's funeral service had been held here. There had been other weddings, other funerals. She wondered why the place felt so strange, so foreign to her. Perhaps the years in California had altered her perceptions? It felt unnaturally cold.

She zoned out from the vicar's drone, her eyes drawn back to the polished wooden coffin. To imagine Sophie in there, rigidly immobile, the lightning sparks of moods and laughter absent, was impossible. *Only the shell of Sophie is there,* Alison thought. *Her spirit is extinguished; all that animation has vanished into the air.* In life, Sophie was never still, always turning, swirling, a dervish of movement, impossible to capture in a sketch—though Alison had tried many times—difficult to capture in a photograph.

Alison had one treasured picture of Sophie. It was taken at a family barbecue moments before Sophie left on the back of the motorcycle of the yellow-haired boy who would become her husband. Alison's mother had taken the picture, calling out *Say cheese, Louise.*

"Can I have this one? Please?" Alison asked, when her mother showed it to her.

"It's not very clear. There are better ones."

"I really want this one."

For the first time in her young life, Alison had liked her own image in a snapshot. In this picture, the sun had shone into the camera, bleaching the edges of the print so that her skin looked white, the freckles gone, her hair paler than gold, and the edges of her body undefined. Liz, shaded by the tree, was just a smudge, a shadow. Sophie was laughing, her fair hair flowing behind her, caught in a flash of sunlight, a gust of wind. Matt leaned against the tree trunk, his eyes crinkled, an elbow resting on Alison's shoulder.

This was the photograph Alison kept by the bed in her shared university room. She liked friends to pick it up, study it. As if they would believe the photograph rather than their own eyes. As if her freckles had indeed vanished, her auburn hair changed color and grown silky. At first, her attachment centered on the fact that she looked pretty in the photograph; later, she treasured it because it showed Sophie's essence so exactly and because it was the only picture she had ever had of Matt.

After the second hymn, the vicar looked across at Mrs. Stuart, leaned forward, and murmured something about eulogies. His words were audible, even to Alison and Liz at the back of the church. Mrs. Stuart shook her head. *No,* she said, and made a sweeping gesture with her hand as if to say *Move on, move on.* Liz uttered a small tutting sound.

"The old bat doesn't want anyone to speak—" she whispered.

"Shush," Alison said, sensing a change in the atmosphere. She turned. A young woman with faded blonde hair, dark at the roots, was striding forward from the rear of the church. She wore jeans and a black denim jacket and returned Mrs. Stuart's disapproving look with a defiant glare. She lifted her chin, addressed her words to the people on the back rows.

"I'm Linda," she said. "Sophie was my friend. She was the best friend I ever had."

She paused.

"But I bet a lot of you think that. She made everybody feel like her best friend. That was one of the beautiful things about her."

Linda spoke for a minute or two longer about how kind Sophie had been, how much fun she was to be around, how she was trying to put her life back together after some really hard times, how she loved her twin daughters.

At this, Alison looked around for the little girls. They were not visible in the church and nor was their father, though he had taken off anyway, when the twins were babies, and had been separated from Sophie for years. Sophie had always refused to talk about him. Alison wondered if he knew that she was dead.

"Sophie wasn't Little Miss Perfect," Linda continued. "She loved to laugh, and she loved to dance, and there was a time there when she liked to get high. And she was always, *always* a right tease." Laughter from the back of the church. "But she was lovely and loving. That's what I'll remember."

The young woman appeared ready to step away, but she stopped, looked back at the congregation.

"A lot of people who cared about Sophie are here today," she said. "But the truth is, she died alone in a hotel room. Waiting for someone. I'm thinking that person must be here, right here in this church. You could tell us, maybe, what happened that night."

She stood still, her eyes moving from row to row. The listening mourners shuffled uncomfortably.

"Jesus," Liz whispered.

"No?" Linda asked finally. "Okay. I'll just say this then. I'll wonder why Sophie died, and why she died all by herself when so many people loved her. And I'll miss her. Every day of my life."

As she stepped down, returned to the back of the church, Mrs. Stuart looked hard at the vicar. Her message was clear now: *Enough. Move on.*

"Please turn to page thirty in your hymnbooks," the vicar said.

FIVE

Well, that Linda girl was a bit of a surprise," Liz said when the ceremony was over and they stood outside the church. A cool wind had started up again; it carried the scent of eucalyptus. "You want to go back to the house for a few minutes?"

"Mrs. Stuart actually invited us?" Alison asked, watching Matt get into a black limousine with his wife and mother.

"No. We should go anyway. Offer condolences to Matt. You don't want to catch up with him?"

"Yes. I do," Alison said. "But—"

Liz gave her a searching look.

"Bit strange to see him again?"

"Just a bit. He looks different. Tidy."

"Yep."

As she began to drive away, Liz asked, "Remember when we all used to play that Gotcha game in the woods?"

Alison blinked. It was the exact memory that had been going through her head that morning.

"Good grief. You *are* a psychic witch. Honest to God, I was thinking about that earlier."

"You were supposed to jump out and shout, *Matt's a big dick*. But you didn't, did you? You said something else. Nobody heard what you said. And Matt yelled, *I can't hear you, Ali. You're out!* And you burst into tears."

Liz shook her head. "Weird kid you were, Ali."

Alison had whispered so quietly under her breath that it could not possibly have been audible: *I love you, Matt.*

And he had looked at her, the blue eyes wide, and smiled, and she was terrified that he had heard, that he might repeat it. She had broken the rules of the game. This was not the rude ragging the game demanded, but instead, a secret so warm and quiet from deep inside herself that she was never able to say it again to him, or admit what she had said to anyone.

"I didn't like that game," she said now. "I was always scared somebody would get hurt."

"Well, they did get hurt," Liz said. "Remember when Jonathon fractured his wrist? Somebody tripped him. We never found out who it was."

"Poor Jonathon. That was the summer he fell out of the tree, too."

"That was Sophie's fault," Liz said.

"Not really. He didn't have to climb up there."

Sophie had been taunting the boys from the highest branches of the old oak, calling down that she was Queen of the World, that she had climbed higher, faster, than anyone had ever climbed before. As Matt yelled at his sister to get down from there, both Jonathon and Ronnie began to climb.

Alison remembered the hard snap of a branch breaking, the skinny body in the dark-blue sweater tumbling, and the ugly, dull thud as he hit the ground. She recalled Jonathon's cry of pain.

"Stupid game," Liz said. "Dangerous. All that gang stuff—really, that's for boys. God knows why you and Sophie liked it so much. Remember when Sophie got caught on the barbed wire on the roof over at the brewery warehouse, and Matt and Ronnie climbed up there to help her, and you went after them? You and Sophie, honestly. You were both idiots."

"We were adventurous," said Alison, knowing that this was only part of the truth. She would have played any game when Matt was involved, followed him anywhere, no matter how dangerous.

～

As they pulled up outside the Stuart house in their old neighborhood, Alison studied the house next door, her old home.

"Wonder who lives there now," she said.

"Don't know. They've spruced it up a bit. Nice conservatory."

"It was a nice house before. Dad was sad to leave it."

"He likes it in Scotland, though, doesn't he?" Liz asked. "So my mum said."

"Yes. I talked to him this morning," Alison said. He had sounded so Scottish again, the lilt in his voice more obvious after his move to the Highlands. "It's a smaller school. And I think he's got a woman friend. Said something about a Clara, an artist. Owns a B&B."

"Really?" Liz said. "And you're okay with that?"

"Of course I am. I'll go up to see him soon. He sounded a bit odd this morning. Evasive."

"Well, that certainly runs in the family," Liz said, locking the car. "Anyway, did you get a good look at Matt's wife?"

"Yes. Looks very French."

"That suit must have cost a bit. And that little feathery thing she's got on her head. You know they can't have kids?"

Alison, halfway along the path to the Stuart home, stopped abruptly and turned to stare at her friend.

"How on earth do you know that?"

"Mum told me. They might adopt Sophie's girls."

"Oh, I was wondering what would happen to them," Alison said, beginning again the walk to the front door. They both hesitated on the step. The front door had been left open; voices could be heard coming from the kitchen. Just inside the hallway was another door that led to the basement.

"Wonder why she isn't holding it down there, in the basement," Liz murmured. "Keep her carpet nice and clean. You know"—her voice dropped to a whisper—"I don't think we've ever been in her living room, have we?"

"Not that I remember. She wouldn't even let me in the house. I was too dirty. In every possible respect. Don't think Matt and Sophie were in the living room too often, either."

"Banished to the basement," Liz said. "Remember how she used to make them change their clothes down there? Whenever they'd been playing outside? Put everything in the washing machine and change before they were allowed upstairs."

"You think we should strip off?"

Liz smiled and moved inside.

Alison looked back through the small window in the hallway into the basement. If Sophie's ghost appeared anywhere, it would be down there. She heard the voice of Mrs. Stuart somewhere inside the house and gave a small shiver.

"Come on, dreamer," said Liz. "Let's get this over with."

~

Alison saw Matt on the far side of the room even as Mrs. Stuart, greeting arrivals at the door, shook their hands in a frozen way and then moved on to other mourners. Matt turned, looked hard at Alison, smiled, and then shook his head, the gesture so familiar from years ago that her jolt of pleasure was instinctive, her own smile immediate.

The light was behind him, creating the fair halo she remembered. *Light is where he stands.* Aware of the clamor, loud in her ears, the quickening of her pulse, Alison stood still. It was insane to feel like this after so many years, she told herself. She was married now. She was an adult.

Matt crossed the room at once. As he approached, Alison took a fast breath. The atmosphere in the room had changed: it felt like the San Fernando Valley in high summer, the air felt dry and harsh, impossible to breathe.

Then he was kissing her cheek. His lips were warm. He smelled of pine-scented soap.

"So, how are you, Ali?"

His voice had deepened with maturity, but she was reminded again of the pleasing timbre of it. Even as a teenager, once he had outgrown the awkward variations of adolescence, she had loved his voice.

"I'm fine. I'm so sorry about Sophie. It's terribly sad."

"Yes, it's tragic. She seemed to be getting herself together at last."

"I know. Her poor little girls. It's awful."

"We'll do our best for them," Matt said.

He stepped back to study her.

"Well, you look very grown-up, I must say."

"You, too. You look prosperous. And your hair is shorter."

"Prosperous? That's the last thing I am. Teachers earn less than a pittance."

"At a French university? I thought the French valued education and culture."

"A pittance. So, what are you doing these days?"

"Struggling in advertising."

He gave her a quizzical look.

"Really? I'd like to hear about your life now. Like to talk. You're staying with Liz? I could call you. How long are you here?"

"A week or so."

"A week? Is that all?"

"I might extend it," she said impulsively. "You can call me on my cell."

She quoted the number to him, and he keyed it into the phone he pulled from his pocket.

"I'll call," he said.

"How long are you home?"

"Not sure. Until we can get the legal aspect of things worked out for the girls."

"You're adopting them?"

"We have to go through some assessments first. But Celine wants to adopt. Make it permanent."

"Celine is your wife?"

"Yes." He turned, waved vaguely into the room. "She's over there. You must meet her."

"I'd love to. Maybe later?"

His eyes scanned the mourners' faces.

"I suppose I should move around a bit. Thank people for coming. Jonathon's here. Did you speak to him?"

She followed his gaze to a tall, bearded man standing in a far corner. He was leaning on a walking stick as he chatted to a young woman.

"He's grown a beard!"

"Yes. He's just back from Syria. He was injured over there."

"Ah, that's why he has the walking stick? He's still working for the BBC?"

"Yes. He needs more surgery apparently."

"Oh, wait. Isn't that Samantha? Is she with him?"

"No. He's involved with a rather accomplished woman photographer, I think. Not sure of the details. Haven't had a chance to catch up properly."

Alison looked again at the ex-Savages across the room. Jonathon's skinny frame and curly brown hair looked the same, but the beard was new. Samantha had been a nervous girl with a pale, closed face and an obvious infatuation with Matt. Now she stood close to Jonathon as if for protection.

Another man had stopped to join them. It took Alison a moment to recognize him.

"And Declan as well?"

Declan, once so ragged in denim, now wearing a sharp, tailored suit, his hair smoothed back from his wide face, was shaking Jonathon's hand.

"He looks spiffy. Bit of a player."

"He's in commodity trading," Matt said. "Or snake oil. Not sure which."

Alison smiled.

"So many old friends. Well, it's good they came."

"Indeed it is," Matt said. He leaned forward to kiss her cheek again. "I'll call you. In a day or two."

Alison watched him cross the room and return to his mother's side. His wife sat on a window ledge, sipping from a teacup. Her silver earrings, set with amethyst stones, caught the light as she moved her head. She was chatting to a man Alison had never seen before. There was something patrician about her posture: she held her head up, shoulders straight, a woman accustomed to being admired. She looked across, saw Alison watching and, eyes narrowing, seemed to be assessing her. Although they had never met, Alison felt that Matt's wife knew who she was, knew all about Alison's teenage crush on her husband.

Alison turned away, searching for Liz, and saw her across the room talking to a man she couldn't name but vaguely recognized. Alison hesitated about crossing the room to them; they were engrossed in conversation. She felt restrictively out of place. It had been too many years. Jonathon saw her then and waved, and so she moved toward him.

"Well, look at you, all adult and gorgeous," he said, hugging her.

"Gorgeous yourself. What's with the beard?"

"No time to shave when people are trying to blow you up. How are you, Ali? Didn't recognize you at first. What happened to the purple hair?"

"I was persuaded to go upmarket."

"New hairstyle and no sketch pad?" he said. "You're a whole new upmarket person."

"The sketch pad was just a prop. Didn't realize it at the time."

"You were good! All those trees and leaves."

"Good at leaves, hopeless at faces. Story of my life."

"Not so. I loved your woody pictures. I kept that sketch you made of our fort all the way through college. Hung it on my wall."

"You did?" Alison said, smiling. "And nobody laughed?"

"On the contrary. Original art? It impressed people. Especially girls."

"Good to hear. But hey, are you okay? Why the walking stick?"

"Bit more surgery required." He hesitated, looked serious. "It's so good to see you. I wish it wasn't—"

"I know. I'm still in shock. It seems impossible."

"It *is* impossible. There's a blank space in the universe where Sophie should be."

"A huge empty space," Alison said. "I didn't see you in the church."

"I was huddled at the back with the, er, alternative crowd." He dropped his voice. "Remember when you wanted a tattoo and your dad wouldn't let you have one? You'd have liked it back there. Some very interesting tats. The guy in front of me had *HATE* tattooed on his neck. Just that one word, in big letters. And his girlfriend had a jagged line on the inside of her arm and the words *Cut Here*. I couldn't stop staring at it."

"Good grief," Alison said, trying to imagine what looking at such a thing every day would do to mood and brain function. "Don't see any of that crowd here."

"Not sure they know this house exists. The guys around me seemed surprised that Sophie had a mother and a brother."

"She probably never told them," Alison said, just as Samantha returned. Samantha nodded and smiled at Alison but turned immediately to Jonathon, murmuring that they should go offer condolences to Mrs. Stuart. Jonathon rolled his eyes.

"Go ahead," Alison said. "See you later."

Left alone, Alison looked around, noticed a gray-haired woman emerging from the kitchen carrying a teacup, and so she walked purposefully in that direction, as if in search of a cup of tea.

In the kitchen she found Linda, the girl who had spoken at the service, slamming cupboard doors and cursing. She looked over her shoulder at Alison.

"You any idea where they keep the booze? I can't drink this stuff. Sherry? Shit."

"Not sure. I've never been in this kitchen," Alison said, looking around at the beige tile and traditional wood cabinets. "Must be wine somewhere," she added. "Try the fridge. Maybe there's some white."

Linda peered into the fridge, made a whooping sound, and pulled out a bottle of Pinot Grigio.

"Yay. Good thinking. Want some? Get a couple of glasses."

Alison hesitated.

"Just a small one," she said, reaching for wineglasses. Linda ignored this and poured two large drinks.

"To Sophie," she said. "Cheers."

"To Sophie," Alison echoed as they clinked glasses. "You're Linda, aren't you? I'm Alison. I used to live next door."

"Ali who went to America? Well, fuck me. Pleased to meet you. Soph used to talk about you all the time."

"She did?" Alison said, ridiculously pleased. "I liked what you said at the service. I feel like that, too. I just want to know what really happened. If she meant to do it, or not."

"I didn't know what to say. Just wanted to say something."

"You got it right."

"Thanks. You know what I was thinking, looking at all the people in the church? I was wondering how many of them really knew her. How many of them took advantage of her. She was so sweet to everybody.

"That ginger bint at the front, wailing and sobbing like she was Soph's best mate, and that weirdo husband of hers, stroking her back and looking tragic? They dossed down at her place once. She only had a bedsit, but she let them sleep on the floor. Anyway, they tried to get into bed with her, and she told them no, thank you very much, so they went ahead and fucked on the rug and ignored her. Afterward, that toerag wiped his dick on the curtains."

"Classy," Alison murmured. "She should have kicked them out."

"Didn't want to wake the babies." Her voice trembled.

"You were good friends?" Alison asked.

"Not good enough."

Alison frowned.

"Feel like it's my fault. I should have—" Linda began.

"Done something? Everybody feels like that."

"No. But I *could've* done something. I was babysitting the night she died. I yelled at her. She called to say she'd be a couple of hours, and then she called again and said she was still waiting. Wouldn't tell me who the fuck she was waiting for. Didn't say where she was. So I told her to stay the hell out. I could tell she was wasted. Too wasted to drive. So I said, *Don't bother coming back. I'll stay with the twins. I'm locking the door.*

"And she didn't," she said, a catch in her voice. "She didn't come back."

"Don't," Alison said, touching her shoulder. "Don't, please. Sounds to me like you did the right thing. She shouldn't have been driving. You were thinking of her safety."

Linda shook her head.

"Was I? I was just so fucking angry. I hated how secretive she could get. It's bugging the hell out of me that I never knew how unhappy she was, that she never told me. And she died all by herself."

"You think it was deliberate?" Alison asked. "The overdose?"

"Dunno. But she'd been cutting down recently, really trying to get clean. Why did she do so much that night? Something must have tipped her over the edge."

She gulped at the rest of her wine. "I'm out of here. I don't want to be in this house. Anyway, see you, Alison," she said as she slammed out of the kitchen.

Alison returned to the living-room window and looked out into the garden. The once-trimmed shrubs looked scrawny and neglected, the lawn patchy and littered with leaves from the oak tree.

The night before he ran away to Morocco, Matt had kissed her as they stood under that old oak. She had been kissed before. After Jonathon's clumsy attempt in the fort that rainy day, she had experienced other embraces—in dark corners at parties and once in a car, as the windows steamed and this strange boy she did not know but had met that evening seemed to move too quickly beyond control and kissed her over and over, his breath becoming more ragged, his hands damp. None of them had mattered after Matt's kiss. It had *felt* like her first kiss.

She recalled the sensation of her body weakening at the core, as if her bones had softened. In her bedroom, later, she had relived those moments over and over again. Her skin felt different where he had touched her, her mouth soft, sensitive.

He had told her he would be back, and she was young enough to thrill at the drama of it—the agony and the ecstasy, the pain of loss, the yearning for him, and then the joy of his return.

"I'll be in touch," he said.

"Please."

She thought there would be letters: e-mails sent from smoky Internet cafés in ports frequented by hookers and sailors, or maybe postcards mailed from cities she could barely imagine. She longed to read those, even as Matt still stood beside her.

Later, as she waited for the e-mails and the text messages that never came, the encounter in the garden and that kiss took on a weighty significance—the kiss against which all others were measured—until finally she accepted that it signified only one thing: her first heartbreak.

Lost in this recollection, Alison jumped when she felt a hand on her arm.

"Ali?"

She turned. Ronnie, unfamiliar in a dark suit, stood beside her. He had been a chubby child, a clumsy, uncoordinated youth, and now he was a huge adult, his face an unhealthy red.

"Just wanted to say hello. I'm not supposed to be here. The old mare didn't invite me."

"She didn't invite anybody. We came anyway. How are you, Ronnie?"

"Gutted," he said.

His eyes were red-rimmed and bloodshot; she could smell alcohol.

"I know how much you loved her, Ronnie. I'm so sorry."

"Wanted to see the basement again," he said. "Best times of my life down there. But it's locked. And I wanted to see who turned up. Glad you came, Ali. Sophie loved you. You and Liz. The three of you. God, I remember. Anyway, gotta go."

She pulled at his sleeve as he turned away.

"Give me your number. I'll call you."

As she put his number into her phone, she said, "Matt's over there. If you want to say hello."

He took a step backward.

"I didn't come to see him," he said, spitting the words out fast, as if they might damage his mouth. "I came to pay my respects to Sophie."

Alison stared. Where had that come from? That anger? He had hero-worshipped Matt when they were younger.

"I'll say hi to Jon on my way out," he said. "Then I'm out of here." Alison watched his wide back as he pushed his way through to Jonathon, saw them exchange a brief man-hug before Ronnie did indeed turn away and head for the door. When he reached it, Alison noted that his face changed as he stood back to let someone enter.

Matt's wife came into the room, holding the hands of two little girls: two identical blonde angels with soft pink faces, blue eyes wide and bright that searched the room. *They're looking for their mother,* Alison thought with a sharp shock. The little girls' faces were physically identical, though one child had a brighter, more alert expression than the other. They both looked lost. They both resembled Sophie. Alison felt a wrench in her chest, like a fist clenching, and thought, *Sophie is dead. Gone. Her little girls will never see her again.* As if this thought had occurred to everyone simultaneously, there was an audible sigh from the mourners as the girls were spotted, and then murmurs of sympathy.

Alison turned to find Liz beside her.

"My God, those kids are adorable," Liz said.

"They're beautiful."

"Well, Sophie was beautiful, wasn't she? Would have been stunning if she'd dressed properly."

"She did dress properly," Alison said, remembering Sophie skipping down the steps to the basement wearing thigh-high leather boots, shorts, a tank top over braless breasts, and a stick-on bluebird tattoo clearly visible on her slender arm. "It was fashionable, that look she had. Well, artsy anyway."

"Oh, darling, please," Liz said. "I was fashionable. *You* were artsy. Sophie's style was something else entirely. Anyway, let's go. We've done the necessary. Did you talk to everyone you wanted to talk to?"

"Yep. Ronnie. Jonathon. That's all, really."

"You see Jonathon's beard? Dope."

"He's been out in the field. He'll probably shave it off now he's back."

"Hope so. You talk to Matt?"

"Yes."

"Me too. And Celine, the terribly snotty wife. She'd like to invite us all to dinner, mentioned you particularly. Said she's heard so much about Matt's old friends." Liz raised an eyebrow. "I wonder what she's heard exactly?"

"God knows. What did you say?" Alison asked.

"I responded like a good, dutiful wife—I said I'd check dates with my husband. Come on, let's get out of here," Liz said. "Enough is enough."

SIX

At the house, while Liz made coffee, Alison stood awkwardly in the center of the kitchen, biting at her thumbnail. In the car, her head had been spinning with only one clear thought: she didn't want to return to Los Angeles, not yet. She wanted to find out why Sophie had died alone in a hotel room. She also, she admitted, wanted to catch up with her old friends again: Jonathon and Ronnie. Matt.

She cleared her throat. Liz looked over at her.

"What?"

"Liz, I think I might want to stay a bit longer."

"Course. You're welcome to stay, you know you are, just as long as you like."

"No. I don't mean stay here. I've been thinking I might rent a little holiday cottage for a week or so. Have a proper vacation. Haven't had one for ages."

Liz's face registered her appalled surprise.

"By yourself? Will Jake come join you?"

"Jake might be too busy right now. And I'd like some time to think."

Alison could not explain to Liz the biting awareness she now felt—common, perhaps, after any accident or death—that life is finite, that time is limited. She did not want to describe, not yet, her need to make changes to the way she was living, to discover if other paths through life were possible. To rediscover, perhaps, the artistic, nonmaterialistic person she used to be.

Her friend regarded her anxiously.

"Think about what?" Liz asked.

"Oh, you know. Life. Death. The great metaphysical questions of our time. Stuff like that."

"Not funny. What does Jake say about this?"

"I haven't told him yet. I wasn't clear until today."

"Hmm. Right. If you're sure that's what you want," said Liz, still looking doubtful. "But—have you thought where?"

"No. Has to be cheap. Not too far away. Maybe Shropshire, Herefordshire. Somewhere like that."

Liz brightened at the thought of this challenge.

"Okay, I'll help you find something."

"First," Alison said, "I have to call Jake."

~

His voice on the phone had an echoing quality.

"Is the phone on speaker?" Alison asked. "Please turn it off."

A click as the background sound deadened.

"So, how are you, sweetheart?" Jake asked. "How was the funeral?"

"Pretty much as you'd expect. Sad."

"You found out why Sophie did it?"

"We don't know that it was suicide. It's not certain. There was no note."

"Accidental overdose?"

"Looks like it. Don't know for sure. Her mother doesn't share information at all."

"Did you catch up with the boy next door?"

"Talked to him very briefly after the funeral," she said. "His French wife is very attractive." She waited a moment, then took a breath and said quickly, "Jake—I might be here longer than I thought."

"How much longer?"

"Not sure. A week or so. I'd like a bit of time to myself. Enjoy the English countryside."

Only the humming of the connection was audible for long seconds.

"And why do you need time to yourself?" he asked finally.

"Just need a break."

"We can take a break later. Together."

"You said that months ago and then canceled Maui, remember. And canceled Big Bear, too, at the last minute. I'd like a vacation. And maybe spend some time with my dad."

"And what about your job? Marcus has called about ten goddamned times. You've got commitments here."

At this, his office phone buzzed.

"You better take that," Alison said, fast. "I'll call you again later."

She heard his sigh, a soft sound along the wires.

After the call, Alison sat for a minute or two, studying the rolling stretch of the long lawns. Liz had left a window open, and the air was cool and fresh, an energizing quality to it. Alison took a few deep breaths of a breeze that tasted damp and green, and then she stood and moved to the window. As she looked out, a sudden shower drenched the garden.

Commitments? And with this, a thought came into her head in a blast of soft color: no more brainstorming sessions, client conferences, idiotic jingles. For the next few weeks she would not need to use words like *brand awareness* and *target audience*. "We have to communicate enthusiasm. That is key," Marcus had told her on her first day. "We need collaboration, cheerleaders, team players."

All the things she was not and had never wanted to be.

So, good. One thing was decided. No more advertising, at least for a while.

She turned back into the room, calling out to Liz.

"I'll be upstairs on my laptop," she said. "I want to check out vacation rentals."

Liz appeared in the doorway at once, leaning on the doorjamb.

"You know you said Shropshire? Well, remember that village where Sophie was in the women's shelter? This gal, Lila, who works with Simon—horsey-looking woman, huge teeth." Liz held thumb and finger wide to indicate the size. "She's got a cottage in that village."

Alison frowned, thinking.

"Near Shrewsbury?"

"Yes. That's it. Little farm cottage. It's empty right now. She's thinking of selling it. She just about destroyed it when she renovated it. Took out all the original features. It's comfortable, though. Got a new bathroom and kitchen. It's cheap. Nothing much in the village. A small shop. Not a bad pub. Maybe too quiet?"

"No. It sounds perfect," Alison said. "Is there a bus? Train service?"

"Local bus. Train service from Shrewsbury."

"Tell her I'll take it."

"But don't you want to look at it first? The village is tiny. You might get—"

"Tell her I'll move in right away," Alison said. "As soon as I can pick up the keys."

SEVEN

Liz drove Alison to the Shropshire cottage late the following afternoon. Dusk was falling on the quiet village, and the lane leading to the cottage was made darker by crowding trees, causing Liz to switch on her sidelights, slow her speed, and sigh out loud. The cottage sat on the edge of the village and backed onto what appeared to be farmland. It looked isolated, hunched there at the end of the leaf-littered lane.

"You sure about this place?" Liz asked, peering out of the car. "It looks so—lonely. And a little bit spooky."

"It's not spooky. It's just dark. It'll be fine when I put the lights on."

"Okay, let's get your stuff in."

Inside, the cottage had clearly been renovated, and although Liz complained again that the original features had been destroyed, Alison, not a fan of dark rooms and old beams, was glad that the French windows opened onto a small garden, that the kitchen and bathroom were tiled in new, luminous ceramic.

"It's nice," she said.

"Shame they've modernized it."

"I like modern. And the furniture isn't too chintzy."

Liz inspected it. The place, furnished with simple Ikea-type furniture, had a polished wooden floor with a shaggy cream rug.

"Bit bland. The sofa looks comfy."

While Liz helped with the grocery bags, Alison carried her suitcase upstairs.

"You want a cup of tea?" she asked as Liz, buttoning her coat, headed for the door.

"No, thanks, Ali. I should get going before the traffic builds up. But look—I'll call you in the morning."

Alison listened to Liz's car drive off, then switched on the kettle, the TV, and all the lights, even the one in the bedroom, dispelling the darkness.

A few hours later, a howling wind could be heard over the sound of the television. It rattled the windows. The sky was black. Before she got ready for bed, Alison dragged the fold-down table from the kitchen alcove, wedged it across the shuddering front door, and placed a dining chair on top before stepping back to study it. Yes, it would stop the door from suddenly swinging open and work as a barrier and a good deterrent to intruders. It looked like some kind of offbeat artistic creation, maybe a submission for the Turner Prize. It had a pleasing symmetry.

Even as she did all this, she felt foolish, telling herself that these precautions were unnecessary, that she was a gibbering idiot. This wasn't LA, where triple locks and alarm systems were common even in gated communities. It wasn't the inner city in one of the UK's trouble spots. It was a tiny Shropshire village, so quiet that even the traffic on the Shrewsbury Road was nothing more than a faint and harmless hum.

She had traveled alone a number of times for agency client conferences, and she loved hotel rooms, the anonymity of them, the juxtaposition of the private and the public. She loved the miniature soaps and toiletries, the tea and coffee and little kettles, the noise and bustle of a hotel world, close enough but separate from her.

This was different. Perhaps it was the howl of the wind or the fact that no other human being was remotely in earshot. Her nearest neighbor was at the very top of the lane. And that flimsy front door! It had an old Yale lock: a determined burglar or, God forbid, a rapist or serial killer could open it in five seconds with one good kick. Tomorrow, she vowed, she would buy a solid bolt for it.

Alison had left the landing light on. In bed that night, the darkness outside was so dense, but the light was irritating, and after a while, groaning, she got out of bed and switched it off, thinking that she would never sleep, never—she was destined to become The Insomniac of Shropshire—and fell asleep, finally, out of exhaustion.

She woke in the early hours, trying to guess the time, shaken by the absolute silence. Standing at the window, shivering in the chilly bedroom, she could see the Shropshire hills, round outlines against a vast sky and a gray horizon. The wind had dropped, the rain stopped. Thin clouds, like shadows, crossed over a pale moon.

"Well, damn, would you look at that beautiful sky," she said aloud, and turned to the bed. For a moment she thought Jake slept there. Confused, still half-asleep, she blinked rapidly, saw the empty bed, and felt a piercing dart of loneliness. The dark hills seemed taller, bulkier than they did in the daytime, and she was reminded of the view of the hills from her California home: magical sometimes, under a full moon.

Alison sighed and slipped downstairs to make a hot drink. As she drank the tea, its warmth seeped into her stomach, soothing her. It was normal to feel lonely in a different bed, she told herself. After seven years of marriage, what could anyone expect? It was a habit missed, that was all. She had no practice at being alone in a strange house.

But the nervy, lost feeling persisted, and when she returned to the bed she made a point of lying in the center of it instead of curling up on the left side as she had always done. She could not sleep again and lay awake, watching the window until the light brightened.

~

In the morning, wearing a long raincoat donated by Liz and clutching her umbrella, she set off to check out the village and find the village shop. The slanting rain, pitting against her face, felt uncomfortably cold. She tried to visualize a summer day in the Hollywood Hills, tried to imagine a California sun, blurring and relentless. In Los Angeles she would think of English rain on her face as a way to keep cool. It did not work then. It did not work now, in reverse.

The compact village, constructed mostly of dark stone, had a squat Saxon church, a central half-timbered pub that displayed a plaque with a sixteenth-century date, a small store, and an old-fashioned tea shop. The main street seemed eerily quiet, the faces she saw oddly homogenous in contrast to the multiethnic neighbors of her Los Angeles life. Here, skin was pale, bluish, like skimmed milk, the voices soft as a few residents wished her a good morning, eyes averted. The villagers could be extras in a movie about retirement, Alison decided. Or a TV murder mystery set in the English countryside.

The village shop was also a post office and carried a good supply of basic foods and, Alison was pleased to note, wine and spirits. She looked around. She could see no hardware items at all.

The middle-aged woman behind the counter, neat in an apron printed with cadmium-yellow sunflowers, looked puzzled at Alison's request.

"A bolt? You mean for a door?"

"Yes. A lock. A big inside one, the kind you just slide over."

"No, dear. Not here. You'll need to go to Shrewsbury for that. Hardware store. B&Q," she said, her voice slightly Welsh, here so close to the border. "We're a food shop. You know. Basics."

Alison nodded, embarrassed, turning to stare at the shelves. She should buy a food item, be polite, though she and Liz had stocked the cupboards. She decided on a small loaf of bread, a can of chicken soup, and two bottles of Merlot.

"Two bottles?" the woman asked.

"Two. Please."

Alison wondered if word would go around the village that the woman renting the farm cottage had a drinking problem.

The wine bottles banged together as she made her way down the hill. As she struggled to rearrange her purchases and reposition the umbrella, she noticed a side street, wide and treelined, curving away from the village. An old house stood on the far corner. Alison remembered the e-mails Sophie had sent from the women's shelter. She had described an old house, had written that it had a magnolia tree in the garden. The house right there on the corner had a huge magnolia tree.

Alison walked toward the building, trying to recall the exact words of the e-mail. And yes, there was the fence Sophie had said was ugly and crap-colored. She said the twins had tried to tunnel under it, like prisoners.

It looked like the sort of place a woman and her children could hide from an abusive husband or lover. Why had Sophie been here? Liz seemed not to know, and Sophie had never explained, never told Alison the details. Somebody must have been stalking her.

Alison turned away, hurrying now, back to the cottage. The rain had started again, harder, the wind had picked up.

Her cell phone began ringing just as she reached the cottage door. Juggling the umbrella, the wine, and the loaf of bread, Alison fumbled for it.

"Alison. Good morning," Matt said.

The sound of his voice jarred her. She struggled clumsily with the door key, and the bag slipped from her hands. A crash before the splintered glass of one of the bottles scattered across the path. "Damn it," she cried.

She took a firmer grip on the key and, hands shaking, pushed open the door and sank to the floor in the hallway, still holding the phone.

"Damn," she said. "Damn."

"Alison?"

"I dropped the wine. It's all over the path."

"But you're okay?"

"I'm fine. Sorry. I should know I can't do two things at once. Ever."
Matt laughed.

"You're still at Liz's house?"

"No. I'm in Shropshire. In a cottage. How are you?" she asked, trying to lower her voice, slow it, as she watched the red wine, now diluted by the rain, meander down the path, turning the thin puddles pink. "What's happening with the twins?"

"We're going ahead with the adoption process," he said. "But, something of a shock, Gary Lewis turned up. And wants custody."

"He can't do that, can he? Where's he been all this time?"

"Absolutely no idea. But we'll fight his application. I saw a solicitor today. There's a preliminary meeting in a week. So, tell me, what are you doing in Shropshire?"

"Thinking. Perfect place for it. It's quiet. The village is tiny. It does have a nice pub, though, if you ever want to check it out."

He did not respond at first, and she felt her cheeks burn. Stupid to put him on the spot like that. His wife might be sitting right next to him.

"And Celine, too, of course," she added quickly.

"Celine's in France for a day or so," he said. "But the pub sounds good. How about tomorrow? Too soon?"

"Tomorrow would be fine," she said, a tremor still audible in her voice.

"Tell me how to find you."

EIGHT

A long scented shower, the decision over what to wear, finally settling on a calf-length skirt, knee-high boots, a soft sweater in a clear cerulean blue, and still Alison was ready a full thirty minutes before Matt was due to arrive. She stood at the window feeling as if her entire body were on high alert, as if watching for Matt required her total attention, as if she must be focused, listening for his car, all senses engaged.

She could not keep still. She paced from kitchen to hall, her boots clattering on the tile, raced upstairs to the bathroom—a forced fast pee, as if it would be a terrible thing to be there in the bathroom when he arrived—and then rushed back to the window, taking slow, deep breaths.

When the phone rang she ran to it, saw Jake's number and snapped it onto "Decline." Not Jake. Not now. What could she say? She did the same thing with Liz, ten minutes later. Her friend might detect something in her voice, a tremble of excitement, of anticipation. During all of this, a nagging internal voice reminded her that she was an idiot. She was having drinks with an old friend. That was all.

At last, a black Citroen pulled to the curb. Alison jumped back out of sight and stood as still as a stone statue in the hall. When the doorbell rang, she took a jagged breath and waited a few moments before she opened the door, smiling a welcome.

She gestured for him to come inside, but Matt paused in the door-way, studying her face with such intense scrutiny that she looked away, her cheeks warm.

"It's still a shock to see you all grown up," he said. "I remember a child, a wood nymph, our own dryad of the trees darting about, and here is this lovely woman instead."

She swallowed, her mouth dry.

"We weren't exactly children the last time we saw each other," she reminded him.

"No, but that's how I remember you best. The games in the woods? A slight girl, so quick and funny."

"I never felt quick and funny," she said, turning to lead him into the cottage.

"No? How did you feel?"

"Odd. Clumsy. Awkward."

He smiled. Inside the cottage, he looked around.

"It's got character," he said. "Isn't that what the agents say?"

"That's just agent-speak for dark and poky. This is nice and light."

"It is. So, how far is the pub?"

"Just down the street. Don't need the car."

They walked fast to the pub. The wind had a bite to it now, a north-easterly edge. As they crossed the street that led to the women's shelter, Alison said, "I think that's the shelter place where Sophie stayed. The big house on the corner."

Matt glanced at it but did not slow his step.

"Not exactly sheltering in appearance," he said. "More like Cell Block C."

"I thought I might drop in, talk to them."

He slowed then, turning to look at her.

"Why?"

"Ask them about Sophie," she said. "See if they know anything. Okay. Here's the pub."

As they entered the busy lounge bar, Matt put an arm around her shoulders, and the touch burned, even through her coat. The pub felt warm and steamy. An empty table was visible near the window.

"Grab that table," Matt said. "I'll get drinks. What would you like?"

She tried covertly to study him as he stood at the bar, noting the changes that had occurred from boy to man. Matt had more physical confidence, perhaps, and a style of dressing that surprised her. It was a cosmopolitan look: he wore a leather jacket over a black, fine-knit sweater and looked rather Gallic.

When he returned, with vodka for himself and a glass of wine for her, he lifted his glass formally and leaned forward to clink it with hers.

"Here's to old friends."

"I'll drink to that."

"You like it here? The village isn't too small?"

"It's fine," Alison said. "It's just right for now. Peaceful. Perfect place to think."

"Think about?"

"Next steps."

"You'll go back to California soon, of course?"

"Oh yes."

"Are you happy there? You said you were in advertising."

"For my sins."

"It isn't what you wanted? I know you studied art."

"I'm a copywriter," Alison said. "I didn't plan it. They didn't hire me for it, either. Apparently I have a knack for it. But advertising involves a whole lot of other things that have nothing to do with art."

"And what does it involve?"

"Persuasion," Alison said, taking a sip of her drink. "Manipulation. Deception."

Matt smiled.

"Sounds challenging. And your husband—he's in the same field?"

"No. He's an executive in a large pharmaceutical company. Decides how funding is distributed, which drugs should have trials, stuff like that."

"Hard decisions."

"No. Half an hour number crunching and he's got it. Big Pharma is all focused on the bottom line. And Jake's company is no exception. Profits not patients, that's the company's motto."

He laughed.

"I almost believed you there for a moment."

"You should," she said. "It's true."

She relaxed back in the chair, calmer now, soothed by the taste of the wine, the warmth of the pub, and Matt's encouraging attention.

"So where did you study, finally?" she asked. "After you abandoned Oxford?"

"Sorbonne. Celine's father pulled a few strings for me."

"Ah. That's where you met her? In Paris?"

Her voice betrayed her. The forced light tone failed.

"Yes," he said. His eyes met hers. Alison was certain that he could read in her face all that she did not want him to know.

"So, tell me what you teach," she said quickly.

His face brightened, and immediately he began to talk in the way she remembered, his passion for the writers he was teaching clear in his voice. She wondered if he inspired his students the way he had inspired her all those years ago when she would race off to the library to check out whatever books Matt had mentioned that day. As he talked, she saw the same boy she once loved: the blue eyes she remembered reflecting light from the curved reading lamp as he lay stretched on the old sofa in the basement of their house, the den that he and his sister had made their own. He smoked then, incessantly, and would turn over onto his stomach to stomp out the cigarette in the ashtray on the floor, talking of Oxford, still to come, or of whatever theory excited him that day: existentialism, deconstructionism, poetics. Alison would listen, then later she would research these topics so that she could share in the conversations, keep up. By then, of course, Matt had moved on to something else.

She was able to keep up with him now: the American authors he taught were known to her. They agreed on Bellow, disagreed about Updike—she could have predicted that—and when he pounded the table to make a point she leaned back to grin at him.

"Why are you smiling?" he asked.

"You're just so *opinionated*."

"But that's good, isn't it?" he asked, laughing.

"I don't know. To be so certain about everything? I still have books you gave me years ago that you said were essential reading.

"Of course," she added, covering herself. "I keep everything. I still have a rose from Sophie's bouquet. She gave it to me. And from Liz's."

"And from your own?"

"Bunch of daisies. No bouquet for me. We got married in Las Vegas, in a wedding chapel. I wore a hippie dress and carried daisies."

"And you kept them?"

"Pressed them. And kept the champagne cork from the dinner afterwards."

"You're sentimental, then. I'm not. Not at all."

"I get it from my mum. She hoarded everything. She had every report card, every Mother's Day card. Her bedroom drawers were choked with stuff I'd made at school."

"She was a nice woman, your mother," Matt said. "Kind."

"Yes. So, is your mother sentimental?" Alison asked, certain of the answer.

"Not at all. She keeps nothing. No report cards, awards, baby shoes. Nothing. It's a matter of pride with her. When Dad died, she had his clothes and all his things bagged up and ready for the charity shop the very next day. Even his fishing tackle. She told us once that when she got engaged to him, his mother gave her an envelope with a lock of baby hair from his first haircut. She took it straight home and threw it in the fire."

"Threw the lock of hair in the fire?"

"Yes. Immediately. Thought the whole thing was somehow distasteful."

Alison shook her head, unable to hide her grin.

"Wow. That's a bit extreme."

"See? We come from opposite ends of the spectrum," Matt said.

She smiled at him, met his eyes. A moment when it would be easy to reach across, touch his hand, hold it, amazed that after all the years she still wanted to do that. Struggling to think of something witty and bright to amuse him, she realized she'd missed his last question.

"Sorry?" she asked.

"Los Angeles—tell me about Los Angeles."

~

When they returned to the cottage, Alison fumbled with the key in the lock.

"Coffee?" she asked when at last the door opened.

"Why not?"

Inside, he did not sit down but walked around, picking up a book upended on the coffee table, studying the cover, and reading the reviews on the back. He was clearly so restless that Alison wondered why he had not simply gone home. But something was holding him there. The air was charged in the small room.

"Does your mother know you're meeting me?" she asked as she reached for coffee and the kettle.

"Told her I was having drinks with an old friend."

"But not which old friend?"

"No."

Nervous, she clanked the mugs, cursed under her breath. When his hand touched her arm, she jumped, startled.

"Whoa, sorry. Didn't mean to frighten you," he said.

"I'm just edgy at the moment."

He took the mug of coffee from her, walked back to the living room, and sat on the sofa, watching her face. Deliberately, she sat opposite him, on the armchair. He regarded her steadily.

"You want to talk about why you're edgy?"

"No. Not entirely sure myself. But thank you. Anyway, Liz and I were talking about the Savages the other day," she said quickly, to change the subject.

"Memories of the crazy gang?"

"We weren't so crazy. And we had a motto. In Latin, too."

"Fortis Fortuna Adiuvat," Matt said. "Fortune favors the brave."

"Why are you shaking your head like that? You chose it!"

"I know. What a pretentious little prick I was."

Alison laughed. He *had* changed. He had never been self-deprecating.

"Sophie loved our gang," she said. Matt nodded. She wondered if he found it hard to talk about his sister—as children they had been so close—but when he spoke, his voice was steady.

"She did. She loved ordering people around," he said. "She loved that she could persuade people to be as reckless as she was. We did some pretty insane things."

"No. Not really."

"Smoked, drank. Tested a variety of street drugs."

"Not all of us," Alison protested. "I never did the drugs. Oh, wait, maybe the occasional drag. Remember the first time Declan rolled a joint for us? We were, what, fourteen?"

"Something like that. Fourteen, fifteen."

Alison remembered Declan's grubby fingers flattening the cigarette paper, tapping in the weed, and then rolling it carefully. He lit it, took a long, important drag, then passed it to Sophie, who, clearly pleased to be chosen first, took a drag and passed it to Jonathon who passed it to Matt. Alison had waited, pulse racing. Would he hand it to her or to Liz? Or to Ronnie? He handed it to her. From his lips to hers. She was high at the very thought, before the drug had time to hit.

"I'd get the giggles when the others were smoking," she said. "Their laughter was so infectious."

"Contact high," Matt said. "No. Your forte was shoplifting. You were *very* good at that."

"Shoplifting? Yep. Because I was invisible. I'd go with Liz and Sophie to that big discount pharmacy, and Liz would be so nervous she would drop things, and Sophie would chatter on and ask too many questions, and the salesgirls and the security people would be so busy watching the two tall, blonde girls who were clearly up to no good that I could just slide up to the counter and scoop away, slip the small stuff into my bag. Mostly lipsticks and mascara. Always had a bit of a stash."

She paused, thinking back.

"I was terrified the whole time," she said. "I was glad when we stopped doing it. Jonathon kept on lifting CDs, remember, until the old downtown store started a new tagging system?"

"True. We were never short of music, makeup, or porno movies," Matt said.

"Porno movies! Oh my God. I'd forgotten about that."

A winter's evening, cold and dark too early. Sophie and Declan had come down to the basement, laughing and noticeably high, carrying a battered box of old videos they'd found in Declan's dad's shed. Sophie had insisted that the lights be turned off. *We need candlelight for this,* she said. Alison recalled her own shock at the images on the screen: a redhead with large, high breasts; a man with a blank, harmless face and a swaying penis so huge and purple that it looked like a weapon. Alison, still a virgin then, had shuddered, bewildered. How could that possibly . . . ? But it did, minutes later, and rammed into the glistening, waiting vagina. She remembered wondering why none of the actresses had pubic hair; she remembered the amplified groaning and screaming sounds from the video and Liz giggling, embarrassed. The boys stayed silent, focused. Alison had looked over at Sophie. Sophie wasn't watching the screen—she was watching her friends. Her eyes, gleaming in the candlelight, moved from face to face. Alison had been relieved when it was over, when she could return to the safety of her own home, her own neat bed with its freshly laundered sheets.

"That first porno flick was a bit of a shock," she admitted now to Matt. "I'd never seen an erect penis before. Really scared me."

"We were young."

"I think Sophie was happy then," Alison said.

"Yes, I believe she was."

"Did you see her at all when you were living in France? I know she was hard to reach."

"She was impossible. She avoided her family. Celine and I visited her years ago in the rehab unit at the hospital in Sussex. She was going through a tough time then. It was a miserable visit. She wouldn't talk to Celine at all, and she wasn't making a lot of sense. She was very shaky, very much on the edge. A nurse gave her a sedative while we were there, and eventually she fell asleep."

He trailed off, thought for a moment.

"We saw her briefly, very briefly, at the service for Dad. Last year."

"Oh yes, I'm sorry about your dad. Sophie came to the funeral?"

"Yes. Didn't think she would. It wasn't a funeral exactly. He'd left strict instructions for a no-fuss cremation. No religious service, nothing." He stopped, took a sip of his coffee. "It was a nightmare. I was certain Sophie wouldn't turn up—but she came late, racing in just when this vicar person had begun to read something about the dead person being in the other room, or in the wind, or some such."

"I've read that somewhere, I think."

"Sophie was so jittery and restless. She said, *What crap*, got up from her seat, and paced up and down in the entranceway. We could hear her footsteps on the stone. Mother was angry and kept looking back there. Then Sophie lit a cigarette. The guy officiating tiptoed to the back and whispered to her, and she said in a loud, furious voice, *No smoking? It's a* crematorium *for fuck's sake!"*

Matt shook his head, raised both hands in a gesture indicating helplessness. Alison laughed out loud.

"That is classic Sophie. Did she put the cigarette out?"

"No."

Matt waited a moment, then looked at her seriously.

"I used to wonder how you were," he said. "If you were happy."

"I thought about you, too. All the time. I'd ask my mum and dad to check with your parents, but they never seemed to know. Or they didn't want to say."

"They knew," he said. "But they were angry with me for leaving. Angry for a long time."

"I suppose I imagined you in Tangier most of all. After the first postcard. I kept hoping you'd come home."

"I couldn't do that."

He put down his coffee cup, looked at his watch.

"I should leave," he said.

He stood. As she stood with him, he moved forward and lifted her chin so that she had to look at him.

"Do you know that out of everyone in my life, you're the only person I have ever truly trusted?" he said.

"Trusted with your life? Bank balance?"

"Everything."

He hesitated for a moment. Alison knew that he was about to kiss her. Later, she would ask herself why she hadn't simply stepped back, turned away, but her heart was racing, and she stood, waiting.

The kiss, when it happened, brought the past, with all its emotion and turmoil, surging back. The touch of his hands on her shoulders, his mouth on hers, felt different from the long-ago kiss in the garden. His body was taller, stronger, pressing against her. But it was the same boy, now a man. Matt. As she responded to him, her hands to his shoulders, he pulled away.

"I'm sorry," he said at once. "I'm really sorry. I didn't mean to—" He looked closely at her face. "I wish . . ." he began, his expression unreadable.

The words hung between them, unsaid.

At the front door, he moved forward to kiss her cheek, a fast, light kiss, a casual good-night. But his hands were warm on her face, and she leaned into him. The longing she felt was so acute that her breath caught in her throat. When he moved away, she was conscious of the cool air on her cheeks, of the darkness around them.

"I'll call you in the morning," he said, so quietly she barely heard.

Alison tried to force calm into her expression.

"Drive carefully."

She closed the door, stood in the hallway, waiting until she heard his car pull away, shaken at herself, at him. How insane to let him kiss her like that. And wrong. She was married to Jake. Celine, Matt's elegant, perfect wife, could be right now returning from France on her way back to him.

He is not for me, she told herself. *It's too late.* She recalled how hard it was: the waiting for just another postcard that would change the day, bring light and joy to it. The hopeless daydreams, the futile miserable dates with guys who did nothing wrong except not be Matt. She had pulled herself out of that, traveled to America, met Jake, began a new life. She had managed to forget Matt. Almost. And now?

He is like an addiction, she thought. *I am setting myself up for months of rehab.*

NINE

In the flat light of the morning, the cottage looked littered and cold. Alison had undressed by the fire, and her clothes were strewed across the sofa. The coffee cups still stood on the kitchen counter.

She switched on the fire so that the fake flames would lighten the room and turned on the radio in an attempt to mask the mutinous silence of the telephone. She had been listening for the phone, waiting for it to ring, since first light. *I'll call you in the morning.* The words had been said quietly, without certainty. Matt couldn't possibly mean them. The radio presenter's voice was a low murmur, forecasting possible economic collapse for what sounded like the entire world, or at least Europe. Alison turned the radio off again. It was stupid to take Matt's words seriously. Why should he call? He would be busy with his work, his legal plans. His wife.

After a cup of coffee and a slice of toast she felt better and opened her laptop. Three e-mails from Marcus, asking where on earth she was, and one e-mail from Jake. Her husband sounded angry: Marcus had called him repeatedly.

"Would you please let that man know what the hell you're doing?" Jake had written. "I don't have a clue what to say to him. And why isn't your phone working? Why does it keep going to voice mail? Call me."

Alison sighed. She would call Jake later, she would, she *must*, e-mail Marcus later, but right now she needed a brisk walk to clear her head. She would take the path behind the cottage. It would lead to the village eventually, curving around a soft hill.

The air outside felt crisp and clean, so she crossed over the wooded dell, enjoying the crunch of leaves under her feet. Eventually, she could see her own road running parallel with the hillside, the small Saxon church at one end of the main street, the pub at the other, in shadow now.

She stopped on the ridge, looking down at the village. It was a soothing landscape. Peaceful. England's growing crime rate, the detritus of poverty and neglect, was not obvious here. It was hidden in the crumbling architecture of its cities.

The village looked unreal. Which was the dream: Los Angeles or this quiet place? The Biltmore evening and all the people at that sparkling party—herself in the jade gown, Jake in black tie—seemed like dress extras in a movie. One viewed in a small art cinema, quite foreign and unknowable in this tiny village under a cold sun.

When she reached the center of the village, she looked inside the empty church and gazed into the window of the tea shop, where three older ladies sat primly around a small table. She noted that the pub closed each afternoon for a few hours.

She stopped outside the shelter. They would remember Sophie here. They might know *something*. Alison, after a few moments of indecision, marched up the path.

The woman who answered the door was middle-aged, wearing tailored tweed clothing. Alison stared, confused. There was something familiar about the face and gray hair.

"I know you, don't I?" Alison said, and then a click of recognition. "You were at Sophie's funeral. I saw you coming out of the kitchen!"

The woman regarded her without expression.

"May I help you?" she asked.

"I'd like to talk to someone about Sophie. I just want to find out why—" Alison heard the catch in her own voice. "I need to talk to someone."

The woman tugged her inside.

"Please. Come in. We like to keep this door locked."

Inside, after bolting the door securely, she turned back to Alison.

"Sophie stayed here, didn't she?" Alison asked. "I know she did. I had e-mails from this place. I just want to know, well, why she was here. Did she have an abusive partner? Was someone hurting her? I don't understand why she died. Sophie had a lot of problems, but she'd never commit suicide."

"You sure about that?" asked a voice behind them. Alison whipped around to find another woman watching her. She wore an apron and had a lined face and tired eyes.

"Deirdre," the gray-haired woman said sharply. "We don't talk to strangers. As you well know."

"I'm not a stranger," Alison said in a panic. Desperate for the women to talk to her, Alison pulled out her passport, her California driver's license, old bills and papers, and spilled them all onto the hall table.

"Look, this is who I am. If you have a computer, I can find e-mails from Sophie. I've got a letter here. See, I kept it."

The table was now a mess of papers.

"I'm Alison Eastlake," Alison said, holding out her hand. "You might remember me from the funeral."

The gray-haired woman smiled finally.

"Vivienne Cameron," she said at last, shaking Alison's hand. "I'm the manager here." Then, her voice softening, she added, "Why don't you go and have a cup of tea with Deirdre? She knew Sophie. Perhaps she can spare a minute to talk to you."

"Thank you," Alison said. "Thank you."

"Back here," Deirdre said. Alison followed her, wondering if she was a domestic helper, maybe a volunteer who lived in. Alison was willing to bet that Deirdre had escaped to this place herself once.

Deirdre led the way along a corridor, then through a large lounge furnished with old armchairs, the floor littered with toys. Four women of various ages sat there, two with children on their laps. One woman was knitting. A television buzzed in the corner of the room. The women fell silent, watching, as Alison walked through, and though she smiled and said hello, only one voice responded to her. She heard whispering, and then a reprimand as a child scampered past, knocking over a pyramid of wooden bricks. A woman in an apron, folding laundry in a corner of the room, looked at her curiously.

They reached an empty room attached to the kitchen, and Deirdre indicated two wooden chairs.

"Sit down," she said. "Take the weight off."

Alison sat, looking around at the bare room: mugs and plates draining by the sink, an empty milk carton on the table. The place smelled of overcooked vegetables. Deirdre switched on the kettle and then sat down opposite her.

"So, fire away," she said. "What you want to know?"

"Why was Sophie hiding here?" Alison said. "Who was she running away from? Couldn't have been her husband. She hadn't seen him in years. Did she have a new partner?"

"Wasn't that," Deirdre said, then leaned back, chewing at her lip as she regarded Alison. "You know she had a bit of a problem?" she asked.

"With drugs? Yes, I know that."

"She tried to get clean. Really tried. But she kept going back. Anyway, she couldn't pay 'em. The people she owed."

Deirdre stood to make tea, returned, and placed the mugs on the table.

"And they beat her up?" Alison asked.

"Yeah. They did."

Alison winced.

Deirdre dropped her voice.

"Not everybody knows about that here. This place is supposed to be for, you know, domestics."

"Okay. I understand. But do you think the people who beat her up had something to do with her dying like that?"

"No. Don't be daft. They just punched her around a bit. Gave her a black eye."

Deirdre's tone indicated that she had seen worse, right here, in this place.

"So you think she killed herself?"

"I dunno," Deirdre said. "It's possible."

"She might have overdosed. She did when she was sixteen," Alison said, recalling her panic at the time, the long minutes outside the Midlands club when she was terrified Sophie would die. "She took a bunch of ecstasy pills at a club in our hometown."

"Yeah, she talked about that once. That *was* an accident. She was just pissing around then."

"So why was she in a hotel room?"

"That I don't know. And I ain't going to guess."

Deirdre hesitated, lowered her voice.

"She didn't always follow the rules, our Sophie," she said. "Not even here."

"Why?" Alison asked. "What did she do?"

"She was always sneaking out. Meeting people."

"Who?"

Deirdre shrugged, looked away, clearly not wanting to give further details.

"All kinds of people. Don't matter now, does it? Anyway, I'm ever so sorry she died. I really liked her. And her two little girls, well, they was smashing. Ever such good kids. Wish I'd helped her a bit."

She stood.

"Got to get on," she said.

Alison followed her through the living room. A toddler on tiptoe, trying to see out of the window, called out to them. Deirdre turned.

"Get away from that window, Josh," she said sharply. As she spoke, a young woman raced to him, pulled him away from the window, and lifted him in her arms. She had long fair hair, blue eyes, and bruises in a riot of purple and yellow around her eyes. Alison caught a glimpse of the woman's frightened expression before Deirdre hurried to them, moving them both toward the corridor that led to the back of the house.

"Sorry," she said when she returned to Alison. "I need to get that lad his tea. His mum's not well."

"Thank you for talking to me," Alison said.

"No bother."

Deirdre walked with Alison to the front door.

"You know you can't tell anybody about this place?" she said. "We got to keep it safe. Some of the people in the village know, but they don't say nothing."

"I won't say a word to anyone," Alison promised.

~

As she walked slowly back to the cottage, Alison tried to imagine Sophie there in that sad house. Beaten up by drug dealers because she owed them money? The prettiest girl she'd ever known, one of the smartest, but always the most reckless. What had Liz called Sophie once: the poster child for self-destruction? That had never changed. But who had she been meeting when she sneaked out from the shelter? A dealer? A lover?

As she made coffee in the cottage kitchen, she remembered Ronnie. He had stayed in touch with Sophie. He might know. Liz had said he lived in Shrewsbury now, he was close enough to meet up for a drink. He didn't answer the phone, but she left a message as if she were simply calling for a chat, then waited. The phone rang a minute later, and it was Ronnie.

"You want to get together for a drink sometime? Talk about old times," she asked. "If you're still in Shrewsbury, I'm really close by. That little village where Sophie stayed in the shelter."

"What you doing there?"

"Just having a break. So? A drink? Maybe lunch?"

"You want to talk about Soph," he stated flatly.

"Well, yes. Don't you?"

"Nope. It doesn't help. It makes me feel worse."

"You stayed friends, though, all this time?"

"Yeah. We were mates."

"You saw her recently?"

"Yeah."

"She was still using?"

"What if she was?"

"For God's sake, Ronnie. I'm not judging her. I just want to know what happened to her. So, you saw her often?"

"Yeah. I did. She was my dealer."

Alison, stunned, gripped the receiver hard.

"She was what?"

"My dealer. She was carrying—oh, fuck, what's it matter now."

"What was she dealing?"

"Nothing scary, Ali, for fuck's sake. She was careful. Wouldn't touch heroin. Nervous of meth. Just regular stuff, easy to shift—weed, E, ket."

"And coke? She was using cocaine again herself?" Alison asked quietly, recalling the white powder on the counter of a club bathroom once and Sophie with a rolled-up note in her hand. Liz had turned away. "So ugly," Liz had said. "That looks so ugly, sniffing like that." Sophie had laughed.

Ronnie's voice had a defensive note now.

"She'd cut back a lot," he said.

73

"Do you know who she got it from? They beat her up, you know."

"Shit, I know that. She didn't pay 'em. Well, they get nasty when they're not paid. She was selling to mates; that's all. Not big amounts. She wasn't some huge fucking regional dealer, Ali. Just peanuts. But they didn't like it. She switched then. Never did find out where she got her gear after that. She kept it quiet."

"God. I had no idea." Alison paused, thinking. "You think Soph was meeting her supplier in that hotel room?"

Ronnie's laugh, high-pitched for such a big man, was loud and immediate.

"Her supplier?" he said. "You meet suppliers in back alleys, Alison. Or loading areas behind pubs, crack dens in Smethwick. You don't pay out for a posh hotel with room service."

"Wasn't it the Regent? By Birmingham Airport? That's not posh, is it?"

"Well, it's big. I drove by it, just to have a look. Wanted to go in but—fuck. What's the point?"

"Who could she have been meeting there, then?"

"Dunno. Wish I did."

Then, quite abruptly his voice changed. "Sorry, Ali, gotta go," he said. And hung up.

Alison stood quite still, holding the phone.

"A dealer," she said aloud. "Dear God."

She found the hotel easily on the Internet. Large, as Ronnie had said, part of a huge international chain. She studied the generic furnishings and the wide lobby. Impersonal, businesslike. A place to meet a lover or to do a drug deal? It was anonymous enough. The bedrooms were neat, neutral, furnished with only basic essentials: the bed, a desk, a landscape picture on the wall. The bathrooms had a clinical sterility: white tile, so cold and clean. Was that the last thing Sophie saw? That blank white wall?

When had it begun, Sophie's addiction? Did she get tired of the weed that Declan brought occasionally to the Stuart basement and want something different, something new? Alison recalled the day Sophie, out on a school trip, met a boy who gave her free samples of pills that were apparently popular in the hottest clubs in the city.

"Look," she had said to Alison and Liz.

Alison stared, surprised by the colors of those pills and capsules held in Sophie's pale, cupped hands.

"You should paint them," Sophie had said. "They're so pretty."

"What are they?"

"Rainbows."

Now, in the Shropshire cottage, Alison wondered why a cycle of addiction had begun for Sophie while the others, although just as enthusiastic about trying these new substances, had eventually gone on to college, found careers. Look at Declan in his tailored suit, now a successful man in the city. And Janine, a member of their gang for one summer, who had seemed so troubled with her cutting and weight issues, had gone on to study economics at LSE and was now married. But Sophie—gradually moving away from her old friends, finding new ones, dangerous ones—had taken a different path. A path that would lead to a lonely hotel room and the end of her life.

Alison snapped the laptop shut. It was unbearable to imagine Sophie dying there. The Sophie she used to know. That warm, colorful, laughing girl, dancing in the basement.

TEN

When her phone rang, late in the afternoon, Alison ran to it breathless with expectation. But it wasn't Matt, it was Liz.

"Please, please come to dinner." Her friend sounded frantic. "Simon will pick you up. He's coming from Chester and it won't be a problem. Please. Tonight. Dinner's at eight. Can you be ready at seven?"

Alison looked at her watch. She had less than an hour.

"Liz, I'm not really up for—"

"Darling, I'm rushing out. Have to drop off Jamie. Simon will be there at seven. Don't have to dress up."

"But—"

"Later."

Liz snapped off the phone. Alison groaned. Damn. She was in no mood for a dinner party with Liz and Simon's cluster of middle-class friends, with their talk of property prices and holidays abroad and the amusing antics of all their beautiful children. Still. Liz and Simon were good friends, old friends, she owed them courtesy, at least. She walked upstairs slowly, reluctantly, to dress.

~

Simon arrived at seven exactly. Alison hurried out to the green Jaguar as soon as it pulled to the curb.

"Do you always give dinner parties at the last moment?" she asked. "I barely had time to comb my hair."

Simon looked harassed as he opened the car door for her.

"Was a bit of a rush, Ali. Sorry. You look very nice, though, I must say."

"Thank you."

He drove cautiously out of the village, heading toward the motorway.

"I hope it's not a big party thing," Alison said.

"Lord, no. Just Matt and his wife, Jonathon, and us three."

Alison took a sharp breath.

"What? Matt and Celine?"

"Yes. Celine called today. There's a problem with the father of the twins. He's creating something of a fuss, apparently. Celine flew over from France this morning."

"You don't need me there, Simon, surely?"

He glanced at her face, frowned a little.

"I think Liz's a bit intimidated by Celine. Needs some moral support. And Celine asked for you, too. You know Matt better, don't you? Knew him before?"

Alison said nothing, her mouth dry. She was wearing the same outfit she had worn to the pub with Matt and was irrationally furious with Liz for not telling her that he was coming to dinner. Simon gave the steering wheel a hard tap with the palm of his hand.

"It might be fun," he said. He didn't sound certain.

Alison glanced at his pleasant face. She guessed that he, too, felt intimidated, not by the French wife but by Matt. Though Simon had attended the same high school, two years ahead of them, neither Liz nor Alison could remember him there. One of the invisible teens, not quite nerdy enough for academic honors, not a sportsman either. It was likely that Matt, who had been on the rugby team and an honor student, made Simon nervous. He remembered Matt at school, Simon had said once, remembered him playing rugby.

"He was impressive to watch," Simon said then, a note of envy in his voice. "But he was one of the school A-listers. I don't think he ever spoke to me."

Simon had gained confidence with age and career advancement. He was proud of the outward signs of his success: the large house; the sleek, expensive car. A likable man, among his close friends he showed a sharp competitiveness. As if he believed that those high school years could be wiped out with one stunning tennis match, one crucial game of pool.

"Fun, you think?" Alison said now.

"Why not?"

Alison, after a surge of anxiety, wondered if it was too late to plead sudden illness. If she bent over with nausea, would Simon take her home? No, he would probably drive on, deliver her into the care of his wife. He was a kind man; that's what he would do. *Just brazen it out,* she told herself. *Get through it somehow.*

"Sod it, they must be here already," Simon said as they pulled into the long driveway of the house. Matt's black Citroen was parked on the far side.

"I thought Liz said eight."

"She did. They must've come early. Bugger. I won't have time for a shower."

"You look clean enough."

"Well, thank you, Ali."

In the doorway, Alison pulled back to let Simon go ahead of her. Nerves were jackhammering her breathing. She could hear Liz's voice, could smell garlic and red-wine sauce. The house felt warm and welcoming; Elgar played on the stereo. Liz was making an effort.

Matt, on the sofa, his wife beside him, stood when they entered.

"Simon. Nice to see you again. And Alison. Hello."

He shook Simon's hand and then turned to Alison, leaning to kiss her cheek. She could smell the sharp pine of his aftershave. Convinced that her entire body was trembling visibly, like a taut high wire, Alison pulled away at once and crossed the room to Celine. The Frenchwoman stood so that they could brush cheeks.

"So nice to meet you at last, Alison," she said. "The funeral, it was so busy. And you disappeared!"

Her English was perfect, just the trace of an accent that gave her voice a smoky, midnight quality.

"I was in the kitchen, perhaps. The garden."

"Of course. I hear about you from Matt for many years. I imagine you as—quite different. You were very young, of course. When you were all friends. *Les sauvages*."

She laughed, her eyes bright with amusement.

"We've grown up a bit since then," Alison said. "I expect Matt told you I looked like a punk rocker."

"Not at all. He said you were an artist."

"I was then," Alison said. "Not anymore."

"But that is something that does not change?"

"Not sure," Alison said.

The Frenchwoman wore a simple calf-length skirt and tunic in shades of caramel and cream with a silk scarf perfectly and elegantly knotted at the neck. Her makeup was carefully applied; she wore diamonds in her ears. Alison felt underdressed and unfinished next to her.

Liz hurried in from the kitchen carrying a glass of white wine and handed it to Alison.

"Thanks for coming, Ali. I know it was short notice."

"I am sorry. That is our fault," said Celine.

"Not at all. I'm pleased to be here," Alison said, noting Matt's eyes on her, the strained smile. "Where's Jamie?" she asked, thinking that the presence of the lively six-year-old might be a useful distraction.

"Overnighter with his best friend," Liz said. "He's gone with a bag full of video games. Ah, here's Jonathon."

Jonathon, clean-shaven now, in crisp casual clothes, was greeted at the door by Liz and came smiling into the room.

"The fuzz has gone from that handsome face," Liz said. "Thank God."

"Couldn't quite pull off the Hemingway look I was aiming for," Jonathon said as he greeted them all, shaking hands with the men, kissing the cheeks of the women. He seemed at ease, glad to see his old friends again.

"Something smells wonderful," he said.

"Oh my God, still the greedy guts," Liz said. "Nothing changes."

Jonathon, pretending offense, looked shocked.

"Excuse me. I am recovering from a war wound. I need nourishment."

"You were always recovering from war wounds," Liz said. "Never known anyone so accident-prone. Come on, guys. Let's feed this poor waif. Take your seats."

Alison, seated next to Jonathon, found herself across the table from Matt at dinner. She was aware of his every movement, every comment. She tried to avoid his eyes and noticed that he, too, addressed most of his remarks to the others. She was grateful that the conversation did not directly involve her for most of the meal. Jonathon described the scenes in Syria and the accident that had damaged his leg.

"Caused by a bomb officially, but actually because the idiot driving the jeep ran into a bloody wall. Lost his nerve."

"Was anyone else hurt?" Alison asked.

"Nope. Just me. Always the lucky one."

"They won't send you back there?" Simon asked.

"No. One more surgery, then it's a desk job for me for a while."

"Where?" Alison asked. "London?"

"Europe somewhere. Maybe Brussels. I've requested Paris but, well—"

"Push for Paris," Liz urged. "We could visit."

"I don't actually have much control over the decision. Cross your fingers anyway," Jonathon said.

Later, the talk was about the worrying silence of the twins and the need to get them settled. When Matt spoke to her finally, when he asked her what she remembered of Gary Lewis, Sophie's ex-husband, Alison answered quickly, her eyes moving from his face to that of his wife.

"I remember his yellow hair," she said. "I remember him picking her up a few times on his motorbike. And at the wedding, of course. Not sure I would recognize him today."

"He's claiming all kinds of things," Matt said. "That he sent Sophie money. Says he has a bank statement to prove it. Says she denied him access to the twins. Moved constantly so that he could never find her."

"He's serious, then," Simon said.

"Very. With his history of drug use we thought he wouldn't have a chance—"

"You've mentioned that to your solicitor?" Simon asked.

"Of course. He's claiming he's clean now, but he'll have to undergo tests. And he's thinking of marrying again."

"Oh, dear," Liz said. "That's not going to hurt his case."

"No. That's the problem. We need—" Matt glanced at his wife, then looked around the table.

"We need character witnesses. We have them in France, of course, but reputable, respectable people here would help our case."

"It is true of course that you feel you do not know me," Celine said quietly. "But you do know Matt. For so many years."

Alison exchanged a quick glance with Liz. Liz looked toward Simon as if waiting for him to speak, but Simon said nothing. Nobody said, as they might have done, that they had not seen Matt for years. Matt waited a moment and then said it for them.

"And I know we haven't kept in close touch. The panel doesn't need to know that. But you do know what kind of person I am. Can vouch for my honesty, integrity, whatever."

He wants us to pretend that we've all stayed close, Alison realized. *He wants us to lie.* Simon spoke up then.

"Wish I could help," Simon said. "But I think you were already living abroad when I met Liz. I don't have the same history. I'm sure the others will be happy to speak for you, however."

Matt looked at Simon, surprised. He had not expected that. He turned immediately to Liz.

"Liz?" he asked.

"How would we do this?" she asked. "Swear affidavits? Write letters?"

"I think a letter would be enough at this point," Matt said.

"I could write a letter," Jonathon said. "No problem. But with the surgery coming up, I couldn't make a hearing of any kind. A letter be enough?"

"I think so."

Alison rearranged the cutlery beside her plate, sipped from her wineglass.

"Alison?" Matt said.

She looked into his eyes, noted something new in his look: pleading?

"Yes. Of course," she said, and saw his face open into a smile. Celine, too, smiled at her.

"Thank you," she said. "And thank you, Liz and Jonathon, so much. I think we will make a good case. I have copied photographs of our home to show them how we live."

Alison, immediately curious, was pleased that Liz, perking up like a flower to the sun, asked to see the pictures, and they were passed around the table. Matt and Celine's home was a stone house with a square frontage and a well-kept lawn, surrounded by walls and yew trees. It looked large, if dark. Alison, studying the photographs, felt a strange disappointment. She had imagined that Matt would live in an old French farmhouse or something low and modern with lots of glass. Something unusual. Something with unique character. This was dull and square. It looked like an English vicarage: well built, well maintained, unquestionably middle-class.

"Nice house," Liz said.

"It's good and solid," Matt said. Alison looked up then, and his eyes met hers. There was a glint of amusement in them, and she returned his smile, relaxing finally, leaning back on her chair.

"It's lovely," she said.

Soon afterward, the conversation turned to talk of movies and books and work. After the dessert, as Liz urged them to return to the comfortable armchairs for their coffee, Alison stood and began collecting plates.

"I'll stick these in the dishwasher," she said. "Then I'll have to think about leaving."

"I would help, of course," Jonathon said. "But my battle-scarred status . . ."

"Good try," Liz said.

"I shall help," Celine said.

"No. Please, everyone," Alison said quickly. "I can do it."

Celine followed her to the kitchen anyway, carrying two plates from the dinner table. She placed them on the countertop and turned to Alison.

"Alison," she said, her voice soft. She was so close that Alison could smell the musk of her perfume. "I want to say thank you for helping us. For helping Matt."

"It's fine," Alison said, obscurely uncomfortable. "Glad to do it."

Then Matt was also in the kitchen, balancing a pile of plates, calling to the women to get out of his way.

"Let the man see the dishwasher."

Celine smiled.

"I heard someone say cognac," she said, turning to leave the kitchen. "And I do not drive tonight."

Aware of Matt close behind her, Alison turned on the kitchen taps to rinse the dinner plates.

"I can handle this," she said.

"But I want to help," he murmured. She could feel his warm breath on her neck.

She shivered, edged away, began stacking the dishwasher, keeping her back to him.

"I've been thinking of you all day," he said in a low voice. "I keep remembering that—"

"Shush, please," she said, her heart pounding. "Please."

She glanced toward the living room. The open-plan style of Liz and Simon's house meant that although the others were some distance away, they were easily visible. Right now, the other four were settling into their seats; Simon's voice could be heard offering brandy. A comment, unclear, from Liz, and then Jonathon's warm laugh.

"You didn't mention our drink to Celine, then?" Alison asked quietly.

He waited until she turned around, until she had to look at him.

"It seemed better not to," he said. "I'm not sure anyone else would understand."

Alison swallowed. He stood too close, his eyes so intently on her face.

"I want to spend some time with you while I can," he said. "Don't you want that, too?"

He seemed unaware of the others talking quietly in the other room, unaware of the proximity of his wife, sipping delicately at her cognac. He smiled, then ran a finger along the line of Alison's cheek. Alison pulled away, shocked, and looked again toward the living room. She saw the slow turn of Celine's head, almost a shadow movement. Celine had been looking in their direction, Alison was certain of it.

Later, much later, when Alison was trying to put the pieces of her shattered life back together, she would recall that look between husband and wife. Had she imagined it? Or had they exchanged a nod, a small smile, a few moments of absolute complicity?

Right then, in the kitchen, her concern centered on her friend. Liz had also looked up. Her eyes scanned Alison's face, then moved to Matt's. She looked puzzled, but there was something else in her face Alison couldn't read: Anger? Fear?

Alison turned away abruptly, wanting desperately for Matt to leave the kitchen. He was blocking her exit.

"Matt. Please."

"Meet me for lunch in Shrewsbury," he said. "Friends can do that, can't they? Have lunch?"

"Matt. Not here."

"I'll be there on Tuesday. At noon. The Black Bull, near St. Mary's Square. There's a dining room."

"Stop," she said urgently, cutting him off. "Stop."

She pushed past him, back into the living room. There, she remained standing, struggling to think of fast lies, easy excuses. She felt as if she could not force enough air into her lungs.

"I'm so sorry. I have to leave," she said, reaching for her bag. "The late trains are unreliable."

"Stay the night," Liz said immediately. "Please. We can have breakfast. Talk."

"I can't. I'm sorry."

"You can't?"

"We can drive you home," Matt said, adding quickly, "Where do you live?"

"I can drive you," Jonathon said. "No problem."

"You're all in the opposite direction," she said, not looking at anyone. "No. Don't worry. The train is easy."

"Well, Simon will drop you at the station," Liz said. Simon stood up at once.

~

On the train heading to Shrewsbury, Alison slumped back in the seat, drained. Lunch on Tuesday? Why hadn't she just said no? It was impossible. So strange those minutes in the kitchen. Amazing that even now, so many years later, whenever Matt stood close to her, the air seemed charged, a force field around him that caused her heart to pound, her hands to tremble.

His touch had always done that. Even years ago, when she was still a schoolgirl. She recalled one afternoon in the basement. Sophie had painted Alison's toenails a bright scarlet and had begun to paint her own, her feet resting on a stool, when Matt and Jonathon clattered down the stairs.

Jonathon threw himself down next to Alison, causing the sofa to sag and squeak in protest; Matt sat on the floor, his back resting on the sofa. Both watched Sophie as she applied the polish.

"What's that color called?" Matt asked. "Hell's Fire Red?"

"It's called Sin," Sophie said, looking up, grinning.

"No, it's not. It's called Scarlet Woman," said Alison.

Matt lifted Alison's bare foot and inspected it.

"The foot of a scarlet woman," he said.

The touch sent a shock through her body, a tingle to the ends of her hair and then centered in a dark place between her legs. As Matt leaned back she could feel the cotton of his shirt, soft against her knees. She could not see his face clearly, dared not look, so instead she gazed at the top of his head, the curls and whorls of his untidy hair. She wanted to touch it. She wanted to touch *him*. She was fourteen years old.

She had felt like a teenager again as Matt stood so close to her in the kitchen. Liz had noticed. Had noticed something. Her puzzlement was all over her face. How on earth did people conduct affairs without giving themselves away, when she felt so awkward, so guilty, after one kiss? Clearly Matt had wanted to keep quiet about the fact that he had visited her cottage. How quickly he had asked, *Where do you live?*

I should have made an excuse not to go to dinner, Alison thought. *I should have stayed home, stayed safe and hidden in the cottage.*

ELEVEN

Liz's predictable phone call—she loved dinner-party postmortems—came later than Alison expected the following morning. She answered the phone nervously, expecting difficult questions about the encounter with Matt in the kitchen. Liz wasted no time in asking them.

"So, what was going on in the kitchen last night? What was Matt whispering to you?"

"Well, hello to you, Liz. Thank you for a lovely evening."

"I'm serious. Why was he whispering? What was he saying?"

"He wasn't whispering. Don't be silly."

"Was he making snide comments about the meal? About my house?"

Ah. Thank God. A moment of sweet relief for Alison. Dear solipsistic Liz.

"Of course he wasn't making snide comments. It was nothing. He was saying he'd never met a woman who could properly stack a dishwasher."

"Really?" Liz sounded unconvinced. A beat, then her voice changed. Alison could detect the excitement in it.

"Well, I've got some news," she said. "Confirmed. A girl! Had the scan this morning."

Alison, surprised, gripped the phone.

"You're pregnant? My God. Why didn't you tell me? I had no idea."

"Oh, you know. Sophie and everything. We wanted to be sure. We've had a couple of close calls over the last few years."

Alison knew how badly Liz and Simon wanted another child, remembered their devastation after an early miscarriage two years ago.

"That's wonderful!" she said. "I'm so pleased. A girl! Oh, that's just—"

"I know. Have to think of names. Victorian ones are the best, don't you think? Anyway, I wanted to tell you last night, but we didn't want to say anything in front of everyone. And look, thanks for coming, Ali. I know it was short notice. They hardly gave me time to cook anything. Was it all right? I know chicken is a bit, well, boring. I expect she cooks all kinds of French—"

"It was delicious," Alison said. "Perfect. Did they stay long?"

"No. Jonathon left right after you did. Wasn't it good to see him? Shame about his knee. But Paris? I hope he gets that post. Anyway, I'm glad he came. Made it a bit easier with the odd couple."

"The odd couple? Come on, Liz."

"Well, they are a bit peculiar."

"How are they peculiar?"

"I don't know. Stiff. Cardboard. It's always been difficult to have a normal conversation with him. I feel like he's laughing at me. Maybe he is. But she's even worse. She's very chic, I'll give her that. I loved her shirt. But she's kind of *frozen*. And not because she's French. Something Stepford wife about her. A French Stepford wife."

"Elizabeth, you are a mean, mean woman," Alison said, laughing. "I thought she was nice, actually. Quite charming. Nicer than I expected."

"They're only being nice because they want something from us."

"Liz!"

"It's true. Though Simon's not going to play that game."

"Yes, that surprised me a bit. When he said no to the reference."

"Surprised *you*? I nearly fell off my chair. You know what he noticed? It is odd when you think about it. They never once mentioned Sophie. They talked about her kids and her ex-husband, but they didn't actually talk about her. When Jonathon started to stay something, Matt cut him off. Simon said maybe Matt found it too painful, but I don't think so. They must be thinking about her all the time. I know I am."

"Me too," Alison admitted. "I keep remembering her in high school. So full of life and such fun. All that hair and her crazy clothes and the fake tattoos."

"She was beautiful then," Liz said, sighing. "Beautiful. So, what are you doing today?"

"Not much. Going to walk around the village. Check out the natives."

"You talked to Jake yet? He's called here twice. Why can't he reach you? He said your phone wasn't working. What *is* going on with you two? You haven't—"

"I'll call him, Liz. Don't worry. It's tricky with the time difference and all. I'll call him tonight," Alison said. "Anyway, I better move. Get to the shop before it starts raining again."

An hour later, in the cramped village shop, she waited as the woman in front of her had a long discussion with the assistant behind the counter. The woman used words Alison had rarely heard in California: *horrid, ghastly*. She thought about *ghastly*. What is a ghast? A ghost of some kind? How can heavy traffic be ghastly?

"Toodle-oo," the woman said as she left, and Alison smiled.

Later, as Alison was leaving the shop, someone called to her.

"Would you hold the door, dear?"

Alison turned to find Vivienne Cameron struggling with two large bags of groceries. A box of cornflakes was balanced precariously on top of one of them. Alison grabbed the cereal before it fell.

"Let me help," she said, reaching for one of the bags.

"Oh, it's Alison, isn't it? Are you walking my way?"

They had reached the bottom of the hill, had turned into the shelter's treelined street, before Alison asked the question she most wanted to ask.

"Mrs. Cameron, was Sophie a problem at the shelter?"

Vivienne Cameron gave her a long look.

"Call me Vivienne. Please. Why would you think Sophie was a problem?"

"I suppose because—well, she was a problem everywhere else!"

Vivienne smiled.

"Ah. She did tend to sneak out. The staff tried to keep it from me. They all loved her, you see. But I knew. In the end, I had to ask her to leave. It was disruptive and made the others feel insecure."

"They wanted to sneak out, too?"

"Oh good Lord, no. Last thing they wanted, actually. Too scared. I had to ask Sophie to find somewhere else to live. She agreed to pretend it was her idea and was very sweet about it. Of course I feel guilty now."

"We all feel guilty."

"Wait. Wait a minute," Vivienne said sharply, stopping abruptly in the middle of the sidewalk. She put down the groceries and took a phone from her pocket. Alison, thinking she was taking a call or checking a text message, waited. But Vivienne Cameron glanced down the street and then consulted something on her phone. Alison turned to look.

"Don't stare, Alison. Please. I don't want him to—"

"Who?"

"There's a man standing opposite the shelter. One of our young residents thought she saw her husband outside the house last week. She's been living in a state of terror ever since. Can't eat. Can't sleep."

Vivienne focused on the photograph on her phone.

"Darn. It looks like him. It really looks like him. But I can't be sure."

Alison, pretending to reach down to lift a grocery bag, risked a longer look. A man in a gray business suit stared at the old house. He carried a black umbrella. To Alison, he had the appearance of a middle-management executive.

"He looks like a businessman." she said.

"Oh. And that means what? Some of them *are* businessmen, Alison. Abusers don't come with horns, unfortunately."

Vivienne stood, biting at her lip, still studying her phone.

"I bet that car belongs to him. The black Beemer at the top of the hill."

Alison glanced up the hill toward the little shop. A black BMW was parked opposite.

"Never noticed it," she said.

"I try to keep track of strange cars," Vivienne said. "And I know every motor in this street. Darn."

"You'll call the police?" Alison asked. "If she has a restraining order against him, maybe . . ."

"No. If he's found her, she's not safe. We'll have to move her."

Vivienne stood a moment longer before making up her mind.

"I'll call our handyman, Harry. He can come a few minutes early. If they see a man at the house, it can act as a deterrent. Or they think they've got the wrong place. I don't want him to know she's here."

"It's happened before?"

"Not often, but yes."

Vivienne turned away then, talking into her phone.

"Harry," she said. "We've got a lurker. A nasty one. Can you come down here? Yes, soon."

She turned back to Alison.

"He's on his way," she said. "Let's go."

When they reached the shelter, the man was nowhere to be seen, but Vivienne was careful to check the street before opening the door. Inside, she called to a young woman in the hallway.

"Wendy, stay back from the windows, dear. Just to be sure."

The young woman with the badly bruised face that Alison had noticed on her first visit stood near the corridor to the kitchen. The girl lifted the toddler, now playing on the floor, and held him on her hip, her arms tight around him. The skin around her eyes and cheekbones was now tinged yellow where the bruises were fading. One eye was shadowed with gray, and her mouth was crusted with healing cuts.

She stood frozen, her eyes wide. Alison had never seen such fear on anyone's face.

"He's outside?" the girl whispered.

"I'm not sure it was him," Vivienne said. "But—best stay out of sight. Just in case. Harry will be here in a minute. Deirdre, help me put this stuff in the kitchen."

Deirdre hurried forward, and the two women carried the bags through to the kitchen. The young woman watched them go, pulling the toddler close, her arms a protective shield. She looked again at Alison as the toddler wriggled and arched his back, wanting to be put down again. Alison moved toward them both.

"Hi, little guy," she said. "What's your name?"

He looked at her, blue eyes wide, then hid his face in his mother's shoulder.

"He's Josh." The girl's voice, trembling, was barely above a whisper.

"He's a cutie," Alison said. "I'm Alison. You're Wendy?"

The girl nodded.

"Are you okay?" Alison asked.

"Was it him? Did Vivienne see him?"

"She wasn't sure. But he's gone now. It's okay. You're safe here."

As she looked again at the girl's battered, terrified face, Alison felt her chest tighten with sympathy and asked quietly, "Did he do that to you?"

"Yes. And—other stuff."

"God, how awful. I'm so sorry."

Wendy hugged the toddler again. Alison saw that she was still trembling badly. The child, as if picking up her fear, began to cry.

"Why don't you sit down for a minute," Alison said. "Until you feel better."

"We got to go through to the back."

"I'll come with you. Get you a glass of water."

Alison followed Wendy to a room at the back of the building with two bunk beds. The young woman offered the chair to Alison and then sat on the bottom bunk. She bent her head to kiss the baby's cheek, and as her hair fell forward, caught in a beam of light from the high window, Alison was reminded of Sophie's hair, the same mix of colors and texture: on top a spun gold; underneath where the sun had not touched it, beige, gray.

"Glass of water?" Alison asked. "Maybe a cup of tea?"

"No. It's all right. I'm okay. Sit down."

Alison sat and smiled at the baby. Josh, chewing at a small gray soft toy, once a mouse, cuddled against his mother.

"He's tired," Wendy said. "When he starts chewing at his cuddly, he's ready for a little sleep."

Sure enough his eyes started to droop. Alison studied the round pink cheek, the damp, open mouth. He would be easy to sketch, just a series of curves.

"Like a little angel," she whispered. "He seems happy. He hasn't been much affected by the . . ."

She faltered, unsure of how to continue.

"You don't have to whisper," Wendy said. "No. Josh didn't see anything. Roger's fits were usually late at night, when he'd been drinking."

"He never hurt Josh, then?"

Wendy shook her head. "No. Oh no. It was just me it was aimed at." Wendy's face was serious, a small frown furrowing her forehead.

"He didn't do it at first, you know. Only after Josh was born. Seemed to start something funny in him. I think he was jealous of the baby, to be honest. I said that to Vivienne, and she said it was possible."

"That's when he started to hit you?" Alison asked. "After the baby?"

"He didn't actually hit me the first time. He—well, I suppose he forced himself on me. Josh was really little. About four, five weeks old. He was breastfeeding. Roger had been out drinking with some of his workmates, and he was well away when he got home. Said all the men were talking about going home to shag their wives.

"I had a rough time with Josh. He's got a big head. Well, you can see." She stroked the baby's head gently. "And he really ripped me when he was born. I had a bunch of stitches and stuff. This night . . ." Wendy's voice was a monotone now, as she remembered it, her eyes staring straight ahead, as if watching it on a screen. "Well, when he came in, all loud and drunk, I was breastfeeding Josh, singing to him. Roger stood in the doorway of the bedroom and he said, *Oh, look at the little virgin Madonna with her kid.* And I said, *Shush, you'll wake him up,* and he went mad. He really lost it. He started yelling at me—*Don't shush me, you frigid little bitch*—then he . . ."

She stopped, swallowed. Alison leaned forward and touched her arm gently.

"It's okay. You don't have to talk about it."

"No. It's all right. Then he just pushed himself into me. It really hurt. Josh had dropped off to sleep, and I moved him across the bed a bit, put my arm around him, and I was biting into his little baby blanket to stop from crying out. And Roger was kneeling up there. Banging into me. It was so—ugly. It was horrible. The baby didn't wake up, though. Isn't that amazing? It was quick. But I remember the taste of that blanket in my mouth, the smell of it—milky smell, baby smell. That smell on a blanket makes me sick now. How sad is that?"

She looked over at Alison and gave a small shrug.

"Good grief," said Alison, shivering. "And you didn't have a clue when you first—"

"Met him? No. He's so sort of polished, you know. A bit posh for me. I left school at sixteen and worked in a shop, and he's been to university and everything and has this good job. I couldn't understand why he liked me."

"Because you're so pretty," said Alison. "And nice."

"Oh, I'm not pretty," Wendy said, but she blushed a soft pink. "I was flattered he noticed me. He used to come shopping with me. Help me pick out clothes. I'd never had anybody do that. You know, care what I wore. Not a boyfriend, anyway. He'd pick things off the rack and wait until I tried them on and tell me which ones looked nice. Told me to grow my hair. He didn't like it short."

"And you thought that was good?"

"Oh yes. I thought it meant he really cared about me. Loved me. You know."

Alison sighed.

"What about your family? Could you—"

"Mum died. Just before we got married. She liked Roger. Thought he would look after me. Don't know my dad. He left when I was three."

"So there was nobody you could—"

"My friend at work. I think she guessed. But I didn't tell her everything."

"But you didn't leave him after that first time?"

"Oh no, not right away," Wendy said. "You always think it won't happen again. Everybody says that. Roger was so sorry afterwards. He'd be in tears. He'd actually cry. Swear it was love, you know, that made him do it. Said his emotions were so powerful, that's how much he loved me. Said there was violence and pain in all the big things, birth, death, love. Stuff like that."

"And you believed him?"

"Oh yeah. At first."

"What made you leave?"

Wendy eased Josh onto the bed, settled the sheet around him.

"He was shaking me. Really hard. And slapping me around the head and face." She grimaced at the memory. "And Josh started to cry, calling for me. And he'd just learned how to climb out of his crib. Just toddling around. And I thought, soon he could walk in here and see this. Soon."

"And that was it?"

"Yeah. I think. And Roger really hurt me that time. Hurt me a lot. I'd taken down this number to call for help. It was on telly after one of the soaps. So I called it. And they gave me another number, and then I got this nice woman, and she said they could help me.

"I'm really glad to be here. I'm lucky." Wendy stopped, inspected Alison's face. "You look okay, though," she said. "For a new girl."

New girl? Alison realized that Wendy assumed she was a new resident. "Oh, wait. No. I'm not living here. I was just helping Vivienne. I'm staying in the village. The little cottage at the end of the lane."

"Oh." Wendy looked disappointed. "I thought you— Your family around here?"

"No. My dad's in Scotland. I—"

"I love Scotland! I went there once."

"It's beautiful. I've got friends in Worcestershire. I came to ask about someone who stayed here for a while. Sophie."

Wendy's eyes widened.

"Sophie? I heard about her."

"I'm trying to find out what happened to her."

"Oh, I heard a lot of stories. When I first came here this girl I shared with, she's gone now, she couldn't stop talking about Sophie. Said she had a millionaire boyfriend. He'd pick her up round the corner in this big car and take her to posh hotels."

"A millionaire?" Alison said. "I don't think so."

"No, well, I bet it weren't true. You wouldn't believe the stuff they say around here."

"I can imagine," Alison said. She thought of the women trapped here, in this claustrophobic place. Of course they would gossip, imagine things, entertain each other.

"I said to her," Wendy continued, "if he was a millionaire, why didn't he buy Sophie a penthouse? Get her a bodyguard? Buy some clothes for her kids? None of the kids here have enough clothes. Josh is wearing pants from the donation basket, and they're too small. Why didn't he buy her stuff?"

"Good point," Alison said.

"She did have a boyfriend, though," Wendy said, dropping her voice. "I heard that from a lot of people. She used to meet him. Must have been married or why didn't he protect her?"

"Well, she might have had a boyfriend, but he wasn't a millionaire, I'm pretty certain of that," Alison said.

"She died, didn't she?" Wendy asked. "Killed herself."

"We're not sure if she killed herself. But yes, she died."

Alison heard Vivienne's voice in the corridor.

"I better go," she said, standing. "I probably shouldn't be back here."

"Thanks for, you know, talking to me."

"Take care," Alison said. "And don't worry. You're safe now."

When Alison reached the hallway, Vivienne Cameron was struggling into her coat.

"Alison. So there you are."

"I was with Wendy. Will she be okay?" Alison asked. "She's so scared."

"Yes. He was rather scary from all accounts. We'll have to move her again, just to be sure," Vivienne said. "Goodness knows where. Everywhere is jammed full." She turned to the front door. "Come along, Alison, we can leave together. Deirdre, lock the door behind us, dear."

TWELVE

Back at the cottage, Alison called Liz.

"You know all those boys' clothes you don't need, now that you know you're having a girl? Will you stuff some in a bag and bring them over next time you come?"

Liz, uncharacteristically silent for a few moments, seemed unable to formulate one question.

"Why?" she asked finally.

"That shelter. Where Sophie was. Those poor kids need clothes. And toys."

She described Wendy and her little boy.

"He's about eighteen months old, I think. I saw a couple of other toddlers, as well."

"Oh, okay. No problem," Liz said. "What about women's clothes? I bet those women ran off with nothing to wear."

"Maybe. But they don't need designer—"

"They must need sweaters. Come on, it's getting cold. I'll bring some. I've got dozens. And nightgowns I've never worn. I can drop the stuff off on Tuesday. We can catch up a bit."

Tuesday? Matt had said Tuesday. In Shrewsbury. She had not said yes. Even so.

"No. You don't have to come right away. Drive all the way over here."

"It's not far! We can go to the pub for lunch."

"Not Tuesday," Alison said, desperate now. "I've made an appointment to have my hair cut. And join the library in Shrewsbury. How about Wednesday? Wednesday would be good."

"Okay," Liz said, sounding puzzled. "Wednesday. Doesn't matter to me. And Ali, will you please, please call Jake. He's called here again. He's getting very pissed off. He said it was important."

~

"My wife! Well, glory be," Jake said when she called him later. "It's a miracle!"

"Sorry about my phone. I—"

"Well, I am just happy to hear your voice. I'd almost forgotten the sound of it. You decided when you're coming home?"

"No, not quite yet," Alison said. "I'll know soon."

"How soon?"

"Very soon."

"Well, I sure hope so because that bed feels very cold and empty without you in it."

"I know."

"So you going to call Marcus? He is driving me nuts. He's called here a dozen times. Yesterday he was actually *hissing*."

Jake, always an excellent mimic, imitated Marcus's voice: *This is most unsatisfactory. Alison's absence is . . .*

Alison laughed out loud.

"Stop it! You sound just like him."

"Look, the guy's an ass," Jake said. "I get that. But he's your boss. It's your job, sweetheart."

"I know, I know. It's just, well, never mind. We'll talk about it another time."

Jake seemed to hesitate, his voice quieter than usual.

"You are one strange gal, Alison. You got any idea what you're doing over there?"

"Not entirely."

"Figured out what you want?"

"Honestly?" she said. "No. But I think I know better what I don't want."

"And that is?" he asked, sharper now.

"Hard to explain on the phone."

"Right. Well, I want to talk to you about that. Don't you think, seeing as you are my wife, and we are, in fact, married, that maybe we should talk face-to-face? Talk properly?"

"Yes," she said. "Perhaps. But—"

"Then I'll come there."

She held the phone away for a moment, the room seemed to be tilting; she was dizzy with surprise.

"You will come here?" she repeated slowly.

"Yes. Meeting with the McCourt Group in London. Lindsay was going to handle it, but he'll trade places for sure."

"Well," she said, stunned. "I hadn't expected—"

"No. I guess not. And God knows, I don't want to put you out at all. Disturb your little UK routine or whatever. But we do need to talk, sweetheart. What's the address out there in the country?"

She stiffened.

"You don't have to come here," Alison said. "We can talk on the phone. Or when I come home."

"Alison, I've already discussed this with Lindsay. I'm coming."

She knew well that stubborn note in his voice. He would not be deflected.

"Okay, but this village is miles from anywhere. I'll meet you in London."

"Fine. I'll book a decent room at Brown's. I'll e-mail details. Around a week. Time enough for you to do your thinking. Okay?"

"A week?"

"Yep. I'll text you details. And for Christ's sake, let Marcus know what the hell you're doing. Okay? I miss you, honey. See you soon."

The phone clicked. She stared at it. Jake to come to England? She was not ready. Not yet.

She moved to the window. She could see fast-moving clouds, a storm brewing. She listened to the wind, then the sound of a train moving toward Shrewsbury. It had a soft shuffling sound, not the evocative rhythmic beat of the steam trains that made men in old movies lift their heads and dream.

She shivered. There was nobody out there watching her, she knew that, but she drew the curtains anyway, shutting out the early damp darkness. In California, the sun would be bright, a clear light. Jake had been in his office, at his desk, when they talked. She had heard the tap of his computer keys. He had probably been there for hours.

His alert mornings used to amaze her. How could anyone rise like that, so eager to embrace the problems of the day? Since the promise of promotion he had been starting work even earlier, leaving later, spending hours in his home office on weekends He loved his job, no question. He had assumed, always, that she loved hers equally. Well, how could he think differently when she had never told him the truth? He heard her sighs and complaints about Marcus, but they had never properly discussed the deeper reasons for her discontent. *We have not discussed anything much for some time,* she thought. *Nothing that matters.* So little time together. And now he was making plans for a trip. Now he wanted to talk. The irony of it. She had pleaded with him to take time off, and she had made reservations in Maui and in Big Bear only to have to cancel them at the last minute because of his work commitments. She would have loved, just months ago, to join him on a London trip. And now? It was the worst possible time.

He had said that Marcus was angry. Well, of course he was. He was probably ready to fire her, and who could blame him? She turned on her laptop, read the news headlines and a recent movie review—both so removed from her Shropshire reality that she felt she was reading news transmitted from another planet—then she checked e-mails. Jake was right: five increasingly irate messages from Marcus.

Alison sat back, thinking. She had made the decision. It was unfair to leave the agency hanging like this. She wrote a short note to Marcus, copied to Human Resources, saying that she would not be returning to her job at the agency. The vacation time she was owed would serve as notice. She did not expect to be paid for the extra days. She hesitated a moment when the e-mail was written. Marcus would be furious. He would likely refuse to give her a reference. Still, a small price to pay. She hit "Send" and immediately felt light-headed with relief. Done. At last. No more advertising. No more jingles and catchy slogans and smoke and mirrors and slippery deceit. Ever.

~

In bed that night, Alison, unable to sleep or read, pulled the duvet up to her chin and gazed into the darkness. A light rain tapped the window. The curtains were thin. Her mother would have lined them, pulling out the old Singer sewing machine, humming as she worked. The women's shelter would be drafty in the winter. Had Sophie been cold there, with her twins?

Both losses, her mother and Sophie, were very different and far apart. And yet—*the rain is full of ghosts tonight.*

Drifting off to sleep, her thoughts melding into unclear patterns, Alison realized that with the finality of giving up her job, something had definitely changed. She felt different, she decided, as her body relaxed into the warm bed. It was as if she had taken off a mask and returned, barefaced, to the world. She did not have to pretend to value a career she did not want, or pretend to enjoy occasions she hated. She was free to do exactly as she pleased. The concept of this freedom should be exhilarating, and yet, and yet—the static state of her marriage, the confusion over her feelings for Matt. She felt as if she were standing at a crossroads. The road looked rocky and windswept in both directions.

THIRTEEN

A few minutes after midday on Tuesday, Alison entered the restaurant attached to The Black Bull in Shrewsbury. The contemporary dining room, a popular addition to the Georgian landmark hotel and known for its Mediterranean-style food, appeared crowded with professional types and tourists. She saw Matt at once, at a table near the window, and he stood as she crossed the room.

"It's good to see you," he said, holding her shoulders, kissing her cheek. "I'm so glad you came."

Her face warm, Alison sat down, fiddled with the napkin, and then looked across at him. When his eyes met hers, she felt the same strange softening and looked away at once, searching for a waiter, longing for a glass of wine, anything that might ease the trembling in her limbs. It had been a rushed morning. She had dithered in a tense funk before deciding that yes, she would meet him, it was just lunch, what harm could there possibly be in that? Then the country bus ride to Shrewsbury, a ride that seemed to take forever. Alison felt flustered and uncomfortable and wondered if her skin was a bright, unbecoming pink.

"White wine?" Matt asked. He seemed amused at her discomfort. "You look rather warm."

"Please."

When the food was ordered, the glass of wine in front of her, Alison took a long gulp, looked at him, and, aiming for a light and friendly tone, said, "So. How are you? What's happening with the adoption?"

"Moving forward," Matt said. "Rather more complicated since Lewis turned up."

"I bet. Amazing how he just popped up like a genie from a bottle. How are the little girls?"

"Lily seems fine. She's lively, a tomboy. Rosie is still worryingly quiet. She talks to her twin, that's about all."

"Lily and Rosie," Alison repeated. "I love their names."

"Lillian and Rosalind, formally."

"Do they have a secret language and signals, like twins are supposed to do?"

"They might. They whisper." He laughed. "They're very sweet. Really."

"So what happens next?"

"The hearing with the panel. Thursday the fifteenth. In Worcester. You'll still be here?"

His face serious now. The hearing was clearly worrying him.

"I could be. Do your—what are we? References? Do we need to attend?"

"Yes, we'll need you there, if at all possible. They might want to question you. Could you have your written statement in by then? I think the solicitor is sending you a letter."

"Of course," Alison said, wondering what on earth she would say.

"They're essential, I'm afraid. And . . ." He paused. "If Liz is busy and thinks she can't make it, could you try to persuade her?"

"Do my best. I suppose Liz's statement might carry more weight than mine? Living in the community and all. A parent herself."

"Possibly. I was hoping that Simon . . . Well, it's his decision, of course." He paused to allow the waiter to place the cold salmon salads in front of them. "Your opinion will also carry weight. You've known me nearly all of my life. We were next-door neighbors. You knew Sophie well. You remember that hoodlum husband and his drug abuse and how he left her. You know what Sophie would have wanted."

Alison realized that, indirectly, he was telling her what she must say.

"What Sophie would have wanted?" she said. "I'm not sure—"

"I think it's important that someone speaks for her," he said. "You're the perfect person to do it."

She thought about that. *Am I?* The perfect person, perhaps, to understand the old Sophie. But how well did she know the young woman who loved her two small children with all her heart and yet had a sideline in dealing cocaine? A woman with addictions and problems who hid from criminals who wanted to hurt her? That was not the Sophie she knew. Or was it? The old Sophie had been a magnet for trouble, too.

"You seem anxious about it," she said now to Matt.

"I am. I'm not at all sure of the outcome."

"Is Celine anxious, too?"

Alison, deliberately saying his wife's name aloud as a stubborn reminder, watched his face. His expression did not alter.

"Celine's quite convinced that we'll get custody," he said. "She seems to think that because I'm a professor and Gary Lewis manages a supermarket the panel will automatically rule in our favor. Consider us superior in some way."

The smug self-deception of the French bourgeoisie, Alison thought but did not say.

"She's sure about the adoption? She wants a family?"

"God, yes. It's what she's always wanted, but, well, it's not possible for us."

So Liz had been right. Curious, Alison looked up from her plate.

"Celine needed surgery a few years ago," he explained. "Made childbirth impossible. Anyway, what about you? No plans for children?"

"One day. Yes. We both want them. We just haven't discussed it recently. The girls will have a charmed life in France, I imagine."

"They will indeed. Celine's already decorated their room. Arranged for new furniture."

"You'll stay in the same house, though?"

"Yes. That house has been in Celine's family for generations. The French don't buy and sell with the same frequency as the Brits or Americans."

Family money, family property, Alison thought. If Matt had been right about earning a pittance, then their obvious wealth must come from Celine and her family.

"Lucky girls to be adopted into that," she said.

"They'll be spoiled, I expect. Celine loves buying them clothes. God knows how many dresses and things they have now."

"That's sweet," Alison said, trying to sound as if she meant it.

"Lily doesn't think so."

"She's the tomboy?"

"Yes. She screamed like a banshee when Celine wanted her to wear something new. Pulled all the lacy stuff around the neck right off. Rosie likes dressing up. Admires herself in the mirror. Has her hair brushed."

Alison could see the picture clearly: Celine brushing the hair of the little dressed-up girl. *Celine's dolls,* she thought, and felt a strange chill.

"Well, let's hope it works out for you," she said, her voice too bright, raising her glass. "Here's to the adoption."

He touched glasses with her but did not smile. They ate in silence for a minute or two. The salmon, poached in something sharp and citrus, tasted acidic, and Alison, struggling to relax, found that Matt's eyes were too often on her face, so that she took tiny bites of the food, sipped frequently at the wine.

"So what are you finding to do in the village?" he asked after a while. "Besides visit the pub?"

She laughed.

"I try to limit the pub visits," she said. "Had an odd experience at the women's shelter. This girl—"

"The shelter?" he interrupted. "What were you doing there?"

"I wanted to talk about Sophie. Met another young woman hiding there."

Matt put down his fork and regarded her seriously.

"Alison, don't go digging through Sophie's life. Please. You'll be very disappointed."

"I'm not *digging through*," she said. "Why? What do you mean *disappointed*?"

"Oh—drugs. Evictions. Toxic relationships. You know all that already. This gossip—it won't help."

"I didn't gossip. Didn't talk about Sophie in the end."

He leaned back in his chair.

"Okay. So tell me what it's like in the wild world of advertising."

"What it *was* like. I gave up my job last night."

"You did? Why?"

"I decided I'd prefer to work in a salt mine."

Wanting to entertain him, she described her first days at the agency and some of her earliest attempts at jingles, exaggerating the embarrassing results.

"I rhyme words differently," she said. "That doesn't help."

"Of course you do. You're a Brit. So, what happened to the painting, the drawing you used to do? Will you go back to that?"

"Not good enough. I learned that at Bristol. I was well outclassed. I love the theory of art, the joy of looking at it, appreciating it. The practice? I'm not as good as I want to be."

"I'm sure that's not true."

When the meal was finally finished, the plates removed, the dessert menu refused, she looked up to find Matt's eyes, intent, serious, on her face.

"It's just so good to see you again," he said, reaching for her hand across the table.

"You too."

He held her hand for a moment, and then, surprising her, he lifted it to his face and kissed the inside of her wrist. A gentle, damp kiss, his tongue curled against the soft and sensitive flesh.

Alison felt a tingling pulse run through her entire body and took a fast inward breath before pulling her hand away. Matt smiled and moved his chair back.

"We should go," he said.

Alison was ahead of him, had almost reached the door of the restaurant, when Matt caught her by the shoulders, pressed her back against him.

"Wait," he said.

Startled, she looked out into the street and understood the reason for the urgency in his voice: she saw Ronnie, head down, slouching slowly past the restaurant. Unkempt in a black T-shirt, his hair long and uncombed, wearing no jacket on this cool, autumn day, he stared at the ground as he walked, vacant, oblivious. He looked so lost, so sad, that Alison instinctively moved forward, wanting to call out to him. Matt tightened his grip on her shoulder.

"No, Alison," he said.

"But he looks so—"

"I know. But he's angry at me. He'll be even angrier if he sees us. He won't understand."

Held like that, pressed against him, as if caught in an illicit tryst, as if in danger, she was aware of her heart thumping hard and wondered if Matt could feel her trembling.

"Poor guy," she whispered.

Ronnie paused on the sidewalk, searched for something in his pocket, seemed reassured when he located it, then looked up at the sky. A strange moment then, as his face lifted, as if he were praying. Alison, on a surge of sympathy for him, tugged open the restaurant door.

"Ronnie," she called. He stopped, appeared confused as he looked around. Then he saw her.

"Ali," he said. The smile began and then faded at once as he registered Matt's hand on her arm, pulling her back.

He pushed past her, straight toward Matt.

"What the fuck are you doing?" he asked, his voice shaking with anger. "What the fuck do you think you're doing?"

Matt took a step backward, but Ronnie—heavier, taller, and propelled by fury—grabbed the lapels of Matt's leather jacket and within seconds had him pressed against the wall inside the entrance of the restaurant. Alison saw that Matt's shock had been replaced by a dark rage. His eyes burned with it. He tried to push Ronnie away, and Alison watched, horrified, as the two men struggled, locked in a clumsy ballet. The air felt scorched, as if they could annihilate each other, as if this was their intention. The idea flashed in Alison's head that serious damage could be done if someone didn't intervene.

"Stop it!" she cried.

Two waiters, both slight, wiry but apparently strong, were there in seconds, pulling Ronnie away. Alison tugged at his T-shirt.

"Ronnie, for God's sake. Stop it. Please."

He looked at her then. Anger blazed in his eyes for a moment longer, and then it was gone. He smelled musty: unwashed clothes, tobacco, old sweat.

"Outside," the older waiter said.

Alison pulled Ronnie away, holding tight to his arm until they were outside the restaurant. Matt remained inside; she could hear him apologizing to the staff.

"This is crazy, Ronnie," she said. "What's the matter with you?"

"Him. He's the matter with me. Him and his smarmy ways."

"What's he done to make you so angry? He loved Sophie, too, you know. He's grieving, just like you are. Just like I am."

"Really? So where was he when she needed help? When she was in trouble? When she was fucking homeless. Pissing around in France, that's where."

"Same goes for me, Ronnie. Where was I? Where was Liz?"

"And where was I?" he said. "Is that what you want to say? I tried to help her, Ali. I did every fucking thing I could."

"I know. I know you did."

She kept her hand on his arm, squeezed gently. Matt, talking over his shoulder to the manager, was emerging from the restaurant.

"Go now, Ronnie. Please," she whispered. "Please. I'll call you later."

He walked away, unsteadily. He was drunk, she realized now. Unbalanced, his gait was all over the place. Pedestrians passing by him moved aside, giving him a wide berth as he made his stumbling way down the busy town street.

"He's in bad shape," Matt said, coming to stand beside her and watching as Ronnie moved farther down the cobbled hill, turning finally into one of Shrewsbury's shuts, a medieval passageway that led to the high street. "He looks dreadful."

She turned to him.

"He's not really angry at you. It's because he misses Sophie. He wants someone to blame. He's just angry she's dead."

"I don't blame him for hating me. I should have done more for her. I know that now." He rubbed at his upper arm and shoulder where Ronnie had pinned him to the wall. "I tried, Alison. She wouldn't listen to me, to anyone."

"I know that. So does he. Really."

"I suspect he's angry at himself. Feels guilty. He probably supplied her. And he started her on drugs originally."

"No. That's not true," Alison began, then stopped, biting her lip. It wouldn't help Matt to know now, when it was too late, that the reverse was true, that Sophie had been the supplier.

"No. Ronnie's not a dealer," she said. "Never was. And it was Declan who first got hold of weed and ecstasy. Remember? In the basement? He had the contacts in the old days. Ronnie never did."

Her bus stop was in the opposite direction. She turned toward it.

"I should get my bus."

"I can drive you."

She shook her head, not trusting herself. Her body had already proved itself unreliable.

"It's okay. The bus is fine."

"Isn't it slow?"

"A bit. But I like it. It goes through a lot of lovely countryside."

"If you're sure? I'll walk with you to the stop."

No other passengers waited there. The wind had picked up and was lifting trash from the overfilled bin and scattering it all over the street. Alison buttoned her coat.

"Look, why don't I just drive you home?" Matt said. "I won't come in. Just drop you outside your cottage. It's cold. The wind is cold."

She hesitated for only a moment.

"Where are you parked?" she asked.

~

At the cottage, he walked with her to the front door and waited for her to open it. When she had done so and turned to him, her smile in place, he reached into the inside pocket of his jacket and pulled out a paperback book. It was a collection of Neruda poems.

"Before I left for Oxford," he said, "we were talking about Neruda, and I wanted to give you this. But somehow, I don't know why—I just didn't. So, here it is now. It was still in my old room at home."

She took the book in both hands, looked at the cover.

"Matt, that's lovely. Thank you."

She placed the book and her bag on the hall table, turned back to him, unsure now. She was touched by the gift, unnerved by his closeness. Then, slowly, he reached for her, pushing her gently inside the cottage. The door clicked shut behind them.

He kissed her for a long time, his hands in her hair. Pressed against him, Alison could feel his erection, hard against her.

"I feel like a schoolboy again," he murmured.

His hands moved down her body, holding her close, and, unthinking, she held tighter. When he reached under her sweater, she felt his palm against the bare flesh of her back, warm, as if when he removed it, the imprint would remain, branding her. At his touch on her breast she registered a shimmer of half-remembered dreams: this is what she had imagined as a sleepless teenager, as a young woman in college, this boy, this man, here, his arms around her. It felt unreal. She was pressed against the wall, uncomfortable. She wanted him now, wanted to lead him, however stumbling and awkward, up the stairs, into the bedroom. Surely it was the only possible next step?

She was about to say so when a sound, so unexpected and incongruous, filled the small hallway. It was the French national anthem, playing on his cell phone.

Alison moved away at once. Matt reached into his pocket for his phone, read the caller's number, then snapped the phone onto "Decline."

"Sorry," he said.

Alison stared at him, the mood shattered.

"It actually played 'La Marseillaise'? That's a bit *camp*, isn't it?"

"Celine chose it. A joke."

He reached for her again, but her desire had faded, leaving only a deep embarrassment. Celine's name said aloud right then, the mention of a joke between them, had cooled the air.

"You should leave, Matt."

He moved away.

"I'll call," he said. "Soon. Alison—I—"

"Bye."

She waved from the door as his car pulled away, then she turned back into a cottage that now felt cold, empty, too quiet. *Is this how it will be,* she asked herself as she switched on the kettle to make tea. *Is this how we will conduct our grand affair? With furtive fumbling against hard walls and the interruption of campy ringtones?*

A seeping uneasiness then, a nausea she knew was caused by her residual concern for Ronnie and the awkward and distressing scene at the restaurant, but also, unmistakably, caused by guilt. She had betrayed Jake most certainly. She could not deny it now. Where was the line between fidelity and betrayal? A kiss? The touch of a hand on breast and body? She would have led Matt willingly, happily, up those stairs if the phone had not interrupted them. She should feel shame, she told herself, and she did, but overriding that, she felt a confusing excitement. Matt. The boy she had loved so many years of her life, pressed against her, excited by her. *I feel like a schoolboy again,* he had said. And, for just a few minutes—before the ringing of the phone brought reality and the outside world into that dim hallway—she had felt like a schoolgirl.

~

That night in bed she opened the book of Neruda poems and read the inscription on the flyleaf.

Don't forget me. I won't forget you. Matt.

He said he had meant to give her the book the day he left for Oxford. She remembered that day clearly. She had tracked him down in the late afternoon, found him lying on the worn leather couch in the basement.

"Last weekend here," he said.

"You don't sound sorry," Alison said, moving to the fridge to help herself to a soda.

"I'm not."

"Oxford might be harder than you think."

"Everything is harder than you think."

"You nervous?" she asked, soda in hand, snuggling down into the old floral armchair. "About Oxford?"

"Not the work. Other stuff."

He looked up at a clattering on the stairs, and Sophie appeared, heading straight for the fridge. She had dyed her fair hair dark at the roots, though it was still blonde at the tips, and she wore tight jeans, leather boots, and was braless under a tiny black tank top. One slender arm sported a tattoo of a bluebird.

"You drink all the beers, bro?"

"A couple left. Bottles."

"Fuck," said Sophie. "Cans are better. For the bike."

"Forget it," said a male voice from the top of the stairs. "Let's go."

Sophie grabbed a couple of beers anyway and raced up the stairs.

"How you doing, Ali?" she called over her shoulder. "Decide where you're going next year?"

"Bristol. Study art."

"Cool."

Matt watched his sister's departure, his eyes dark. Alison knew there was no point in asking where Sophie planned to go to college. She was failing in school. Liz, in the same classes, had reported that Sophie, despite being in the gifted tier and ahead of her peers, had inexplicably failed her math and science A levels.

"The assistant head said to her, *Sophie Stuart, are you trying to fail on purpose?* I mean, it's so weird. She could pass those exams in her sleep."

"Maybe she doesn't want to go to college just yet?"

"Well, she could do a gap year for God's sake. And she's skipping school all the time. Why is she doing that? She's crazy."

Alison wondered about this as Sophie raced back upstairs, calling to the boy who waited at the top.

"That the same guy Sophie was with at the barbecue?" Alison asked Matt, as the sound of a motorcycle drifted down to the basement. "The one with the short yellow hair? Didn't get a look at him."

"Who knows," he said. "They all look the same."

"Is he the reason she's skipping school? Is that why you don't like him?"

"Not just him. She is, as the parents say, going off the rails. Veering off them at speed."

"She'll get back on track," Alison said.

"Don't say *track*," Matt said.

"What?" Alison felt a cold shiver. "She's not using—"

"No," he said. "Not yet."

Not yet.

He did something strange then, something so un-Mattlike, that years later she could remember exactly how he looked. He walked to the fridge, reached in for a bottle of beer, and slammed the fridge shut. Then, he punched it hard, with the beer bottle still in his fist. The glass smashed, beer spouting up like a fountain. There was a dent where his fist had hit the door.

"Fuck," he said. "Fuck it."

He looked, stunned, at his bleeding hand, and Alison rushed to him, grabbing a paper towel and holding it to the cut. The smell of beer filled the room. It had soaked his shirt. His hand was red and already beginning to swell. She glanced up at him and saw that he had tears in his eyes.

"Hope nothing's broken," she said.

"I don't break."

He was struggling with the makeshift bandage and Alison reached to help him, wrapping the paper towel carefully, then looked up at his face.

"What's up, Matt?" she asked gently.

He took a breath, seemed to waver for a moment.

"Long story. Improbable. Impossible."

"I've got time. Imagination."

He breathed out a sigh.

"Ah," he said. "Nothing. Nothing."

~

When she left, sometime later, Alison passed Sophie on the stairs. Sophie's face was flushed, her hair damp in wisps around her face.

"He still down there?"

"Yep."

Sophie clattered down, her wedge sandals scuffing against the wood. Alison, blinded by the sun, had reached the street before she realized she had forgotten her sunglasses. The basement, always dim, looked shadowy after her brief exit into sunlight. From the top of the stairs she could make out the figures of Sophie and Matt at the far end of the room. She paused for a moment, watching them. Sophie was inspecting Matt's injured hand. She lifted his hand in both of her own and made a joking gesture of kissing it better. Alison smiled at this and then jumped, startled by the crash of the front door, the dropping of bags, and Mrs. Stuart's piercing voice.

"What are you doing here, girl?" Thelma Stuart asked.

"I left my sun—"

"Why do you all think you can just walk into somebody's house without warning, without invitation? Do you think you have—"

From her vantage point on the stairs, Alison was able to see both Matt and Sophie as, heads lifting, they stiffened at the sound of their mother's voice. Matt turned away; Sophie stood quite still, frozen in place.

"Never mind. I'll get them later," Alison said, turning fast, brushing past Mrs. Stuart, unable to look at the woman's face, before hurrying to the calm and safety of her own home.

FOURTEEN

Good grief. What a miserable-looking place. Doesn't it make you think of the Bates Motel?" Liz asked, staring at the women's shelter. She had arrived just before noon with two boxes of the promised clothes and a bonus box of toys. Alison, looking with Liz at the forbidding building, wondered if she should have warned Vivienne that they were coming. Liz had opened the trunk, was pulling at one of the boxes.

"Don't you dare lift anything," Alison said. "I'll go knock. Wait here."

"Oh, for God's sake. You're worse than Simon. I'm pregnant, not a bloody invalid," Liz said, but she waited nevertheless, watching.

Vivienne looked surprised to see Alison on the step. Alison explained about the clothes and toys.

"I don't know if you accept . . . ," she said.

"We accept everything we're offered, Alison," Vivienne said. "And thank you."

"Could you help me with them? Liz is pregnant. Don't want her lifting—"

"Of course," Vivienne said. She shook hands with Liz, thanked her, and within minutes the boxes were inside the hallway, and Vivienne was waving from the door. Liz, craning her neck to see inside the house, pulled a face as the door was firmly shut.

"What a depressing place. God. Hate to think of Soph there."

"So do I. But where else could she go? Her mother? Come on."

"I know. I wish . . . ," Liz began, then made a *tsssk* sound, shaking her head. "Anyway, let's have lunch."

In the pub, Alison led Liz to a table by the French windows. Here, a soft breeze wafted through the rooms, lifting the edges of the curtains, rustling a newspaper lying open on one of the bench seats. At the bar, she ordered them both sandwiches as a group of rowdy Australian hikers entered, pressing up to the counter. They were followed by a young couple and a number of single men. When Alison returned to Liz, with drinks and food, the place was crowded.

"Quite the little social scene," Liz said. "Nice atmosphere."

"Isn't it? Real pub, too. Proper food. Fresh."

Liz sipped her orange juice.

"God, that shelter place. Those poor women."

"I know."

"Why *was* Sophie there? Did you find out?"

"Some hoodlums beat her up, I think."

"Drug related," Liz said.

"Looks like. Someone told me she used to sneak out to meet a boyfriend. I'm guessing she was meeting her dealer."

"Probably. Oh, that girl. Why didn't she just . . . Well, I suppose she tried to get clean."

"Addiction, Liz. Not easy."

"I know that."

Liz took a bite of her sandwich, a gulp of her juice, then asked, "So, Ali, what's happening with Jake? Did you talk? Why couldn't he reach you?"

Alison didn't know how to answer.

"We did talk. He's coming to the UK next week," she said after a moment.

Liz regarded her, eyes puzzled.

"That's good, isn't it?"

"Not really. I'm not ready yet."

"You're not *ready*? He misses you. He wants you home."

"I know."

"So? Will you go back with him next week?"

"Not sure."

"Why not? What's going on, Ali?"

"Oh God, Liz. You have no idea how confused I am."

"But what's happened? What's changed?"

Alison looked away, shaking her head.

"It doesn't make a lot of sense, but I finally realized I'm living a life I hate."

"What's wrong with your life? You love California, don't you? You're doing well. You've got a good marriage. Jake loves you. He acts like he does."

"Yes. Well, he loves some version of me. I'm not sure it's the real one. The professional woman who wears the right clothes to corporate functions? That's not me."

"But he loved you before all that," Liz said. She thought for a moment and then asked in a quiet voice, "The big question is—do you love him?"

"I do. Yes, I think I do," Alison said. "I'm just not sure it's enough."

"It has to be enough," Liz said. "There's nothing else that matters."

"True. Could be that I don't want to be . . . that person. Maybe it'll be different now that I'm not."

"What person?" Liz asked, sounding bewildered.

"That Executive Wife person. The sharp advertising person. I really, really hate the presentations, the getting up in front of the client like a performing monkey and lying through my teeth."

"Well, you always did hate being the center of attention. Remember at Cross Street primary when you were a shepherd in the holiday pageant and pulled your hood so far down over your face you couldn't see anything, and you tripped over the baby Jesus in the manger and went flying."

Liz laughed merrily at the memory.

"Oh, fine for you to laugh, Miz Liz. You just had to sit there and be the Virgin." Alison bit her lip. "It's not that. It's the fake enthusiasm and selling the client some false, fabricated idea so they can sell it to consumers, and it's all based on lies and smoke and mirrors. It's just a slippery form of deception."

"So, don't do it. Do something else."

"I wish I knew what. I just gave up my job. Sent Marcus an e-mail."

Liz put down her drink, sat back on the padded seat, her mouth a small circle of surprise.

"You're kidding me? Just gave notice?"

"Yep. Have to find something else."

"Well, you will," Liz said firmly. "You're smart. You love art, don't you? Design?"

"Not much help when it comes to career choices." Alison sighed. "God, Liz—my head's all worms and black holes. Total confusion."

"Take more time, then. Wait till you're sure. It's not like Jake can't support you while you look around."

"Jake supporting me isn't the answer," Alison said, then stopped, aware that she was saying too much. She stood. "I'll get you another drink. Orange juice?"

"Juice would be great. And bring me back one of those sexy Aussies from the bar," Liz said, eyeing the hikers.

"Down, girl. You're a respectable married woman. And pregnant."

When Alison returned with their drinks, she smiled at her friend.

"The Aussies all have previous engagements. Drink your juice and behave."

"It's definitely the hormones, you know. I was like this when I was pregnant with Jamie. I wanted to bonk every fit male in sight. I would not throw that tall, fair one out of bed for starters."

"You wouldn't—I mean, actually?"

Liz looked at her and laughed.

"No! Not in real life. Just in my head."

"You've never?"

"Been unfaithful? Nope. Of course not. Nor has Simon. Well, I don't think so. No. He would never . . . Why? Have you?"

"No, not me," Alison said, lifting her wineglass to hide her warm face. She could not look at Liz. "Anyway, I hope Simon is benefiting from these hormonal surges."

"Naturally. He gets a bit confused by the mood swings. And the desire for macaroni cheese at three in the morning. He's so sweet. Pregnancy makes him awestruck. He treats me like some strange creature from another planet."

Liz, as if remembering something, gave a start and reached into her purse. She handed a tiny picture to Alison.

"We asked for extra copies. This one's for you."

Alison stared at the small scan picture, studying the swirls and curves. It looked like a sandstorm but inside, curled, complete, and recognizable, a baby. She felt a hard jolt of something then: envy, longing. This tiny embryonic baby girl. A sister for Jamie. She would look like Liz, probably. She would be beautiful. Liz and Simon would have the perfect family.

"She's a stunner already. Look at her lovely long legs."

"And long fingers. Artistic. She'll be an artist. Maybe a musician."

"She'll be gorgeous," said Alison. "And loved."

"Loved indeed. That's the secret, isn't it?"

Liz tucked her own copy of the scan back into her purse.

"You and Jake ready for kids yet?"

"We haven't talked about it recently."

"Don't do it just to—you know. If you're not sure."

"I'm not that dumb, Liz."

"I know. I know."

Liz took a gulp of her drink, then looked back over at the bar.

"Cute tall guy is giving you rather obvious looks."

"He's more likely looking at you," Alison said.

"Possible. But I don't think so."

"I do," Alison said. "I have years of experience. I know when I'm with you, or whenever I was with Soph, I can just blend into the furniture as far as men are concerned. When I walked to school with you two tall blonde goddesses, I felt like the troll under the bridge."

"Rubbish," Liz said. "You were a pretty little thing. So fierce and passionate about stuff. Sophie used to get a lot of attention, though. Got to admit that. From everybody. Men and women."

Liz thought for a moment and then gave a small cough.

"You don't think Matt's wife is bisexual, do you?"

Alison, sipping from her glass, almost choked on a mouthful of wine.

"Celine? No. Of course not. What makes you—"

"Just something a bit odd about her. About the two of them together. You didn't see it?"

"No. She's reserved maybe. She's French."

"I was thinking they might have some kind of marriage of convenience. Wondered if they were both gay. I mean, he never had any long-term girlfriends, did he? Not really? Just occasional dates, nothing serious. You were his only girlfriend really. And that wasn't physical. Well, I don't think so. Was it?" She looked at Alison, smiling, already sure of the answer.

"You know it wasn't."

"Okay, well, I just felt there was something about them. I can't explain it. Maybe it's him. He's a bit cold physically. He hates to be hugged. You noticed that? He goes all stiff. Maybe that's it." Alison, her cheeks warm, took another sip of her drink, unable to look at Liz.

"Maybe."

"Funny when you think how different Sophie was—always kissing and hugging people. What was that poem she used to quote? Something about if you've given all your kisses you haven't given enough?"

"You're mangling it. It's Propertius. *If you have given all of your kisses, you have given too few.* Sounds more like Matt, actually."

"Matt? When did he ever kiss anyone?"

"No. I mean, it's a classical quote. He loved reading that stuff."

"Well, he might have been reading it, but Sophie was living it. Remember when she kissed the head girl, the batty one, kissed her right on the mouth. Poor thing nearly passed out."

Alison smiled at the memory.

"She kissed me on the mouth a few times," she said. "Always took me by surprise. But it seemed so natural from her. It would have been strange from anybody else. She was a great hugger. Physical. Throw herself onto the sofa between people and link arms with them both. Remember how she would do that? Put her head on your shoulder? Just to watch TV. Or listen to music. She couldn't sit next to anyone without hugging them close in some way."

"She got a bit too huggy with Simon once, and I told her to cut it out," Liz said. "He was always tongue-tied and nervous when she was around."

"She was huggy with everyone. She used to curl up next to my mum on the sofa sometimes, snuggle up next to her like a cat."

"She loved your mum," Liz said. "Wanted her for herself."

"Yes, she did," Alison said, remembering a very young Sophie in the McDonald kitchen, watching as Alison's mother made gingerbread men. Alison had begged for dough to make her own figures, and Liz and Sophie were given a lump of dough, too, and the three girls made a mother and a father each. Liz's were carefully fashioned: a skinny man, a curvy woman; Alison's gingerbread mother had a clearly identifiable curling smile, the father a thatch of unruly hair. The face on Sophie's gingerbread father was blank; the mother had tiny, almost invisible eyes and a mouth that was a short, straight line of hard black licorice.

Alison, thinking of Sophie's playfulness, her flirting with everyone, male and female, understood then, with the hindsight of maturity, that beneath the spirited teasing was a neediness none of them had recognized.

"I wish we'd understood her better," she said. "Maybe she wouldn't have—"

"I don't think we could have made a difference," Liz said.

At that moment, Alison's phone rang. She pulled it from her bag and stared at it. The Stuart house. Matt's number. She clicked it off. She could not talk to him right there, with Liz listening.

"You're not switching Jake off?" Liz asked. "Because really, that's not fair. You need to talk—"

She leaned forward and took the phone. She was so fast that Alison, shocked, released it without thinking. Liz studied the screen.

Alison, wanting desperately to grab the phone back, bit her lip savagely, praying that Liz would not recognize the number. She did. Of course she did. The same telephone number from their childhood, Sophie's old number, Matt's number. The Stuart household.

"What the—Mrs. Stuart isn't calling you, is she?" Liz asked. Then her face changed, darkened. "Wait a minute. It's Matt? Right?"

Alison nodded.

"It's just a—"

"I knew it! I knew it when I saw you both in the kitchen." Liz's eyes met Alison's. "You said it was nothing."

"It *was* nothing. We're just going to meet for drinks. He wants to talk about the hearing."

"Oh, sure," Liz said. "Come on, Ali. Is that why you don't want Jake to visit?"

"Don't be ridiculous. No. Nothing to do with Matt."

"Really? So why the secrecy? Oh, for God's sake. Do you think I'm totally stupid? You're going to sit at his feet and adore him, aren't you? Just like you did before?"

Liz stood, picked up her coat.

"I don't understand," she said, her voice breaking. "What is it—what *was* it—about those two that makes everybody lose their bloody heads. Do stupid, stupid things. Risk everything. Him and Sophie. I swear—"

She had paled. Alison, scared for her, took her arm.

"Liz, don't get upset. It's nothing."

"It's never nothing when the Stuarts are involved. Don't risk everything for him, Ali, please. Please."

"I'm not. It's just—"

"Oh, never mind. I've got to get home."

~

The light was already changing, the sky darkening, when Alison said good-bye to a still worried Liz. Inside the cottage she closed the drapes and switched on lamps. The noises in the cottage, the fridge, the hum of the television recorder, felt vaguely menacing. Alison wondered irrationally why everything seemed to echo and repeat. She could not shake off the feeling that she was far removed from the rest of the world and yet not safe from its dangers.

She had tried to reassure Liz, had said that her chats with Matt were not serious, just meeting for drinks, just catching up, but her friend had not believed her.

"If that were true," Liz had said, "you would have invited all of us. Me and Simon and Jonathan and maybe Ronnie, too. You've still got a stupid crush on him, Ali. Admit it."

Now, Alison thought over her words. A stupid crush? Was that really all it was?

When the phone rang later in the evening, she jumped.

"I called earlier," Matt said. "You didn't answer."

"I was having lunch with Liz. She picked up the phone, Matt. She recognized the number."

"What did you tell her?"

"That we might have a drink together. Catch up."

"And why shouldn't we? The hearing is so close. We need to talk about it."

"Is that why you called?"

"No. I called to tell you that I was thinking of you," he said.

Alison leaned back on the sofa, closed her eyes. Damn.

"You must be alone. Where's Celine?"

"France."

Alison sighed. How shabby this was. How ridiculous.

"I can't do this, Matt. I'm sorry. I can't be furtive and sneaky like this. Wait until your wife is away. Lie to my oldest friend. I feel like some kind of criminal."

"We can talk, can't we? Have a drink together?"

"Then why do we have to be so secretive about it? Friends can have a drink together, can't they? We don't have to pretend. It was so awkward with Liz. And with Ronnie, well, it was horrible."

"I just want to see you," he said. "Talk with you. Look at you. That's all."

She allowed the words to register fully, her heart lifting, and she could think of nothing to say in reply.

"I must go," he said. "That sounds like Mother's car. We'll talk soon."

Alison closed her phone. Mother's car. Jesus.

~

In the shower the next morning, the shampoo a helmet of suds over her hair, Alison heard the phone ring once and then ring again. Ten minutes later, still wrapped in the bath towel, she checked the messages. The first was from Liz.

"Ali? Are you there? Where the bloody hell are you? Listen, got a phone call from Celine this morning. She wants us all to have dinner. At Mrs. Stuart's house. Call back right away, Ali. Please."

Alison's reaction was clear and immediate. No way. She could not survive another dinner with Matt and Celine, and certainly not in that house. The very idea of it was appalling: To pretend good cheer and concern about their problems when she was weighted with her own? To face Matt across another dinner table? No. Her discomfort would be clear to everyone, most particularly to Liz. And Mrs. Stuart? No. Never. She could not face any of them.

The second message was from Matt.

"Just wanted to say hello again," he said, his voice warm. "I hope you'll be joining us for dinner."

Us? Of course he would use that word. He was one half of a couple. Just as she was.

She erased the messages, then thought hard for an excuse. It came to her with a second cup of coffee. It was extreme, but necessary. Dad. She would visit her father immediately. An hour later, she took a long breath before she phoned Liz. She had her excuse ready: she had called her father and told him of her arrival in Scotland that evening.

"Did you get my message?" Liz began.

"I can't make it, Liz. Sorry. I've arranged to go see my dad."

"What? When did you decide that?"

"This morning. Thought it would be a good time to do it. Before the hearing. And before I meet Jake."

"So when are you leaving for Scotland?"

"Late this afternoon," Alison said.

"Today! Sod it, Alison. They're your friends. Well, Matt is. Your very special friend, I believe. You should be at the bloody dinner. You can't face his wife, is that it?"

"No. It's nothing like that," Alison said. "Look, I'm sorry, but I can't disappoint Dad now. And I've booked my ticket."

"Well, maybe we can postpone the thing?"

"No. Don't do that. It'll be fine. You'll see."

"Well, easy for you to say, isn't it? Bugger."

Liz hung up. Alison stared at her phone. Liz was clearly furious. Well, too bad. She felt a smidgen of guilt. Mostly she felt relief. She stood slowly and stretched before she looked out of the window into the Shropshire garden. The light splintered over the leaves, littering the lawn after last night's gale. There was no traffic this morning, no sound at all, apart from a dog barking somewhere in a far farm and the wind rustling in the trees.

Scotland. Yes. A trip would surely help to clear the buzzing confusion in her head.

FIFTEEN

A rare day: a mackerel sky earlier, then scudding clouds, and now a sky as blue as a harebell and the loch to match. Alison walked with her father along the bracken path at the lake edge. He broke off sticks, chewed at a piece of grass; he seemed entirely at home, here in the Highlands.

"So gorgeous here, Dad. You're lucky."

"Suppose I am. You're seeing it at its best. Winter days can be raw and dark. Still lovely, though," he added.

"It's peaceful. How far is the school?"

"Twelve miles. But it's a quiet road. And a straight one."

"It's a smaller school?"

"It's not so wee," he said, a defensive note in his voice. He prided himself on handling large classes of unruly teenagers without ever losing his temper. "About the same size as the school I attended when I was boy."

Her father had grown up in Fife, in a charming village called Crail. Alison had been conceived there, a fact Alison's mother had shared on Alison's eighteenth birthday when, giddy with champagne, mother and daughter were giggling in the kitchen.

"Behind the pub," her usually reticent mother confided.

Alison had stared, openmouthed.

"I was conceived behind the pub? But weren't you staying with Gran? Why not in the bedroom? In the bed?"

"We felt, well, embarrassed in the house."

"But you were married!"

"I know it sounds silly. It's just we felt—well, never mind."

She giggled again, her cheeks pink.

"You really got carried away behind the pub?" Alison asked, grinning.

When Alison visited her grandmother shortly afterward for what turned out to be the last time—the old lady died some months later from a massive stroke—she shared this piece of information with her, just for the pleasure of seeing her grandmother's amused face.

"Ach, what a daft couple of buggers," Agnes had said.

But she took a photograph of her granddaughter outside the pub, and Alison mailed it to her parents with an inscription on the back: *Alison Agnes McDonald, eighteen years and nine months later.*

"Have you been over to Crail?" Alison asked her father now.

"No point, really. Not with Ma gone."

"But it's so pretty there."

"It's pretty here."

They edged the water; it lapped quietly, losing its color on the stones. Alison was reminded of her mother's funeral and her father's pellucid tears. She had never seen him cry before—she had never seen any grown man cry—and she was struck by how differently his tears appeared on his face: they were transparent, the pallor of his skin showing through. Compared with her mascara streaks, her father's tears were almost invisible, his grief inaudible. He stood silently, his hands clasped in front of him, clenching, unclenching.

Three years ago. She had thought he would never recover, and yet here he was, settled into a new home, with, it appeared, a new woman friend.

"You want to meet Clara?" he asked Alison after they had walked for a while.

"Of course I do. Where does she live?"

He waved vaguely in the direction of the village.

"Near the pub."

"That's useful. Is she a good friend?"

"Yes. I would say so."

He said nothing else, and Alison did not press. It was not her business after all. She had never doubted that he loved her mother, but he had spent enough time alone.

~

In the cottage guest bedroom, Alison, preparing for dinner, pulled out clothes from the suitcase and laid them on the bed. Then she stopped, surprised: the patchwork bedspread, with its odd mix of fabrics, was the very one her mother had made for her. Her father had carried it with him, then, from the old house. She didn't think he noticed such things. This one was definitely hers: patches from a blue gingham dress, a soft red coat, the blanket from her old doll, the silk nightgown her grandmother had given her with the lace edge. A hodgepodge of fabrics that Alison had loved. Her mother had stitched them together carefully, and the bedspread had remained on her bed until her teenage years. Then Alison, imagining that visiting friends might laugh, had hidden it away and displayed the *de rigueur* black-and-purple or raspberry-striped bedspread instead. Alison sighed, smoothed the cover, visualizing her mother on the old Singer sewing machine, her head tilted. She dreamed when she sewed, one could see it in her eyes. Alison sat on the bed for a while, stroking the cover, then finished dressing and headed downstairs to join her father.

He was pouring himself a scotch and lifted the bottle to show her.

"Aperitif?"

"Not scotch, thank you very much. White wine?"

"Cooling in the fridge. With your name on it."

While they sipped their drinks, she fielded her father's inevitable questions about Jake.

"So why did you come ahead without him?"

"Nothing to worry about. Just taking a break."

"Ah, well, it's good that he's coming to join you."

"Yes."

"You always seem so happy together," her father said, eyeing her over his glasses. "Jake—so enthusiastic, so interested in the world. I like that about him. His joy in things."

She looked up, surprised.

"Yes. I like that, too."

Her father gave an odd shrug.

"Try to look at the balance of it."

"The balance of it?" she repeated.

"Yes. If you can. Anyway, let's get moving," he said. "Don't want to keep Clara waiting."

~

Clara, a small, dark-haired woman in her fifties, had eyes brown and bright like a bird's. Her voice delighted Alison; it was soft and clear with the accent of the Highlands. She was born on the Isle of Skye, she told Alison; her brothers still lived there. Alison must visit.

"I'd love to," Alison said.

"We could all go," her father said. "Family thing."

Alison noted his glance toward Clara, the shared smile.

Clara urged them back for coffee at the B&B after their meal. Alison had imagined a stone cottage, but the place was a huge Victorian mansion with wide bay windows, high ceilings, original tiles in the entrance hall. Clara's own watercolors hung on the walls of the large sitting room.

"You're good, Clara," Alison said, standing back to admire a misty loch scene. "I like this."

"Ach, I just play. Your Da says you used to paint. Draw all the time."

"I did. I wasn't any good, unfortunately."

"Nonsense," said her father. "Your mother and I thought you were very talented."

"Course you did. My teachers didn't agree with you."

"Do it because you love it," Clara said. "I do."

"I might give it another try," Alison said, taking a seat by the stone fireplace. "This place is awesome. It's really special."

"Lot of work," Clara said. Alison noted again the look between her father and Clara.

"We're thinking I might move in, help out a bit," her father said. "With the garden anyway. Maybe do a few of the chores. The girl who helps with breakfast is leaving."

His eyes on her face, he waited for a response. Alison, taken by surprise, tried to look enthusiastic.

"Good idea. How many guest rooms do you have, Clara?"

"Four. Doubles with en suites. Not always full, of course, but we do quite well. My quarters, right here. And a couple of rooms and a bath at the back for the helper."

"It's a great place," Alison said. "I can see why it's hard work, though. Your helper is leaving?"

"Aye. She's marrying an Englishman. A wee bit of a merger. He's a widower, three children. She has the one daughter."

Alison smiled at this. *An Englishman.* Said with the same mockery she remembered from her grandmother.

"And moving away?"

"Down to Leeds. We'll have to find somebody else for the work."

The idea came to Alison a few minutes later, as Clara handed her a cup of coffee.

"It's okay, then, for your helper to have a child?"

"Ach aye. No problem there," Clara said. "None at all."

"Well," Alison said slowly, "I think I might know someone."

She thought of Wendy, the young woman in the shelter, could still see clearly the absolute fear on the girl's face. Slowly, she told Clara and her father about the situation there. She described the bruises, the stalking husband. She told them about Josh.

"Would she want to move all the way up here?" her father asked. He looked doubtful.

"Why not? She'd be safe. He'd never find her."

Her father took a white handkerchief from his pocket, removed his spectacles, and began to polish them. A ritual she recognized instantly. He was thinking. Alison waited for the question or pronouncement she knew was coming.

"Why are you so anxious to help this girl? Did you know her before?" he asked finally.

"No. Sophie's the only connection really."

"And you couldn't help Sophie, and so you feel . . ."

Alison felt the same irritation she had felt as a teenager when her father offered complex theories for behavior that she believed was perfectly simple and obvious.

"Look, I just want to help a young woman who's in danger. There's nothing complicated about it."

"It would be fine with me," Clara said quickly. "We could mebbe try it for three months. See if she likes it?"

"Thank you. I'll ask her as soon as I get back. How about if I get her to call you? Talk about it." Alison turned to Clara then, smiling. "So long as you don't mind that she's an Englishwoman?"

"Ach, away wi' ye," Clara said, laughing.

~

Later, in the single bed in her father's cottage, Alison woke to hear the banging of an open window and the patter of rain. The sound of the soft midnight shower filled the room; the breeze moved the curtains, swirling pale ghosts against the silver of the sky. Alison listened for a while; it was so British a sound. In Los Angeles, rain came in winter, hard rain, drumming the earth. The winds, in their elevated neighborhood, could be disturbing and raw, shaking windows, piling trash onto their wrought-iron fence. This Scottish night was cold and fresh, the rain like a blessing. She breathed in deeply—the earth smelled rich, the scent of damp leaves in the air. She watched the window for the clouds to drift away, for the moon to emerge.

She heard her father moving around, heard the creak of a floorboard and then the sharp crack as the window was closed. He would not lie awake listening to the rain falling on the Scottish moss outside his window—he would be used to it by now, the pleasure of it taken for granted.

She sighed, turning over, thinking about what her father had said about her marriage to Jake. The balance of it? He was right. They had been happy in the early days. As newlyweds, their physical attraction sent them racing from the restaurant to the nearest bed before they had finished dinner. They laughed a lot, worked and played hard. Both were beginning new careers. Jake's rise to the top was fast; Alison's was slower, as she struggled with early advertising projects. They even laughed, then, about those. Her first television commercial used a visual of a pork sausage with a Hula-Hoop against a background of disco music. Jake, the first time he saw it, laughed so hard he could barely speak and called it The Dancing Penis. That commercial became the benchmark for subsequent projects.

Doesn't have the drama of the dancing penis, Jake would say when she shared her later efforts with him.

When did he stop watching her commercials? When had she stopped telling him about them? Maybe when her assignments shifted to cosmetics and perfume, became female focused. But she had stopped taking an interest in his work, too. He did not discuss drug trials these days, perhaps because she was cynical about Big Pharma. They didn't talk much about anything that mattered, she thought. Their conversations focused on domestic matters: who would pick up the dry cleaning; whether her car needed servicing; how long he would be away for the latest conference, when he would be back. The large number of friends from the early days of their marriage had dwindled as babies were born and free time became scarce. Arranging even a simple birthday dinner out was complex and dependent on work schedules and the availability of babysitters. *Life as an annotated spreadsheet,* Jake had said once.

Decisions must be made before she met up with her husband, she concluded as the rain began again, a soft tapping against the bedroom windows. She needed to be clear what she wanted, for Jake's sake and for her own.

∽

"Walk around the loch with me," Alison's father said after breakfast the next morning. "You've got time before your train."

The loch was misty; her father walked slowly, sighing occasionally. Alison had felt his eyes on her over the last couple of days, quizzical and worried.

"I like Clara," Alison said. "She's warm and cuddly."

"Yes. She is."

"You must like cuddly women."

He laughed.

"Doesn't everyone?"

This clearly triggered some memory or other, for his next words were of Mrs. Stuart.

"I'm glad you came back for the funeral, Ali. Poor Thelma. Well, I can't imagine what she's going through."

"Yes. She seems to be holding up, though. Stiff upper lip and all that."

Her father gave her a long, sideways look.

"Hmm. You always were a wee bit wary of her."

"Wary of her? She terrified me."

"Not the easiest woman, I know. Did you meet up with Matt?"

"Yes. Liz invited him and his wife for dinner last week. Jonathon, too."

"She did? That was nice of her. Matt was your pal, though, mostly. Wasn't he?"

"I suppose."

They walked in silence for a while.

"He was a sturdy lad," her father said. "Clever, too. So was Jonathon. Very bright boy. Jonathon still a beanpole?"

"He's filled out a little bit, but yes, still skinny."

"Never seen a lad eat so much. Your mother loved to feed him. I remember when Matt and Sophie moved in next door. You were so excited. New kids to play with. We were glad you had friends so close by. Hated you chasing off on your bike, at the mercy of drunken drivers and other eejits."

"They all spent a lot of time at our house."

"Aye, they did. Well, they loved your mother's cupcakes."

"Naturally. Matt and Sophie weren't allowed cakes at home. And they could drop a crumb at our house without being yelled at. Or banished to the basement."

"Not that bad, lassie, surely?" her father said, chiding. "Interesting to watch them grow up. I always felt Matt would make a success of his life. An ambitious lad. Determined. Sophie, too. I thought she was a plucky wee thing. Your mother worried about her."

Alison turned, surprised.

"Worried about Sophie?"

"Yes, thought she was a troubled child. Always putting herself in jeopardy. Seemed to seek out danger."

"She liked challenges," Alison said, remembering Sophie leaping from the top of the old oak tree on the rope swing, giving an exuberant jungle howl. "Mum was right to be worried. Liz called Sophie the poster child for self-destruction once. She got that right."

She paused.

"Did Mum ever talk to Mrs. Stuart about Sophie? Her mother was so mean to her. Really mean. Well, she was nasty to both of them, but Sophie was convinced that Thelma hated her."

"Ach no. She didn't hate her," her father said, looking away. "Thelma's not an easy woman, I know that. A woman with impossibly high standards. Behavior. Housekeeping. It was just—"

"Just?" Alison asked, urging him on.

"Never mind. None of our business."

"Dad! Come on."

"Family matters are best kept within a family."

"Please."

He seemed to be thinking.

"You won't go running off and tell Liz? Because if she tells her mother . . ."

Liz's mother was known as the Town Crier by some of their old neighbors.

"Of course not."

Alison tugged her father's arm, pulled him to the low stone wall that ran alongside the path to the loch, and sat down next to him.

"Spill," she said.

He shook his head.

"Thelma didn't hate Sophie. She worried that Sophie might get out of control like—"

"Like . . . ?"

He sighed.

"I really shouldn't be telling you this."

"Dad! Go on."

"Doug told me once, on one of our fishing trips. The only time that poor man ever talked. Thelma had a sister. Joanna. A bit of a wild child. Younger than Thelma. Your mother saw a picture of her once. Said she looked very much like Sophie. That same full head of hair." Her father gestured, his hands making curling movements around his head. "She ran away from her home in Wales and lived with Doug and Thelma for a while when Thelma was pregnant with Sophie. Thelma had a tough time with Matt, and the second pregnancy, so very soon after the first, was difficult. Joanna was supposed to help out but—I don't know what happened. It got rather complicated. Thelma asked her to leave."

"Asked her to leave?" Alison said. "You mean she kicked her out?"

"Well, yes. The poor child got into drugs, bad company, killed herself when she was just a wee bit older."

"*Killed herself?* Oh my God. And Mrs. Stuart thought Sophie was like her?"

"Possibly. She was scared she might follow the same pattern."

"Well, she did follow the pattern, didn't she? The exact same pattern. No thanks to Thelma Stuart."

"Alison," her father chided, but there was no real anger in his voice, only sadness.

"Why didn't Mr. Stuart speak up? Tell Thelma to lay off Sophie a bit."

"Doug was— Well, he did his best," her father said. "Under the circumstances."

He was silent again, looking out at the scenery as if it held some quiet secret he might learn. He was not going to say more. She was sure he knew more. But that was his way. If he had promised to keep a confidence, he would keep it. Her father stood again, brushed at his pants.

"So Doug used to talk to you on those fishing trips, did he?" Alison asked.

"Didn't talk much. But fishing, well, it's a lot of hours sitting by a river. We chatted a bit."

He mused for a moment.

"Like driving. People often talk frankly in a car. Not looking at each other. Back and forth. The only time to talk to a teenage girl is in a moving car, I can tell you that from experience. No eye contact."

Alison laughed.

"So that's why you always drove me to school when I was worried about something?"

"I enjoyed those times," her father said quietly.

They resumed their walk up the hill. At the crest they halted, taking long breaths. The air was so clean Alison could taste it in her mouth. It was like fresh spring water.

"You think Clara is sure about taking Wendy on?" she asked. "And Josh, too? He's just a toddler."

"She'll love it," he said. "Frankly, so will I. Nice to have kids around."

Alison caught his look.

"Liz is having another baby," she said.

Her father turned to her. His eyes were soft with something she couldn't read.

"That's good news."

"Yes. A girl. She's really pleased."

He reached to touch her cheek. She blinked, close to tears. He seemed about to say something, changed his mind, and turned to begin the walk back.

When they returned to the cottage, Alison made coffee and carried it through to him. He took a sip, then picked up his book to resume his reading. Alison smiled. Jake, when he first met her parents, had been amused at the way they sat in silence, reading in armchairs on opposite sides of the fire. Bach on the stereo and the rustling of pages: one of the key memories of her childhood.

She remembered Jake in the bedroom of the old house as he shrugged off his shirt. She was already in bed, and he turned to look at her.

"They're really nice and all, your parents," he said. "But holy shit, they're quiet. I've never met a couple as quiet as they are."

"They're not like your parents, certainly."

Jake's parents were Palo Alto suburban: a mother coiffed and styled and pressed. Her skin was constantly tanned; she wore the right sunglasses. His father was a gruff man who played golf. Nice people. Pleasant. Thin and transparent. As light as air, as clouds.

"I don't think yours are like anyone else on the planet," he said.

"Nobody is like anyone else on the planet."

"Oh, that's so deep," he said. "Come here, my little one-of-a-kind."

He climbed into bed beside her, tugged her against him.

"Remind me why you're so special," he said, rolling her on top of him.

Alison lifted a hand to hold the headboard steady, to keep it from tapping the wall. Jake shook his head, his eyes glowing.

"They'll never hear us," he said.

"Shush! They might," she whispered. "It's not a big house."

"Okay. Solution. That nice big blue rug."

And they slid out of bed, onto the rug, laughing like children.

~

"Penny for them, Ali?" Her father had put down his book and was studying her face. Alison attempted a bright smile.

"Not worth a penny."

"You seem a bit preoccupied."

"I need to make some decisions," she told him.

"Take your time and make sure they're the right ones," her father said.

SIXTEEN

The Virgin train was new and sleek. Alison found a seat by the window and settled down for the journey to Shropshire. She knew it would seem endless, despite the props she had brought along to shorten the time: one newspaper, a glossy magazine, her Kindle in her bag. She carried, too, a large bag from the toy-and-crafts shop just outside the station. There she had found crayons, a coloring book, and a fat red train for Josh, and then, at the last moment, she caught sight of a large sketch pad on the top shelf and had added it, Winsor and Newton willow charcoal sticks, and some pastel chalks for herself.

"That's good to see," her father had said, approving of her purchases.

"Inspired by Clara," she said. Not true, but it made her father smile.

"Safe journey," he called from the station platform as he waved her off. "Call when you arrive."

The journey became a fog of memories as the train sped through the drab Northern cities and eventually neared the Shropshire hills. Alison, thinking back to Sophie's troubled relationship with her mother, decided that her father's explanation did little to clarify it. So what if Sophie looked like this Joanna girl? That was no excuse for Mrs. Stuart's relentless cruelty to her daughter. She remembered Sophie dancing in the basement one day after school, twirling a pretend baton like a cheerleader, singing along to the music. Any random onlooker might have been amused. Alison, watching from the armchair, laughed at her friend's pouty faces and high kicks. Liz was searching the fridge for a cold drink; Matt and Ronnie, at the far end of the basement, were sharing a cigarette. Sophie, as she danced, pulled off her school cardigan, making wild movements with her hands. She looked so funny. There was nothing disturbing, to Alison's eyes, in her dancing. But somebody had left the door to the basement open. Matt insisted always that they keep it closed. Later, they blamed Ronnie.

So they were not prepared for Mrs. Stuart's high-pitched scream from the top of the basement stairs.

"Stop that, you little tart. Stop it!"

Sophie froze. Matt looked up. Liz and Alison exchanged startled looks.

"We have to go," Liz said. "Come on, Ali."

They had to pass Mrs. Stuart at the top of the stairs. Alison remembered the woman's face, white, pinched, her eyes like slate. Sophie followed behind, calling for them to stay, and then as they reached the front door, they heard the chilling, echoing sound of a hard slap, an open hand on Sophie's soft cheek, followed by their friend's cry. Alison noted Matt's shocked face and the cigarette still in his hand. She questioned then, and was to wonder again later, why Mrs. Stuart had not been angry about *that*.

It was not the first time Mrs. Stuart had slapped Sophie. Her friend often had dark bruises on the back of her knees. A hairbrush, Sophie had said. The Mark of the Brush. Once, Liz had noted the black fingerprint bruises on Sophie's soft upper arm.

"How did you get those?" she'd asked.

"Mother trying to keep me in place while she yelled at me."

Later, after the basement slap, Alison, pretending innocence, though she knew very well, asked her parents what it meant to be called a tart. Did it mean someone was evil?

"Not evil," her father said, smiling. "Just a little free with your favors."

"Is Sophie free with her favors?" Alison asked.

Her father's face changed. A look passed between her parents.

"Did somebody call Sophie a tart?" her mother asked in a quiet voice.

"Her mum did. Because she was dancing."

"I'm sure she didn't mean anything by it," her father said, after a silence.

Later, she heard her parents whispering in the kitchen. Her father's steady murmur and then her mother's voice, rising: "To her twelve-year-old daughter?" her mother asked.

She hadn't told them about the vicious slap or the regular bruises. She wished later that she had.

~

Alison took the long walk back to the cottage. It had been stuffy on the train and worse on the bus, and here, though the air was cold, it felt so crisp and fresh that she crossed over the wooded dell to take the hillside path home. Impatient to talk to Vivienne and Wendy, to describe the opportunity in Scotland, she stopped first at the shelter. Vivienne answered the door.

"Hi there. Sorry to barge in," Alison said. "I need to talk to you. If you've got a minute."

"Of course," Vivienne said. "Come back to my office. It's down here, out of the way."

The room that led to the kitchen looked crowded. One woman, middle-aged and well-dressed, stood apart, clearly uncomfortable. Her wrist was tightly bandaged. When a woman with two missing front teeth approached her, she shrank visibly, shaking her head.

151

"She'll learn," murmured Vivienne, noticing this. "All in the same boat."

"Must be hard at first."

"Oh, it is. For everybody. Here's my office. Would you like me to close the door? Is what you want to discuss private?"

"Yes. Well, it is in a way."

In Vivienne's cramped office, Alison explained about her father's new life in Scotland. She described the Victorian B&B, the two rooms for Wendy and Josh. Then she handed Vivienne her father's number and Clara's number, too. Vivienne listened carefully, without interrupting.

"My dad's a teacher, so he's well used to children," Alison concluded. "And Clara seems like a lovely woman. Very warm, very capable."

Vivienne sat back in her office chair, nodded.

"It does *sound* rather good. It's rather a long way from the areas she knows. And I would want to call your father, of course. To discuss it with him. Wendy must do so, too. Before she makes any decisions."

"I know. I thought I should tell you first. In case you felt she wasn't ready, in case she should stay here a bit longer."

"To be honest," Vivienne said, "we'll be glad of the bed. We need to take some of the Birmingham overspill. They're bursting at the seams over there. We've got to move her anyway. If he *has* found her, she's no longer safe. This could be a good opportunity for her. And for Josh."

"Okay. Will you tell her?"

"Why don't you describe it to her first? And I'll talk to her later. Be prepared, though, for some resistance on her part."

"Resistance?"

"A new place. Leaving a safe place. Living alone. It can be terrifying."

Vivienne was right. Wendy accepted the toys with obvious surprise and pleasure, settled Josh on the floor with the red train, but did not look as glad, nor as grateful, as Alison had expected when told about the job in the Highlands. Her brow furrowed. She sat on the bottom bunk, and as she listened, her fingers plucked and tugged at the duvet cover.

"You sure they're okay about Josh?" she asked.

"Of course. My father will love him."

"But—you sure I'll get the job? How can I work when I have to take care of Josh?"

"There's a play school in the village. And you only have to help out in the mornings. Breakfasts. Maybe change the beds. My dad might help with that, too. Not sure what his jobs will be."

"I'm a rubbish cook. I never got the eggs right for Roger. Never."

"You just have to help out a bit, set tables, make toast. I think Clara does the actual cooking."

"It's so far away."

"I just came from there! Fast trains. It's not so far at all."

Wendy shook her head slowly.

"I don't know."

"It would be safe," Alison said gently. "And Josh would be safe."

Wendy looked away.

"I know. But . . ."

"But?"

"It's Scotland."

She looked so doubtful that Alison thought that they could be discussing the far side of the moon.

"You said you loved Scotland. It's beautiful there."

"I only went there once. When I was a kid. I don't know anybody."

"You'll know my dad. And Clara."

Wendy looked at the floor.

"I'm scared to go somewhere new," she admitted. "I've never lived by myself."

"I know," Alison said, taking her hand. "The idea is scary, but once you try it, you'll be fine. And you have to move on."

"How? How can I move on?"

Wendy's mouth trembled. She looked like a little girl. There was something already defeated about her. Alison squeezed her hand.

"Just think about it," she said. "Okay?" She fumbled in her bag to find a pen. "Here's my dad's number. Call and talk to him. And here's my number if you want to ask questions. And talk to Clara, too. She's lovely. Really sweet. You don't have to go if you don't want to. They'll understand if you don't like the idea."

Wendy took the numbers, stared at them doubtfully. Alison moved to hug her.

"Give it a shot," she said. "You might love it."

SEVENTEEN

In the cottage, after a shower, tea, and a sandwich, Alison pulled out the sketch pad, the charcoal, and the chalks. The solid feel of the charcoal held firmly in her hand, the powdery residue on her fingers, were instantly familiar, and she attempted a leaf, and then a tree, and finally, focusing memory on a face, tried to draw Sophie. A young girl in high school, laughing. Frustrated at her first attempt, she tore off the page, crumpled it, and began again. She could not capture it, the laughter, not exactly. *Just play,* she told herself. *Just play, draw a face, any face,* and saw, some minutes later, that instead of Sophie she had drawn Josh. So what did that mean? A message from the subconscious? That she wanted a baby was not something she had ever hidden from herself, or from Jake. Smiling, she studied the sketch, shaking her head. Those curving cheeks!

Later, she rinsed her hands before bed and found that removing the residual charcoal and chalk felt oddly soothing. It had not vanished then, the pleasure of it. In her dreams that night she sketched faces that vanished into curving trees and cumulus clouds.

∼

Alison telephoned Liz the next morning, wanting news of the dinner with Matt and Celine, prepared for some residual resentment from her friend.

"I'm back," she said. "My dad sends love."

"How is he?" Liz asked, her voice cool.

Alison related news of her father's good health and his relationship with Clara. Liz, obviously still sulking, said *Interesting* in such a snippy way that Alison sighed.

"Okay, okay. Look, I said I was sorry. I would have come to dinner if I could, you know that."

"Oh, sure, course you would," said Liz. "Except it might have been a bit awkward flirting with Matt with his wife right there."

"Don't be ridiculous. I just wanted to see my dad before Jake arrived."

This, she knew, was guaranteed to distract Liz. It did.

"Right. When's he coming?"

"In a couple of days. I'm meeting him in London. At the hotel."

"You're not going to do anything stupid, are you? Something you'll regret?"

"No. We'll talk. That's all. We need to talk about a lot of things. Anyway, how was the dinner party?"

"Tedious," Liz said. "Celine was charming enough, but I got the feeling she didn't really want us there. That the whole thing was Matt's idea. She looked good, though. Classic dress in that great jersey fabric that drapes well, makeup on, hair just so."

"Really?" Alison said, responding to this image of the elegant wife with a hollow mix of both envy and relief that she hadn't been there to witness it.

"She did the cooking as well," Liz continued. "Not a bad cook. Did a passable fish dish and a nice crème brûlée. You know she comes from one of those old semiaristocratic French families? Her father's some kind of judge. Commissionaire? Whatever they're called."

"No surprise. She has that patrician look. Did you see the twins?"

"Oh yes. They are beautiful. Their hair looks curlier somehow, little curls around their faces. They look so like Sophie. Except they're angelic. Celine paraded them through for us just before dinner. Had them dressed up in these old-fashioned nightgowns. The kind you see on antique porcelain dolls. High, tight necks and very pretty but—well, they can't be comfortable. Lily, the livelier one, hated the nightgown."

"She's the rebel."

"Yep. She tugged and tugged at the neckline, and then when she was climbing over the back of the sofa to get to Simon—you know how kids really take to Simon, and heavens she really reminded me of Sophie, the way she could climb—anyway, one of the buttons popped off. Well, you should have seen Celine's face. She gave this little yelp. Apparently the buttons are expensive. A button, for God's sake!"

"Expensive buttons on kids' clothes?" Alison asked.

"I know. Stupid. And dangerous. I started to tell her how buttons like that are a no-no for little kids. They'll swallow them, or stick them in their ears or up their noses, but Simon stopped me with one of those *Mind your own business* looks. You know how he does when I launch myself into the conversation with advice that people don't want to hear."

Alison, wanting to ask about Matt but unable to find the words, asked instead, "And how was the old witch?"

"Witchlike. Went on and on about how Sophie had spoiled the girls and how she believed in a healthy diet and discipline. Lot of stuff like that. She talked at me until I just about lost the will to live. Then they discussed the hearing for hours. They really want us to be there."

"Well, we will be, won't we? We did promise."

"I suppose. I don't feel qualified to give an opinion, honestly. I haven't seen Matt in years. I don't know Celine. How can we say she'll be a good mother? Do you know she never once went up to check on the girls? She kept talking about how much she wanted to adopt them, but apart from their little fashion parade, she didn't go near them all evening so far as I could see. Mrs. Stuart put them to bed and looked in on them later."

"Maybe Celine feels awkward because it's not her house?"

"Perhaps. Anyway, I suppose better her than Mrs. Stuart."

"God, yes. Mrs. Stuart's too old, surely? And in poor health."

"You never know what they'll decide when it's a committee decision. The panel might feel it's best not to uproot them. Especially to a foreign country. Can you imagine having to live with that woman? Banished to the basement. Just like Matt and Sophie."

"Matt and Sophie got to like the basement," Alison said.

"Yes, well, they did later. But when they were little kids? You know, I was thinking about that birthday party Sophie put on for herself in the basement. Remember, when she was ten?"

"And invited all the kids from school and her mother didn't know about it so there was nothing to eat?"

"Yes. Well, she *had* asked her mother if she could have a party, apparently. She told me so years later, and her mother said no. So Sophie just went ahead and had it anyway. Thought that games and all that lemonade she'd pinched from somewhere would be enough."

"It *was* enough, actually. I remember that party was fun," Alison said.

"True. And she did have a nice cake. That was pretty strange when you think about it. Her mother must have got that, at least."

"She didn't!" Alison said. "That was Mum. I went back home to borrow some paper cups for the lemonade and told Mum there was no food, and she said, *Not even a cake?* And I said no, and she said, *Come back in fifteen minutes.* So I did, and she'd rushed to the shop and bought this cake and some paper plates, and she said, *Don't ever, ever tell Mrs. Stuart I got this. Don't tell a soul. If it ever comes out, say you and Liz bought it with your pocket money.*"

"You're kidding," Liz said, sounding peeved again. "I never knew that."

"Well, she swore me to secrecy. Of course it didn't matter, because Mrs. Stuart never did come down there and see that cake. They never had a birthday party, did they? Either of them."

"She was a mean old sod, their mother," said Liz. "Well, she's still a mean old sod. No wonder Sophie was such a flake, with a mother like that."

"Oh, don't say that. She wasn't a flake."

"Crazy, then?"

"Crazy for sure."

Alison took a sip of her coffee. "I miss her," she added quietly.

"So do I," Liz said. "You know what's funny? I miss the thought of her. Of her being somewhere in the world. Laughing. Dancing."

"We'll remember her like that," Alison said. "Dancing and singing along with the music. You got a cup of tea? We'll have a toast."

She leaned forward to clink her coffee mug against the phone.

"Here's to you dancing, Soph," she said.

She heard the tap of Liz's teacup against the receiver.

"Dance on, Sophie," Liz said. "Show those angels your moves."

~

Alison had just hung up the phone, was still holding her coffee mug, when the doorbell rang. Frowning, she looked out of the cottage window. Matt's Citroen was parked at the curb. She stared, disbelieving. Matt. Here.

She opened the door, barely able to breathe.

EIGHTEEN

Matt stood on the step, his coat collar up, his hair blowing back in the wind. His expression was serious as he regarded her.

"I missed you at dinner," he said. "I didn't mean for you to run away."

"I didn't run away. I just went to see my dad. Come in."

He stood in the cottage hallway, awkward, his hands loose at his sides.

"Take off your coat," she said. "The kettle's just boiled. Make yourself coffee while I comb my hair. I look like a wreck."

Upstairs, Alison raced around the bedroom, giving herself a fast spray of cologne, a touch of mascara, attacking her untidy hair with the hairbrush. Concluding that she would look like an idiot if it were obvious that she had changed her clothes, she replaced the sweater she was wearing with a fresh, newer one in a similar shade of blue.

When she came back downstairs, breathless, Matt was standing in the kitchen, stirring his coffee.

"I worried you would stay in Scotland," he said.

"And miss the hearing? I wouldn't do that. I wouldn't let you down."

"I thought I must have scared you away."

"Of course you didn't. Come sit down."

He sat on the sofa. She sat opposite him, leaning back in the armchair, trying to look calm and in control.

"So, everything's in place?" she asked. "The solicitor is confident?"

"Pretending to be. I'm not so certain. Gary Lewis seems quite determined to get custody."

"He abandoned the twins. He abandoned Sophie. Surely he doesn't have a chance?"

"He was married to her."

Alison thought back to the basement party after Sophie's wedding. The young groom drinking beer and laughing with his mates in the corner while Sophie danced alone in the middle of the room. They had all been so young.

"I never could figure out if Sophie really loved him," Alison said. "She never said she did. She was pretty wild in those days."

"Who knows?" Matt said, just as Alison's phone rang, loud in the small room.

"Liz, most likely," Alison said.

"You should answer it."

"Be quiet, then."

"Silent as a stone."

Alison answered the phone with a question in her voice.

"We're packed!" Wendy said. "We're ready to go tomorrow. Just wanted to say thank you."

"Already? Wow, that was fast."

"Vivienne needs the bed. And your dad said he would meet the train. I talked to him on the phone. He seems ever so nice."

"He is. He's lovely. Are you leaving from Shrewsbury?"

"Yes. Harry's going to drive us to the station."

"What time are you leaving the shelter?"

"About eight."

"I'll try to be there. Wave you off. I'm so pleased, Wendy. Really."

She hung up the phone, smiling.

"Not Liz, then?" Matt asked.

"No. A girl at the shelter."

"You're still involved over there? Why?"

"Not involved. I was just so curious about Sophie. I'd feel better if I knew—" She wavered for a moment and then asked, "Was it an accident, Matt? Have you any idea?"

He shrugged, looked away.

"I don't know. I suppose we'll never know."

"I wish I'd been a better friend. Supported her more."

"Everyone says that, but really, she had more friends than she needed," he said.

Alison, surprised by the hard note in his voice, wondered if he was referring to Sophie's drug contacts. He seemed uncomfortable. Alison struggled for something else to say.

"My dad was telling me about the fishing trips he used to take with your father," she said at last. "How they both enjoyed them."

"Really? I think that was the only time he was happy, when he was out all day on the banks of the Severn."

"My dad knew about Joanna," Alison said. "Not much. Just that your mother had a sister, and Sophie—"

He turned fast to look at her.

"Jesus. He told your dad? I never knew they were such good friends." He sighed. "Well, it's good he could confide in someone. I think his guilt just weighed him down."

"Guilt?"

"Mother never forgave him," Matt said. "She was always throwing it back at him."

Alison blinked. A moment of blank confusion before his words made a real and wrenching sense. So that's why Thelma had thrown her sister out of the house. Doug Stuart must have had an affair with the teenage Joanna. Just after Sophie was born. The young woman was supposed to be helping to take care of the newborn. Alison thought about it, baffled. An affair seemed so out of character for the mild-mannered man she had known.

"Do you know what happened to her?" she asked finally. "To Joanna?"

"Not sure. She died; that's all I know."

Alison stood.

"Strange how our parents remain a mystery to us," Alison said. "Even when we grow up."

"Ah, but you loved yours, didn't you?"

"I did. I do."

"Relationships," Matt said. "They're always complicated."

Alison lifted his coffee cup.

"I'll make you some fresh coffee."

In the kitchen, she made the coffee, recalling Mr. Stuart. A mouse of a man compared to his strident wife. His wife's anger toward him must have been deflected to Sophie. Alison wondered if Sophie had ever understood that, had ever learned the details. She had never spoken about it.

In the living room, Matt had relaxed back on the sofa. He took the coffee from her.

"Come sit down here," he said, patting the seat beside him. She felt her breath catch, placed her own coffee on the small table, and sat down next to him. His eyes met hers. He seemed more at ease now. He reached to stroke a strand of hair from her face. A moment later, he was kissing her, holding her hard against his chest. She felt his hands on her shoulders, then her breasts.

He did not pull away this time, nor did she. His touch was tentative, but the soft stroking had an arousing effect, and Alison felt the curl of desire growing slowly in her belly. She clutched him tighter, wanting his body against hers. The discomfort of their position, pressed together on the narrow sofa, caused her to pause. His breathing was ragged.

"Matt. Not here," she whispered. "Come on."

And felt courage enough to lead him up the stairs and into the shadowy bedroom, dusky, soothing in its quiet. They undressed quickly, frantically, urgent hands helping each other and themselves, their bodies hot and reaching, until the smooth blending of skin on skin against the crisp cold cotton of the sheets. Matt made love to her carefully, deliberately, studying her face, gauging her responses. Made shy by this close scrutiny, Alison could not relax, and finally when she felt he must be getting impatient, tensed and cried out, faking it. She did not want to disappoint him now.

He held her close, whispering into her hair.

"Why did we wait so long?" he asked. "For that particular teenage fantasy to come true?"

She smiled.

"My fantasy. Not yours, I don't think."

"Oh yes. I always wanted you."

"But you left. You could have stayed in touch."

He leaned up on one elbow to look at her face.

"I sent postcards!"

"But only postcards. I never knew where to find you. Never knew where to reply."

"I meant to come look for you. One day."

"I hoped you would," Alison said, pulling him back onto the bed so that she could rest her head on his shoulder. "That was my one small hope for years. The day you left, I thought my heart would break. Felt like I had a heavy weight on my chest all that day. Sophie's wedding day. I could barely smile. But I thought—sometime in the future, maybe when I was in college, you'd come back."

He traced her mouth with a finger.

"I did," he said. "And here we are."

"Here we are indeed," Alison whispered, wanting him again, stretching so that her body was full against his, her mouth soft against his neck.

He held her for a few moments longer, then, sighing, moved to the edge of the bed.

"I should shower," he said.

Cold with disappointment, she took a moment before she spoke.

"Fresh towels in the cupboard behind the bath."

Alison moved to sit on the edge of the bed and listened to the cascading water in the bathroom, unable to think clearly. Minutes later, she watched him dress.

"Do you have to go so soon?"

"I do. But I'll be back."

At the front door, he leaned to kiss her cheek.

"We'll talk soon," he said.

When she had closed the door, listened to his car engine starting up, the car moving away, she stood quite still in the hallway.

Here we are, Matt had said. But where was that exactly? And where could they go next?

During the rest of that evening, and whenever she woke in the night, Alison flashed on fragments of their encounter and shivered as she remembered Matt's hands on her body, his eyes watching her as she sighed and moaned. She tried to banish these images, these tactile memories, but they returned constantly in a flood of both longing and embarrassment so that her cheeks burned each time she thought of Matt.

And how to face Jake with these images in her head? An unfaithful wife. She had never considered herself the type, and the stark, cold fact of that made her question everything she had ever believed about herself. It was hardly a casual fling, she told herself. She had loved Matt Stuart all of her life. Surely that made a difference?

Now she *must* make a decision about her husband, about her marriage. Jake could not have chosen a worse time to come. She had been confused enough before; she was a mess of fears and insecurities now.

Maybe all this will clarify when I see Jake, she thought. *Maybe when we talk about the way forward, it will be obvious.* It seemed unlikely.

NINETEEN

The next morning felt different from other Shropshire mornings: the musky scent of sex on the sheets, a sensual sensitivity on her skin—these were new in this environment. Her body had not felt like this—slightly bruised, used—since California, after lovemaking with Jake. Alison lay still for a while, reliving the physical details, Matt's hands on her, his intense attention, his eyes on her face. She shivered. Those images would remain with her when she went to meet her husband.

Tiptoeing back mentally through the rest of the evening, Alison remembered the phone call and sat up with a start. She had promised Wendy she would be at the shelter to wave her off.

At ten minutes to eight, Alison left the cottage, hurrying up the lane, slipping and sliding on the leaves. A few yards from her house, she stopped dead. A black BMW was parked there, a man visible in the driver's seat. Wendy's husband. He was parked under a full evergreen, must have chosen that spot deliberately: he had view of the shelter, but because of the angle of the street and the drooping tree, he would not be visible from any of the shelter windows. They would not see him until they were outside the front door, walking toward the car. But he would see them.

Alison, cursing, reached for her phone to check the call log. Wendy had called last night from the shelter. Please, God, that number was not unlisted. But no. There. There it was. She pressed "Dial," whispering, *Answer, answer, answer*. After what seemed like a lifetime later, she heard Vivienne's voice. Alison spoke fast, her voice low.

"Vivienne, don't let Wendy leave yet. Her husband is in my lane. Watching your building."

"What?" Vivienne said. "Oh, darn it. Really? They're ready to go. Harry is here, waiting to drive her. Her train leaves in . . . Are you sure it's him?"

"Positive. Black BMW. Look, I'll distract him."

"Alison don't do anything that—"

"I'll distract him. Wait one minute, then get her in the car as fast you can. Make sure her hair isn't visible. Have Harry carry Josh to the car. I'll hold him up for a minute or two."

"Now, please don't put yourself—"

"Give her a hug from me. And Josh, too. I'll call my dad later."

She clicked off the phone before Vivienne could protest further, took a breath, and walked fast toward the BMW, stepping out into the center of the lane, as if avoiding the banks of leaves, skidding a little on them. When she was in front of his car, she pulled out her phone and stopped dead as she fiddled with it.

"Sod," she said. "Sod it."

Then, turning as if seeing him inside the car for the first time, she said, "Oh. Sorry."

He rolled down the car window.

"You okay?" A normal, friendly voice, concerned.

"Fine, thanks. Well, no. My stupid phone. Lost the map thing. The app. I can't find the address."

She looked hard at him.

"Are you local? You know where Chestnut Drive is? I think it's Chestnut Drive. I remember the number. Same as my birthday. Number four. I should be there by now."

He leaned out of the window, looked at her, puzzled. His white shirt had a pressed, starched look, fresh from the laundry; she noted the precision knot of his tie. A clean-cut, fair-skinned male, thinning a little on top. She was surprised at his pleasant expression.

"Sorry," he said. "I don't know the area."

"Well, I don't suppose you have a map? Nobody does these days, do they? Funny. But wait—is that a sat nav? Could you look it up?"

"Pardon?" he said. "What did you say?"

If he was irritated, he didn't show it.

"Maybe check on your sat nav? Or on your phone?"

He frowned, looking unsure and then, with an obvious sigh, lifted his phone from the seat beside him. Alison risked a glance at the shelter. A gray car was now parked in front of the building. She took a breath.

"Number four," she said. "I'm pretty sure it's number four. Chestnut Drive."

"Postcode?" he asked.

"Oh, damn. Wait. Wait."

She bit at her nail, thinking hard. She could give him the postcode of the cottage, change the end digit. She recited it as he typed it in.

He shook his head.

"Not valid," he said. "Sorry."

"Maybe I've got the wrong tree," she said. "Can you try something close? Hazelnut? Something like that."

"Hazelnut?" he asked. He seemed amused. "You'll need a valid postcode."

"And maybe a six at the end?"

He tapped in the new numbers.

"No. Afraid you've got it wrong," he said. "Sorry I can't help."

He placed the phone back on the passenger seat deliberately, clearly dismissing her.

"I'm almost sure it's Chestnut," she said. "I should go back home and check. Or ask at the village shop. They might know. So sorry for bothering you." She stayed in his line of sight as she pushed her own phone back into her bag, fastened the bag slowly, and placed it over her shoulder. "Just been one of those mornings. Late night. And, well, way too much wine."

"You need to stay hydrated," he said. "Drink lots of water."

His voice was soft and warm, and she was thrown off-balance for a moment. If you didn't know—you would never know. He seemed like a gentle character.

"I will. Thanks. Have a good day," she called, turning back toward the shelter. The gray car was pulling away. She began to walk slowly down the lane, keeping to the middle of the road, her eyes on the shelter. As she watched, a white car pulled in just as the gray one left, and parked. No. God no. Could this, this white one, be Harry's car? Wendy's husband must have seen it, too. She heard his engine revving up behind her. Heart pounding, Alison continued to walk slowly down the center of the lane. She fumbled for her earbuds, put them in her ears, pulled out her phone again, and studied it like an oblivious teenager. The car was close behind her now. His horn blared. She ignored it. She watched the white car. Someone was getting out of it. At the same moment, the door of the shelter opened.

Behind her, his horn sounded again, louder, longer. She heard the car window roll down.

"Would you get out of my way?" His voice had changed; she could hear the anger in it.

She turned, frowning.

"Sorry?"

"Get out of the way," he yelled.

She saw in his face the rage that Wendy had seen so many times on those nights when he talked to her with his fists.

Alison swallowed hard, moved fast to the side, as his car screamed past. She waited, holding her breath, expecting at any moment to see Wendy and Josh emerge from the door of the shelter. Instead, a woman in a mackintosh and carrying a doctor's bag, locked the white car before walking briskly up the path to the shelter. Someone, vague, shadowy behind the door, greeted her. The door slammed shut.

Thank God.

When Alison reached the end of the lane, the BMW was parked halfway up the hill. She turned the corner, and there was Deirdre at the edge of the sidewalk.

Alison hurried toward her. The adrenaline rush, now fading, had left her feeling shaky, her mouth dry.

"They've gone?" she asked.

"Yep. Safely on their way."

"He's up there. Parked."

"I know. I saw him. The scrote."

"Vivienne didn't say anything to Wendy?"

"What? No. She would have been too scared to leave the house. Funny, I thought I saw his car the other morning in your lane. He must come before he goes to work." She looked at her watch. "He'll be on his way soon. Tomorrow we can have one of the local cops ask him if he's lost. Don't matter if he knows that we've sussed him now that she's gone. Anyway, I better get back. The doctor's here."

"Someone's hurt?"

"New girl. Addicted to painkillers. Having a right tough withdrawal."

"God, how awful," Alison said. "I suppose addiction isn't uncommon?"

"Course not. Painkillers. Antidepressants. Anyway, that was nice of you, Alison, holding him up like that. See you."

She patted Alison's arm, headed back inside the shelter. Alison waved good-bye and walked slowly toward the village shop. Inside, as she placed cheese and grapes into her basket, she saw the black BMW pass on its way out of the village.

"Good," she said aloud.

The woman in the floral apron looked over at her, gave a small, confused smile.

~

In the late afternoon, Alison heard from her father that Wendy and Josh had arrived safely in Scotland. Wendy was thrilled that she had her own bathroom, her father said, amused; she'd never had one to herself before. And Josh was excited by the chickens. They would be fine, he said. They promised to keep in touch. Relieved, Alison decided to head out for a walk. She had been restless all afternoon, edgy after her encounter with Wendy's husband, tired of the scene with Matt playing in an endless loop in her head and the looming prospect of meeting Jake. She would follow the ridge road, she decided, and then walk back in a semicircle to the cottage. It was the perfect day for it, cold and clear. It would do her good, clear the cobwebs, and get the blood circulating a bit. Her body felt heavy and tired; a dull headache throbbed behind her eyes.

The early part of the walk through the village was easy, and Alison moved fast, but on the steep uphill section she was soon out of breath, cursing the fact that she was so out of shape. She would join a gym, she vowed. She would take up jogging.

At the best vantage point, she stopped to admire the view of the village and her own cottage. Then she froze, staring at the point where the lane met the village road. A blue compact car was parked outside her cottage. Not Liz's car. Not a car she had ever seen in the village before. Wendy's husband back in a different car? But he would not park right outside her cottage. Parking was possible along the entire lane. It was someone who had come to see her, had hoped to find her in. She squinted, trying to make out the figure in the driver's seat. Could

Matt be driving a compact? It seemed unlikely, unless he was driving Celine's car. A thought, then, that chilled her. Could it be Celine, come to confront her?

She moved forward, fearful, trying to see better, felt her foot slide on the damp undergrowth, and immediately jumped backward. At the same moment, she heard a noise behind her.

"Watch it!" a voice yelled, too late.

She turned. Vivienne was on the ground, her bicycle next to her. She had tumbled sideways in her attempt to avoid hitting Alison.

"Oh God. I'm so sorry," Alison said. "Didn't see you."

"Obviously," Vivienne said.

She stood, brushing at the dirt on her pants and jacket, then bent down to pick up the bike, straightening the pedals, shaking it into shape. "I knew this old bike was a mistake," she said. She frowned at Alison.

"You jumped back awfully fast," she said. "Why were you hanging over the ridge like that?"

"I wanted to see—" Alison began. She longed to look again over the edge of the ridge, check out the occupant of the blue car. She noted the field glasses Vivienne carried around her neck.

"Vivienne, would you do me a favor?"

"You just knocked me off my bike and now you're asking for a favor?" Vivienne asked, though she was smiling. "Shameless behavior."

"I know. Would you, though?"

"Of course. What?"

"Look down onto Church Road with your binoculars and then up the road to my cottage. There's a blue car parked there. Would you take a look at the person driving? Is it a dark-haired woman? I can't see well enough to be sure."

Vivienne rested her bicycle against the trunk of a pine tree, then moved to the edge of the ridge.

"Darn," she said as she fumbled with the glasses. "These bird glasses are older than I am. Ah, right. Got it. Oh, sorry. Can't tell. They're driving off. Here, take a look."

She handed the glasses to Alison. It took her a moment to focus them, to center the picture she needed. She saw the back of a blue compact turning onto the main Shrewsbury Road, heading out of the village. Through the rear window, the shape of a driver's head and shoulders, indistinct, was just visible. Celine? It was possible. She shivered.

"Gone," she said. "Whoever it was."

"Shame," Vivienne said.

"Just as well," Alison said, trying to keep her voice steady. "I'm not really up for company."

But Vivienne wasn't listening.

"Look to your left," she said. "Starlings. Doing their thing."

Through the glasses, Alison caught a smudge in the sky, spreading. She lowered the glasses and looked hard: yes, the starlings were massing in the sky. She had noticed them, their amazing synchronized dance, one evening through the bedroom window.

"We'll see them clearly in a moment," Vivienne said. "Just to the right of the ridge."

They stood, watching together. It had amazed Alison at first, what seemed like many hundreds of birds gathering together in full view of her window. Each time it felt like a cinematic display for her entertainment alone. The light was perfect right now, ethereal, and the hills dark, so that when the starling formation dropped lower to the ground, the actual details faded, and the hills looked as if they were rippling, coming alive. Then the birds, in tight formation, moved up into the silver sky.

Alison stared, entranced at the symmetry of it, those geometric edges, triangles, the dense pyramids. Then, suddenly stretching out, changing shape, the birds created an undulating flowing form, like butterfly wings, a floating image now, on the darkening sky. It thrilled her each time, this display. She knew the villagers complained—the starlings were loud birds, and apparently their droppings, on parked cars and carefully tended patio gardens, irritated some residents. But Alison liked to watch as new flocks from the north or south joined the main body, blending into the perfect synchronicity of the dance. Then it was over.

"Amazing," she said, turning back to Vivienne.

"It is. A murmuration. Isn't that a perfect word? Not accepted by scholars, unfortunately."

"For what? The dance?"

"Dance?" Vivienne said. "No, the name for a flock of starlings. The collective noun."

"Like a murder of crows?"

"Yes. A parliament of rooks. An exaltation of larks."

"Exaltation? That sounds wrong."

"Why?"

"It sounds too loud and exuberant."

"Larks *are* loud and exuberant."

"Are they? Oh well. A murmuration," Alison repeated. "You're right. It's perfect." She turned back to the path. "I should start back. It's getting dark."

"And I should return this poor bike to the shed. Which way are you walking?"

"Across the ridge, then back down onto the road."

"I'm just up here. The gates on the left."

"I heard from my dad," Alison said as they began the walk along the path. "Wendy arrived safely. Sounds fine."

"I know. She called me. Josh was very taken with the chickens, apparently."

They laughed.

"Such a sweet girl," Vivienne said.

"I imagine she was an easier resident than Sophie."

"They had different problems."

"Vivienne, was Sophie clean when she was with you?" Alison asked impulsively.

The older woman thought for a moment, as if unsure of how to answer.

"Yes," she said, at last. "Tried to be. I worried when she crept out that she was using again. But she never seemed affected. Not when she was with us. Maybe I should have been more vigilant." She sighed. "Of course I feel guilty about that now."

"We all feel guilty," Alison said, and then, as a thought occurred to her: "Did she meet up with a big guy, heavy, red faced?"

Ronnie, with his huge bulk, would be easily remembered.

Vivienne shook her head.

"We never saw the person she met. She was careful about that. Don't know if it was a man or a woman."

Alison blinked.

"A woman? You think she might have—"

"It's possible," Vivienne said. "Sophie loved to tell stories about past lovers, male and female. She could keep that entire sitting room entertained for hours."

Alison laughed.

"Not sure how much of that was true," she said, adding, "Wendy said there was gossip about a big car."

"A millionaire?" Vivienne smiled. "Yes, I heard that one, too. I can't give you answers, Alison. I wish I could."

Alison thought about this as they walked. So Sophie might have been meeting a woman in the hotel that night? She ticked through possibilities in her mind: Linda. No. She had been babysitting the twins. Liz? Alison recalled Liz's distress in the pub when they talked of Matt and Sophie. But why meet in a hotel? No. The very idea was ridiculous. More likely a man, Alison concluded. Probably a sleazebag dealer. Someone she had never met and was not likely to meet. So much of Sophie's life would remain a mystery.

Vivienne had stopped at a set of wrought-iron gates.

"This is me," she said.

Alison looked through the gates to see a low, modern house, all glass and local stone, so carefully designed that it seemed to merge into the hillside.

"Wow. That's a beautiful house."

"It is rather splendid, isn't it? My husband designed it. It's perfectly situated."

"He's an architect?"

"Was. He died two years ago. A stroke."

"I'm sorry. But what a lovely legacy. I imagine the views are wonderful."

"Yes. From every room. We lived on the plot for a few weeks, in a motor home. Took note of the light and temperature changes. Decided where we wanted the big windows. It was enormous fun."

"I bet it was. Where were you before?"

"Vancouver. We lived there for twenty years."

Alison turned, astonished.

"Twenty years! Really? I thought you'd lived here all your life! Your husband was Canadian?"

"Half. He moved there in his teens. His mother was English. From the next village. We both missed England when we were there, and we missed Vancouver when we were here."

"I know that feeling."

"It's common to all expats. Rushdie wrote about it, the homelessness of the expatriate. You must miss California."

"Yes. I do."

"And what do you do over there?"

"Advertising. I spend my days trying to persuade people to buy things they don't want or need and can't afford."

"Hmm. Interesting?"

"No. Not anymore. I've just given up my job. I know I could find another in advertising but—"

"You don't want that?"

"No. No. I really, really don't."

Vivienne laughed.

"You sound very sure."

"I am. It's all lies. That milk on the cereal is white glue, so the cereal doesn't go soggy. Steaks get their healthy, appetizing gleam from shoe polish; the pink ice cream that looks so delicious is mashed potato and food coloring. And the models—filmed through gauze, painted and starved and treated like objects to be bent and stretched and arranged, and their faces, their real faces, hidden behind makeup and shot through filters."

The older woman looked amused as she listened.

"My goodness, I think it's time for a career change for you," she said. "Is advertising what you wanted originally?"

"No. I suppose I wanted to be an artist, but I wanted to be a *good* artist. Not a doodler, a player. But—no. Just don't have the talent. I'm a fair designer. I'm a fairly good copywriter. Not brilliant at either. I wish I had the talent to be a real artist. But I don't."

Vivienne didn't demur, say that she was sure that Alison was talented. She nodded, believing her.

"Why not do it for fun? Do it because you love it. It doesn't have to be a career."

"Yes," Alison said. "I guess I know that now."

She thought for a moment.

"I'm wondering whether to rethink the whole thing. Teach instead. Maybe art or art history, teach kids to appreciate it." As she said the words, she realized that she meant them, though she had not consciously given that particular career path serious thought.

"At university I considered it but—well, both of my parents were teachers. My father taught high school, still does. My mother taught kindergarten, though honestly I never thought of her as a teacher. I saw her as someone who looked after the little kids."

"And you wanted something different?"

"I did then. Now—well, it seems like an option."

"If you love art and can engage your students, you'll give them a gift for life," Vivienne said. "It's like reading. Teach a kid to read and you give him the world."

"You're right," Alison said. "You're absolutely right."

At the sound of their voices, a golden Labrador came bounding from the other side of the house, leaping across the lawns, tail wagging with joy. Vivienne opened the gate, and the dog ran around them both, its entire lower body moving with the wagging tail.

"Calm down, Mavis. Please," Vivienne said.

Alison bent down to pet the dog.

"She's beautiful."

"And she knows it."

Vivienne turned to her.

"We can walk you down to the village if you like. It's getting dark. That path can feel a bit isolated. Mavis would love a walk."

"That would be nice. Thank you."

They walked down the hill, pausing often to wait for the dog to finish her exploration of various bushes, stones, unidentifiable little heaps of earth.

"Will you be staying long in the village?" Vivienne asked, after they had been walking for a while.

"Don't know. I'm all upside down at the moment. London tomorrow. I'm meeting my husband."

"Your husband's in London? I thought he was still in California—"

"He was. He's here now. We had a little break. But we need to, well, I need to, decide—"

Vivienne was silent for a few moments.

"I'm sorry," she said. "He didn't want this break?"

"No. He did not."

"He's in advertising, too?"

"No. Pharmaceutical company. That's part of the problem. He loves his work, works all the time. Recently he's been gone so much. Conferences all over the place. We never take vacations. We never talk or just—" She shook her head. "We used to have fun together."

"It's good that he loves his work, surely?" Vivienne said. "Why don't you join him at some of the conferences? Take vacation time." She sighed. "This must be an odd limbo for you. You can't try to figure it out together? I've never thought that separation helps much. Maybe a week. But a long separation? No. How can anything be resolved if you're apart? You need to work on problems while you're in the same house, the same room, the same bed.

"Just my opinion," she added. "Everyone is different."

They had reached the bottom of the hill.

"I'm fine from here," Alison said. "Thank you for walking me down. And thank you so much for the chat. It really helped."

"It did?" Vivienne said, smiling, surprised. "Good luck tomorrow."

TWENTY

The lobby of the London hotel, with its subdued lighting and low armchairs, hadn't changed. Alison walked through it quickly, surprised at how easily she remembered the way to the restaurant. They had stayed here years ago, when Jake attended a meeting of a huge Europe-based consortium, and Alison had joined him. Her mother had just become ill—though they did not know then, and were not to know for some weeks, the seriousness of her illness—and so she had visited her parents and Liz, met Sophie for a fast drink in a local pub, and then returned to London to window-shop on Oxford Street and Bond Street, shocked at how impossibly expensive England had become. They had dinner together, she and Jake, on their last night at Brown's, she remembered that evening. They had both been tired, and they had taken a bottle of wine back to the room and made love with a lot of teasing, a lot of laughter. *Such a long time ago,* Alison thought, as she located the corridor leading to the restaurant. *A different life, a different marriage.*

In the restaurant, she saw Jake immediately. He sat at the bar, reading a newspaper and sipping a drink. He looked up, saw her, and smiled. She noted, with a shock, how attractive he looked. He brought the signatures of California with him: the tanned skin, the confidence and vitality.

"Hello, beauty," he said, kissing her cheek, hugging her. He appeared at ease as he stood back to study her. "You look good."

"Thank you. I've never had so much fresh air in my life."

She had expected to feel a return of the guilt and confusion, but for those first moments, something shifted. It was like meeting an old friend in a foreign city, when a shared history creates a bond. He looked so familiar, so known, tall and tan, glowing in the dim autumnal light.

She turned away.

"Shall we find our table?" she said.

A waiter came to settle her into the seat and hand menus to them both. When the young man had left, Jake said, "You traveling back with me?"

The question, so quickly, unnerved her. She chewed her lip, stared at the menu with ferocious concentration.

"No. I promised to attend this hearing, Jake. Custody hearing. I think I told you."

"You did? What custody hearing?"

"Sophie's children. Her twin girls."

"I don't remember you saying anything about this. Who's claiming them?"

"Sophie's brother, Matt, and his French wife."

"Oh, right. The boy next door?"

"Yes. But now the twins' father wants custody."

"The father? Well, I guess he has rights."

"He abandoned them. He hasn't seen them for years."

"He wants them now, though?"

"Yes."

"Stable home life?"

"Apparently. But—"

He shrugged.

"You could be on the wrong side here, sweetheart."

Jake looked up as the wine waiter appeared.

"Just one glass for me," Alison said.

"Why? Let's get a bottle. I've cleared the afternoon. We can relax," Jake said, looking again at the wine list.

"One glass. Please. Chardonnay."

She noted Jake's puzzled look as the waiter nodded at her request. When they had ordered their food, Jake leaned back in his chair and scrutinized her. She could not read his expression with any certainty. Concern, perhaps. Doubt.

"You caught up with your dad?"

"Yes. He's fine. Likes his new life in Scotland."

"And all your old friends and boyfriends?"

"Of course. So," she said quickly, "how are your meetings here going?"

Jake shook his head.

"The company guys are okay," he said. "But the lawyers involved? Jesus. British lawyers were put on the earth to drive the rest of us crazy. The senior barrister is fine, just a regular guy, but the young turk? He's really got a pole up his ass. Thinks he's some kind of goddamned superior being. He's as dumb as a post, but he hides it with a lot of fancy talk and a mouthful of marbles. I keep thinking he's kidding."

She smiled then.

"He's probably intimidated by you."

"Me?" His face showed genuine amazement. "I'm a pussycat. Who could be intimidated by me?"

When the food arrived, they ate in silence for a while. Alison picked at the sautéed trout with no appetite. Jake looked over at her.

"So, after this hearing, you'll come home?"

She took a breath. She could prevaricate no longer.

"No. Not yet."

He put down his fork slowly, stared at her.

"What? Why?"

"I need some time to think. More time to myself."

"More time to yourself? You've had weeks to yourself."

"You don't see that we've been having problems? Not just recently but for some time?"

"Problems? No. No, I don't. Nothing major, for Christ's sake. I know I'm busy. I'm late. I know you hate the damn dinners. Well, so do I."

"It's not that. We've grown apart, Jake. We never talk. Not about anything important."

"That's not true. We're busy; that's all. We've been married for—what, how many years? Six? And you suddenly decide that—"

"Seven. Our lives have shrunk. Mine has. Marriage shouldn't diminish us like this. I think a separation—a short one—" she added quickly, "would be good for us. Give us time to decide what changes we could—"

"Exactly what kind of changes do you have in mind?" he asked, edgy now.

Alison bit her lip, trying hard to formulate in words what she needed him to know.

"I don't understand what happened to us," she said. "The people we used to be. Remember when you hung all my sketches in the canyon flat? We never hung them in the new house. What happened to them? What happened to that part of my life? Our life is just work and nothing else these days. No vacations. No time together. Why? To buy a big house and two ugly cars?"

Jake sat up then.

"The cars are too ugly? The house is too big? Not dark and small and fusty and English enough? The house has got to be old and falling apart with crumbling beams and a smell like rotting burlap. Is that it? Why didn't you just speak up, for God's sake, if you don't like the house? Not polite? Maybe everything is just too loud for you? Too American?"

"Don't be ridiculous. I don't mean that at all. And you have a nerve talking about loud. You were the one who tried to tone me down."

"Holy shit. What are you talking about now?"

"You criticized my purple hair. You didn't like the way I dressed."

"I loved your purple hair! I didn't think you needed to hide behind all that goth makeup; that's all. Your skin's so beautiful, and the natural color of your hair is amazing, and I said if you wanted to get the job, then maybe you should try a different look. You seemed intent on shooting yourself in the foot before you even arrived at the goddamned interview."

"Maybe I didn't want the job."

"So why the fuck did you take it?"

Alison stared at him.

"I don't know," she said.

Silence. They looked at each other across the restaurant table.

"Of course we've changed, Alison," Jake said finally, his voice quieter. "You think I don't miss our old life, too? I do. I miss the hikes, the outdoor weekends we used to have. I miss camping."

She stared, astounded. He had never told her that. *Too late,* she thought. *Too late.*

"Other things got in the way," Jake continued. "But—we can get that back, maybe. I can't promise you hearts and flowers all the time."

"I don't need hearts and flowers all the time. I need proper communication. And it's not just the old life. The free weekends. We should be thinking about a family. But we don't, do we? We used to talk about it. We don't anymore."

His face changed then. She saw a hopefulness, a lightening of his expression.

"I thought you wanted to get on with your career first. But look, okay, we can make a few changes."

"No," Alison said sharply. "No."

He looked hard at her, startled.

"It's more than *a few changes*," she said. "For starters, I've given notice. I'm not going to work in advertising. Ever. Not anymore."

"Are you serious? You're good at it. I know Marcus is a pain in the ass, but there are other agencies."

"It's not just Marcus," Alison said. "I hate the work. I've always hated it."

"What? Why? You never said."

"I tried to tell you. Sometimes I just couldn't explain how bad it made me feel."

She thought of the humiliations of past failures. The embarrassment she felt at some of her successes. The filmed commercials that made her cringe. The jingles she never admitted to creating. The young models she befriended who worried and depressed her, with their overwhelming fears of weight gain, of aging, of lost contracts.

"So why did you keep doing it?" Jake asked.

"Because I'm stupid?" she said. "I have no idea. Maybe it's a kind of hair-shirt thing, an odd perception that hard things must be good for me. I seem to have spent my life doing whatever other people expected of me."

Jake studied her face. She could see the bafflement in his eyes.

"What is going on with you?" he asked, in a gentler voice. "You been hiding out here, listing all the things you hate in your life? You think a new career will make you happy, then fine. Do it. I'll support you every way I can. I've always supported you. And, if it's what you want, we can make a baby. We can make lots of babies if you like."

Alison looked at her husband for a long time. He returned her look, unflinching. He pushed his plate away, looked at Alison's food, barely touched, and then looked up at the waiter, hovering close to their table, before he took a long swallow of his wine and got to his feet.

"I don't see why we have to share this discussion with half of London. Let's go. We can take a walk by the river. Eat later."

Alison glanced up, surprised. Jake was not one to leave a meal half-eaten, a wineglass half-full. He signed the check as Alison gulped at her drink. She felt off-balance now, unsure of what was to be said.

"Got to get my coat from the room," he said. "Too damn cold out there. Come on."

She followed him, unthinking, into the elevator. In the room, she realized that it was not a walk by the river that Jake had in mind.

He came toward her, pulled her against him. His cotton shirt felt soft against her face and smelled of fabric softener and deodorant soap and faintly, beneath that, a smell that was so familiar, that was uniquely his own and so evocative to her that when they were first married and he was away on business, she would come across one of his worn sweaters, hold it to her face, breathing him in. She could seek him out and find him in a crowd of millions, if she had to, by his scent alone.

The comfort, the familiarity of it, confused her. Her body, attuned to his, responded as it always had, and she found herself tightening her arms around his shoulders, needing the reassurance of his body hard against hers. She knew then how easy it would be to sink onto that bed, to make love. It would be easy to pretend, afterward, that everything was fine. To begin a different life, maybe a family with a child. A baby.

But. But. Matt.

She stepped back.

"You said something about a walk along the river."

"Afterward," he said softly, reaching for her again.

Her voice was sharp when she moved away.

"That's the only way you can communicate, Jake? You think sex will make it okay? No. Not this time."

Her words seemed to hang in the air of the dim room.

"So go ahead," he said at last, an edge to his voice. "Communicate."

Alison took a long breath.

"Not here."

She walked to the door and opened it.

"Is there a coffee shop somewhere?" she asked.

"Oh, for fuck's sake, Alison. Okay. Let's get a drink."

∼

The hotel bar was dark, cave-like, with low copper tables and plush bench seats. Jake waited until she was settled at one of the far tables by the window, ordered scotch for himself, a gin and tonic for her, then sat on the opposite chair.

"Okay, okay," he said, his voice normal now, the anger gone. "Tell me what you want and let's discuss it. I miss you, Alison. I want you home."

She sighed.

"A few weeks ago I would have asked that we go on vacation and yes, later, maybe think about a baby. That would have been enough."

"And you don't want those things now?" he asked, attempting a smile. "Why not?"

She did not smile back.

"I feel like I'm living someone else's life, Jake. I don't like the person I've become. I used to be an artist. Now I'm—I don't know what I am."

"You've got sketch pads on the top shelf of the closet, you've got paints in the garage. You don't touch them."

"I don't seem to have time anymore."

"Look, we're busy for a few months and you get all bent out of shape? Come on."

"Okay," she hesitated, thinking. "I feel that all the dreams I once had have been—"

"What dreams?"

"Will you just listen for a minute? Stop interrupting."

He leaned back, groaned. "Okay. Shit—that's fine. You wrote the script. You play both parts."

"Don't be silly."

"Look, for Christ's sake. You want to paint—so paint. You want a baby. Okay, sure. Honest to God, so do I. You *know* I do. Let's make one."

"It's not working, Jake."

"What? Why? You want me to tell you I love you every five minutes? I do. You know that. Is that what you want to hear?"

"You loved me. Once. And I loved you, too. But—"

"You used the past tense."

She looked at the table and then out of the small window. It was getting dark out there, had begun to rain. People were scuttling past, eager to get inside and out of the wind.

"Maybe our marriage is past tense. That's really what I came to say."

Jake stared at her for a few moments, disbelieving.

"The boy next door have anything to do with this decision?" he asked, his voice icy.

And there it was, out in the open. Alison realized as she hesitated, lowering her eyes, that she had deceived herself almost as much as she had deceived Jake. Matt was at the heart of her confusion. It had always been so.

She hesitated a little too long. It was too long for Jake. He stood so abruptly that the table shuddered.

She looked up, startled. The pain in his face was so raw that she caught her breath.

"Then there's nothing more to say," he said.

He walked to the door, stared for a few moments into the rainy London street, then he turned on his heel, not looking at Alison, and strode fast to the elevator, heading back to his room.

Alison felt the cold tremble of shock at so clear and unequivocal a response. She waited a suspended, unsure time, wondering if he would return to the bar, or if he would come back to the doorway and gesture for her to follow him so that they might talk further somewhere else. She looked through the thick glass of the window and sipped at her drink, feeling strange and conspicuous in the once quiet bar, as stragglers, sheltering from the rain, hustled inside, bringing conversation and laughter, shaking raindrops from their hair and umbrellas.

After a while she understood that Jake would not return. He was in his room, perhaps. Or he was out walking the London streets. Her marriage was over. The enormity of this hit her as the waiter came to the table and indicated her empty glass. She shook her head.

My God, she thought, *what have I done?* She lifted the check still lying on the table, looked at it for a moment, then waved for the waiter.

TWENTY-ONE

Alison expected Jake to call the next day. In her head, she tracked where he would be and visualized what he might be doing. She understood his bewilderment. She had given him no warning of what was to come, and she could not shake the scene in that dim bar from her memory and kept seeing again and again the shock and pain on his face. She imagined him at the beginning of his work day, lying on the bed in that plush hotel room, hands behind his head, staring at the ceiling, and she wanted to call and say, *I'm sorry. I'm so sorry for hurting you.*

For most of the morning, she sipped coffee and stared out of the window at the tiny cottage garden, littered with leaves.

Now that her marriage was essentially over, she was, or soon would be, free. She did not feel free, she admitted. She felt strangely untethered and lost. And ashamed. She had hurt Jake. She had handled the entire thing badly.

Intermittently, she thought of Matt—at home, preparing for the hearing, with his wife, with the twins—and she mentally rehearsed how she might share the news of her marriage breakup. Would he feel pressured? She wanted him to say something, do something, that might indicate his feelings for her before she told him, and she felt a return of all that buried adolescent insecurity. She had no idea, she realized, what he wanted from her. Her head teemed with questions.

Where would she live? Where was her home? With Matt? Not here, not in this village, waiting for occasional visits. The mistress in the country. A London flat? A Paris flat? A home together. Maybe with the twins and perhaps, later, children of their own. Here, she hit a mental wall. She tried to imagine it, shaken by how impossible, how wrong it seemed. Whenever she thought of children, it was Jake she had always visualized as their father.

"I want you and a home, and I want to spend weekends in forests and by oceans, and I want to carry our children on my shoulders," Jake had said, in the early days of their marriage when she asked him what he wanted from his life. He laughed after he said it, mocking himself.

"That sounds so lame. Okay. Add a Nobel prize and a Maserati."

"Forget the Maserati," she had said, kissing him. "The rest sounds wonderful."

When the phone rang in the late afternoon, she jumped and hurried to it. It was Liz. With the custody hearing so close, Alison had been expecting her to call, but Liz's first questions were about Jake.

"So?" she asked, without preamble.

"So what?"

"Jake? What happened?" Liz lowered her voice to a whisper.

"Liz, why are you whispering? You are talking on the phone. *In your own house.*"

"Oh, he's not there, then. He didn't come back with you? How did it go? Did you fight? Is it resolved?"

Alison hesitated. She did not want to describe those final moments in the bar. Maybe later, after the hearing, she would confide in her friend.

"We chatted. We didn't fight. We were civil and calm," she said.

Liz sighed.

"So where is he now?"

"He's still in London. He has meetings."

"You'll see him again, though? Before he goes back?"

"Maybe," Alison said. "Don't worry."

"Well, excuse me for being concerned. I just don't want you to do something stupid. If Matt—"

"Liz, I appreciate your concern," Alison said, interrupting. "Really. But first things first. We've got this hearing tomorrow. You ready for it?"

"Oh, damn the bloody hearing. You sure we won't have to speak?" Liz asked.

"God, I hope not."

"Because I really, really do not want to speak. I wish we hadn't agreed to this."

"We promised, Liz. We can't back out now."

"We shouldn't have let ourselves be bullied into it," Liz said, then added, "And Simon says he's too busy to come to the thing, so it's just you and me, and I'll have to race off afterwards to pick up Jamie. You're okay getting there on the train?"

"I'll be fine. I'll meet you outside."

"And what about getting back?"

"I'll be fine. I'll get the train. Liz, stop fretting about it."

"It's a damn nuisance. Why didn't they get other people to give them references? Why us?"

"We're old friends. Look, do it for Sophie. And her twins. She'd want us to help her brother."

"Maybe," Liz said, still unsure. "Okay. See you tomorrow."

A few minutes later the telephone rang again, and at the sound of Matt's voice, Alison whipped around, turned off the kettle, moved to the sofa, and sank onto it.

"Just thinking about you," he said.

"You too."

"The timing is rather difficult right now, of course," he said. "With this hearing coming up. But soon—we'll get together. Perhaps a weekend by the sea? We'll arrange something when it's over."

"By the sea? Oh, I would love that. I really would."

"Then we'll be sure to make it happen," he said, his voice soft. He created an intimacy on the telephone that somehow didn't work so well in person. She wondered about that—the timbre of his voice. Low, secret.

She took a breath.

"I met up with Jake yesterday."

"Your husband?" A different note. "And how was that?"

"It got a little complicated towards the end."

"This is hard for you, Ali. I know that. We'll talk about it properly, when we meet."

"Yes. Okay."

Another silence. Alison waited.

"Well, I need to check that everyone can make it for the hearing," he said at last. "Does anyone need to be picked up? You? Liz?"

"We'll be fine," Alison said. "We'll be there."

"Good. I can't tell you how—"

His voice changed then; somebody had obviously entered the room.

"Good, good," he said in a formal voice. "Shall we meet outside the building, then? About thirty minutes before it starts?"

Alison closed her phone. How wary he had sounded when she talked about Jake. She was an idiot. She should have waited until they met in person.

She stood abruptly, returned to the kitchen to make the tea she had abandoned. As the kettle boiled, she recalled an old saying her father used to quote to her: *Take what you want and pay for it. But first,* he would add, *you have to decide what you want.*

If I want a life with Matt, then I must find the courage to tell him so, Alison thought. *And if the price is losing Jake, then I must be willing to accept it.*

Vivienne had called this an odd limbo, this time in the village and the uncertainty about a direction. It felt that way. A weird space between worlds. *Something has to give here,* she thought. *Something has to crack.*

It cracked an hour later when two people appeared on the doorstep of her cottage.

TWENTY-TWO

Alison saw the blue car as it turned into the lane. Instinctively, she jumped back from the window, out of sight. It looked like the same car she had seen from the ridge. The ringing doorbell, a minute later, confirmed it. Celine? Please, no. She could stay silent, not answer the bell. But what if the caller was Matt? She took a long inward breath and opened the door.

A man and a woman stood on the step. The man was tall, thin, his face vaguely familiar. Alison, tussling with memory, searched for a name.

"I'm Gary Lewis," he said. "Sophie's husband. I need to talk to you."

Alison stared: an ordinary face, a tidy man, thinning on top. She could detect only the faintest trace in his features of the young rocker with yellow, spiked hair she remembered from years ago.

"I shouldn't be talking to you," she said.

"Please."

"It'll only take a minute," said the woman with him.

Alison noted the anxious look on the woman's face and held the door open. They stood in the center of the small room, making it feel claustrophobic and airless.

"Please sit down," Alison said.

After some shuffling indecision, they sat close together on the sofa. Alison took the chair, facing them.

"This is Gillian, my girlfriend. Well, fiancé, really," Gary Lewis said.

Gillian, a small woman with a pink, pretty face, nodded. "Pleased to meet you," she said solemnly.

"What's this about?" Alison asked. "How did you find out where I live?"

"Your address was on your statement," Gary Lewis said. "Our solicitor gave us copies."

"Oh. So you know where I stand on this. Why are you here?"

"We want you to ask Matt Stuart to withdraw his application," Gary said. "Or for you to tell the truth."

Alison looked hard at him. "I told the truth. Matt and Celine will make excellent parents. They're devoted to the girls."

"Tell the truth about him and Sophie," said Gary. "The court might think different then. If he wants to stop it all coming out, he better withdraw now. Drop his claim. All that crap he's told the Social about me doing drugs, that's not true. Tell him that. He won't talk to me. He might listen to you."

Alison, confused, felt a flash of fear. His face was so stiff, his eyes cold.

"I don't know what you're talking—"

"Yes, you do. We could tell them, no, we *will* tell them about how Matt abused his sister."

A chill, a cold shiver began at the base of Alison's spine.

"You'd tell them *what*?"

"Matt had sex with Sophie when she was thirteen years old. And this is a man who wants custody of two little girls?"

"You'd tell vindictive lies just to win—"

"Not lies. You know that. Sophie told me you nearly caught them out once. You were with them on a camping trip. She was in a tent with Matt."

"I don't know what you're talking about," Alison said.

"Oh yes, you do. Their sick relationship."

Gary looked so serious, leaning forward, staring into her face, that her uneasiness intensified. She didn't know these people. She should not have let them into her cottage.

"I'd like you to leave," she said, getting to her feet.

"We're asking you to do the right thing," he said. "We'll be good parents. You wouldn't be doing anything to hurt the girls. He's got no right to them. That's a fact."

"Please go," Alison said.

"Listen, I want my daughters. He's not entitled to them." Alison heard the anger in his voice. "He can't take everything."

She met his eyes, tried to hide her fear and discomfort.

"I've made my statement," she said. "Matt and Celine love the twins. They'll take good care of them. And you shouldn't be here trying to intimidate me."

"Okay. Have it your own way. I'll tell them the entire bloody truth then and make sure you get called to the stand," Gary said. "You get up there and lie, that'd be perjury. You could go to prison for that."

"It's not a court of law. It's an adoption panel," Alison said, turning toward the door. Her hands trembled now, and nerves caused her breath to catch in her throat.

"Sophie wanted to live with him," Gary said. "Live with Matt, just the two of them. That's all she ever wanted, all her life. I bet she told you that?"

"No. She never told me that."

Alison paused. What did this man know about Sophie that she didn't? He had been married to her. He had known her during the difficult years. She sat down again on the armchair, wanting, despite all of her fears, to hear what he had to say.

Realizing he had her attention, he spoke quickly.

"She married me because she was pregnant," he said. "You were there."

"Yes. I remember."

"Then Matt takes off, the day of our bloody wedding, and she's upset, but she thought he'll go back to Oxford and then he'll come stay with us for weekends and so, when we get our own flat, she started making plans. A sofa bed for him for when he comes to stay. All this stuff for *him*. She hardly made plans for the baby. Then he writes to her from some foreign place."

"Tangier," Alison said softly. He looked at her sharply, nodded.

"That's it. Tangier. And he said he's not coming back at all. So she goes fucking crazy. Takes off on my bike. She could ride it, you know, used to switch places with me soon as we left her house, me on the back, her steering the bike. It was a heavy sucker, too. Anyway, she takes off on the bike, and she hits the curb and she's thrown off. She's okay, basically, a sprained wrist, but she loses the baby."

He was silent for a moment, thinking.

"When she comes out of the hospital, she don't want to be married anymore. Said there's no point if we don't have a baby. Said she was going to live with Matt. And she waits around the house, moping, smoking God knows what, until he writes and tells her no. He don't want her to come out there, wherever the hell he was, and he's not coming home. Well, she's gutted. She's in bloody pieces for months. Doing all kinds of dope, not taking care of herself. This went on for ages. Then she OD'd one night and wound up in intensive care, and after a bit they shifted her over to the rehab place."

"I remember that," Alison said, trying to speak calmly. "I talked to her there. I was in my second year at university. She never said anything to me about going to live with Matt."

"No. It was their dark little secret. She only told me once when she was really high and out of it and mad with me.

"Anyway, he visits her there, during her rehab, took this Frenchwoman with him, and apparently Sophie went ballistic, but eventually she came out, and we started again. She was clean for a good while. Got a little job and everything. Took care of herself. Then she got pregnant with the girls, and she tried to be straight and healthy, and she was doing well. Really well. She didn't do any dope; she wouldn't even have a beer. He'd write to her. But he never came back to England, and she had the girls and everything was okay, and I thought we was happy. We had our babies. We had our little flat.

"Then he called. Said he was married. Had married the Frenchwoman. She went batshit crazy again. She wanted to go to France. She wanted to talk to his wife and I said no and we had a big fight and she told me to piss off and I was so bloody mad I did. For a week. Went to Brighton on the lash. When I came back, she'd moved out of the flat.

"I thought she'd gone back to her mother's, but she hadn't. Took four weeks to find her, and we talked and she said she didn't want to live with me anymore, didn't want anything to do with me. I said I wanted to see my girls and she said okay—but that was a lie. Didn't know it at the time. I said I would put money in her account for them.

"And that was the last time I saw my daughters. I put money into her bank account that month—I've a got record of it, the solicitor's got it—but when I tried to transfer more after, the account was closed. She kept moving around, one place to another. She never paid rent properly. Lived with different men, lived with this woman for a bit, drew social security illegally. All kinds of shit. I didn't know what the hell to do. I didn't want to grass her up, get her into trouble with the Social or nothing, because what good would that do for the girls, their mum in prison? But I tried to find her, and then I learn from a friend that she's carrying for Zak."

"Carrying?" Alison interrupted. "What do you mean *carrying*?"

"She was a drug courier for Zak. Using, too. He paid her in dope. She sold some of it to her mates."

He stopped then.

"She must have been carrying when she went to that hotel."

Gillian moved to touch his arm; the distress in his voice was audible now.

"But you can see, can't you, how her fucking brother destroyed her life?" he asked. "And mine. All she ever wanted was him. All she ever cared about was him."

"But it's not his fault," Alison said, "that she loved him."

"Love? It wasn't love. Obsession, more like."

"You don't know that."

"I'll win this, you know," Gary stated. "I can show that I tried to find her. And if I have to bring up the weird stuff that went on with them when they were teenagers, I will. I swear. And I can tell you this, he'll regret it. His fine reputation, his nice career."

Alison stood then, wanting them to go away, get out of her cottage.

"Vindictive nonsense," she said. "Everyone will know you're lying."

"Really? You know I'm not." He shook his head. "I don't want to bring it up. I don't, honest. I don't want something on the record the girls might see one day. Things about their mum."

Alison stared at him. *He means it,* she thought. *He doesn't want this to come out. He would have said something sooner.*

"But if I have to—I will," he added. "Tomorrow. Promise you that."

"Please go," Alison said in a determined voice that shook only slightly.

She walked with them to the door. In the shadowy light of the hallway, they both looked older, exhausted. Gary Lewis turned to her as he stood on the step.

"Please," he said. "Think about it. Talk to him. Sophie used to say you loved him. Think what this would do to him if it all came out."

Alison watched them as they walked to their car. When they had driven away, she dropped onto the sofa, shock causing a fine trembling throughout her body. After a while, she stood and stared out into the garden, her thoughts scrambled, waiting for the shaking to stop. She should call Matt. *Must* call Matt. Must warn him of Gary's malice and intent.

She hesitated a minute longer, then dialed his cell phone and groaned out loud when it went straight to voice mail. With clumsy fingers, she dialed the Stuart household and sighed with relief when Matt answered.

"I must talk to you," she said at once. She described how Gary Lewis and his fiancé had turned up on her doorstep.

"He's saying some very damaging things, Matt. And unless you withdraw your petition he's threatening to say them tomorrow. Publicly."

"What kind of things?"

"About your relationship with Sophie. He said, well—look, can we meet? Maybe tonight? I can explain to you—"

He had turned away from the phone. She heard him call *In a minute* to someone.

"Sorry, Ali," he said. "No, not tonight. We're preparing for the hearing. He's just trying to upset you. I'm sure of it. Forget it. Whatever he said, forget it."

"But what if he says those things tomorrow?"

"Then we simply deny them," he said. "Don't we?"

She swallowed. He had not asked for details. As if he knew already what Gary Lewis might say.

"Matt. Listen. He—"

"Alison, please," he said. "Just do it. Please. Say only what you've agreed to say."

A beat. Silence.

"Fine."

"See you tomorrow. Okay?"

A number of things haunted her as she moved edgily around the cottage, replaying Gary Lewis's accusations in her head. Matt and Sophie. Sophie and Matt. In childhood, in the teen years, their names were always said together.

Then, a series of snapshots: images that had seemed only slightly odd, out of focus at the time, now looked different from this new angle. Sophie and Matt in the basement after he hurt his hand. Sophie holding his hand so gently, kissing it. The time when Sophie took too many ecstasy pills in the club in town and said, *Call Matt.* And so they waited outside, Sophie chattering and shivering, hugging Alison for warmth, saying she was thirsty, thirsty. Just as Matt arrived in a cab, she collapsed. He carried her straight into the taxi and took her to the hospital. As he lifted his sister in his arms, Alison thought, *He looks like Rhett Butler carrying Scarlett.*

Before that, yes, long before that, a night camping in the woods. Like a soft light on the horizon, on the very periphery of her memory, brightening, Alison recalled pictures of times when she knew her friends had a closeness she never really shared. That camping trip was the first hint of something she did not understand.

Four of them had arranged to camp in the woods: Matt, Sophie, Jonathon, and Alison. Sophie and Alison shared one tent; Jonathon and Matt had single tents, on each side of the girls.

"To protect you," said Jonathon. Matt laughed at this.

It had been Sophie's idea. Alison's parents were informed that they were setting up camp in Jonathon's garden. Jonathon's parents were told they were camping at Matt's house. A sequence of lies the adults never discovered. They were too young then, around thirteen and fourteen, to be allowed to go camping in the woods without an adult.

The three tents were set up on a patch of soft grass in a clearing. They made a fire, but it kept going out, and eventually they slid into their tents, into the warmth of their sleeping bags, calling to each other, telling silly jokes, giggling, falling asleep one by one. In the middle of the night, Alison woke to find the tent empty and Sophie gone. Terrified, she lay quite still, listening, a series of frightening scenarios playing in her head. Then she heard quiet voices somewhere, soft sounds. Alison, motionless, heard Sophie's whisper, heard Matt answer her. Jonathon, on the other side, snored in a gentle rhythm. In Matt's tent, she heard rustling, and a minute or two later, muffled, dark cries. She could not differentiate the voices, could not tell one from the other.

"Sophie?" she called into the darkness. "Matt?"

Silence, then Matt's voice.

"It's okay, Ali. Sophie had a nightmare."

Sophie came back into the tent a couple of minutes later and slid back into her sleeping bag.

"I was scared," Alison admitted. "I didn't know where you were."

"Don't worry, I'm here now," Sophie whispered.

"Why didn't you wake me up if you had a nightmare?" Alison asked, disappointed that she hadn't soothed and comforted her friend. Sophie who was always so resilient, always so brave.

"Didn't think," Sophie said.

Alison never spoke about it again to Sophie. For what was there to say? *Remember when we went camping and you crawled into Matt's tent in the middle of the night?* It seemed odd, but as an only child, the bonds between brother and sister were unknown to Alison.

Now she thought about it carefully. So much in their teen years had been unclear, had never made complete sense. Matt's anger at Sophie's yellow-haired boyfriend on the day he smashed his fist into the fridge. His running away the night before her wedding. The camping trip. How old had they been when they camped out that time? Early teens? But even if, even if . . . No!

A low and howling wind rattled the windows as Alison struggled with memories that now began to reshape themselves.

She recalled the night before Sophie's wedding, the night Matt ran away from home. She had been waiting the entire day for him to turn up. He had been away at Oxford for three months. She sat on her bedroom window ledge, looking across to the Stuart yard until she heard a familiar sound, the creak of the old swing. And there—the light she looked for; a cigarette glowing in the darkness. Alison pulled a denim jacket over her shoulders. At the edge of the yard, she faltered. She could see the swing moving, see Matt's lounging form. She hesitated for a moment.

Matt's voice came out of the darkness.

"Ali? Hi there."

Alison moved toward him, sat on the step as she used to do when they were small children, and watched him. He liked to swing with the seat tucked way back so he could see the sky. He ground out his cigarette with a toe, then tilted the swing. His face was hidden.

"All set for the wedding?" she asked.

"They are. I'm not."

"They haven't roped you in for best man or something? Some vital role?" she asked.

"No. They seem to expect me to turn up and wear a suit."

"So? That's no biggie. How's the blushing bride? She nervous?"

"I suppose."

"My mother's been fussing about dresses," Alison said. "I thought Sophie wanted it small?"

"She did. Mother didn't."

There was something different in his voice: more than anger, a kind of disgust.

"What's he like?" Alison asked. "I've only seen him a couple of times."

"Thick as pig shit," said Matt. "IQ of an avocado."

"Why is she marrying him, then?"

"You can guess," he said.

Alison took a moment to think about this.

"She's pregnant?" she asked, amazed.

"Yep."

"She never told me! She's been acting like she wanted to be married."

"She doesn't know what she wants."

"You don't have to get married these days just because you're pregnant."

"She thinks she does. Mother thinks she does."

"A baby," said Alison, shaking her head. "Damn." Then she added, grinning, "You think it will have yellow hair?"

The swing slowed, and he looked over at her. His face was unreadable, shadowed.

"Ali," he began. "Look I—I wanted to tell you—"

She picked up his cigarettes. Placed one experimentally in her mouth, pretended to smoke it. Then put it down. She could feel her heart thumping.

"Yes? What?" she asked. "What do you want to tell me?"

A long silence. She thought he would never answer.

"I want to say good-bye. That's pretty much what I want to say."

"Good-bye?" she echoed, whispering the word. The world stalled. A number of questions screamed like frightened seabirds in her head. "Why?"

"I might go away for a while. Go abroad."

"But where will you go?"

"Not sure. France, Spain, Morocco maybe."

"But why? Why now?"

The swing slowed, but did not stop. Creak, creak.

"Mother. Father. The whole family thing. I feel stifled here. I'm suffocating."

"But you're at Oxford. You've already left home."

"Haven't gone far enough. I can't do it, Ali. Sorry."

The swing stopped. He sat upright and looked over at her.

"I've got to go."

"Tonight?"

"Yes."

"Have you got money?"

"A bit. I was going to ask you if—"

"I've got a few quid. Not very much."

"Anything."

"Hang on," she said. "I'll get it."

She had raced upstairs to her room, pulled out the hidden stash she kept for emergencies and the secret savings for the leather boots—thigh high, black leather—she had coveted for months and almost had enough money to buy. Rolling the notes tightly, holding them in her fist, she slipped out of the room. Her parents' bedroom door was closed. She tiptoed, barely breathing, back downstairs, across the gardens. Matt waited by the step. He pocketed the money quickly, without counting it.

"I owe you, Ali. Thank you."

"I wish you wouldn't go. I wish you'd explain. I might be able to do something. I feel—helpless."

His eyes were dark, unreadable.

"I don't think you'd understand," he said. "Nobody would."

His voice was quiet. He leaned to kiss her then, a soft kiss, gentle, that grew in intensity as she clung to him. He held her for a while, his chin on her head, as if resting.

"Wish I could come with you," she murmured.

"I'll be back," he said. "I'll be in touch."

She believed him, imagining their reunion, the joy of it.

Too soon, he stepped away. He seemed about to add something, then looked toward the road, his face changing. Alison heard the sound of a car, then wheels on gravel.

"Shit, the parents are back. I have to go, Ali."

She nodded.

He made a fist, touched her cheek so gently she barely felt it. Then he turned, took the steps to the house fast, avoiding his family.

The next morning, she woke to the sun on her face and her mother's voice in the kitchen, and somebody else—a woman. It sounded like Matt and Sophie's mother.

Alison jumped from bed. Downstairs she found her mother pouring tea for Mrs. Stuart.

"Oh, Alison. I was just coming to get you," her mother said.

She explained that Matt had left the house sometime in the middle of the night, taking only his backpack, his passport, some money he had taken from his father's wallet, and his own credit card. He had written a note apologizing to his sister for missing her wedding.

"And that's all. Have you any idea why he left?" her mother asked. "And where he's gone?"

"No idea. He was around in the afternoon. Talking about the wedding. That's all."

"And what about the wedding, Thelma?" her mother asked. "Will you change the plans?"

"Of course not. It's all arranged. It's all paid for."

The wedding went ahead without Matt. It was all so precisely planned that Alison wondered if anybody even noticed his absence. At the reception in the Tudor House Hotel, Alison sat with her parents and watched the bride and groom, self-conscious, begin the first dance. She glanced over at the Stuarts. Mr. Stuart, usually solemn and impassive, looked animated tonight. He was smiling proudly at his daughter. Sophie was a beautiful bride. A round of applause started up from the guests as the young couple circled the floor. Mrs. Stuart also watched Sophie and her new groom. It took Alison a moment to identify the emotion that showed on the older woman's face: relief. The relief of a burden lifted and gone.

After the formal reception, the young people gathered in the Stuart basement. All the Savages were there and some school friends. Sophie and her new husband were pouring drinks and dancing, and someone lit a joint and passed it around, and it seemed to Alison just like a regular party.

She was reaching into the fridge for a beer when Sophie came over to her. Sophie had removed her veil and taken off the white jacket of her wedding dress so that her smooth shoulders were bare. To Alison, suddenly, she looked like an adult.

"You know where Matt's gone, Ali?" Sophie asked.

"No. Maybe France? He'll be back soon, I'm sure."

Sophie's eyes met hers.

"You think?"

"Yes. Anyway, Soph, congratulations," Alison said. "I hope you'll be happy."

"Happy? Yeah. Wouldn't that be cool?" Sophie said, and returned to the dancing.

A few months later the first of the postcards arrived for Alison. It showed a marketplace in Tangier. On the back in a sloping hand it said only *A suitable place for savages.*

The postcard was unsigned.

~

Now, on this cold Shropshire evening, Alison, still trembling with shock, stared out of the window. The tree at the edge of the small garden was almost bare now; the wind had whipped the leaves from its branches. The ground was carpeted red and gold.

She replayed the entire conversation with Gary Lewis in her head. Could it be true? Could any of it be true? Matt and Sophie had been teenagers, she told herself. People did crazy things when they were young. Perhaps some silly, experimental play? Or maybe Sophie had lied when she told Gary about her relationship with Matt, just to rile him? She was capable of such mischief.

But it would still be damaging if Gary brought it up in the formal atmosphere of the hearing. Even if the arbitrators chose not to believe him, even if they thought he was simply being malicious. If the arbitrators did not believe it, then others might.

And what if, as she stood there on the stand, they asked her directly? Would she lie, say she didn't remember a camping trip?

Alison struggled for most of the evening, wanting desperately to talk to someone. Not her father. No. Nor Liz. She no longer had the right to talk to Jake. As she paced further, she thought of Jonathon, in the hospital in Birmingham. She couldn't tell him about Gary's accusations, but she longed to hear his sane voice, his kind voice. He had known them all well in the Savages years.

Jonathon sounded slow and groggy when he first answered his cell phone; she realized he might have been given meds to help him sleep.

"Oh God, I didn't wake you, did I?" she asked.

"Ali! No. I'm watching *NCIS* with the sound off. That show is nothing without dialogue. Fact."

"Use the earbuds. Put the sound up."

"The nurse confiscated them."

"Why? Oh, you're supposed to be sleeping? Damn. I'm sorry. I just wanted to wish you good luck for tomorrow."

"Aren't you supposed to say break a leg or something?"

"No. That's for your debut acting role at the RSC."

"Oh, right. The op will be fine, Ali. No worries. So how are you?"

"I'm okay. Jon, you know this hearing tomorrow, for custody?"

"Yeah. You're a witness, aren't you? Character reference?"

"Yes. I met Sophie's ex-husband tonight. Gary Lewis. The father of the twins. And his fiancé."

"Really? How come you . . . ?"

"They came to the cottage."

"They shouldn't do that. Did they try to—"

"No. No. They were fine. He really wants custody." She trailed off, unsure of how to continue.

Jonathon, too bright to be fooled, asked quietly, "And now you're having doubts about Matt and Celine?"

"No. Of course not. Matt and Celine will make good parents. Don't you agree? What do you think?"

Jonathon was silent for what seemed like a long time. Alison wondered if he had drifted off to sleep.

"Jon?"

"I'm here. I'm thinking. Okay. Celine? I don't know. She's a bit off-center somehow. Polished. But. Not very warm. I'm not sure she's very motherly. Matt? He'll be protective. He was very protective of Sophie."

"Overprotective?"

"Possibly. Certainly if anybody stepped out of line with Soph, they'd be in deep shit with him."

"Deep shit how?"

"Oh, punished in some odd way. Cold shoulder. Even some kind of physical punishment."

"Physical?" Alison asked, surprised. She had never seen Matt in a fight of any kind except the altercation with Ronnie at the Shrewsbury restaurant, and even then he had remained physically passive, despite the anger in his eyes. "You mean a fight?"

"No. Just an *accident*. A trip in the woods, maybe."

"That time you came down on that rocky patch? That was Matt?"

"Yep. Certain of it. I recognized his sneaker. I'd made a bit of a pass at Sophie the day before. Stupid. She knocked me back, of course. She must have told him about it."

"Really?"

"Yeah. It took me a while to understand that she told him everything. Always."

"They were very close," Alison said carefully.

More silence from Jonathon.

"I suppose in a family like that—" he said at last.

"Tell me," Alison said. "What do you think Sophie would want? Do you think she'd want Matt and Celine to adopt her twins?"

"I suppose so. I don't know. They were estranged for years, weren't they?" He sighed. "For all her apparent frankness," he added, "Sophie was very hard to read."

"You loved her, Jon. I know that."

"I think we were all just a little bit in love with both of them," he said.

He groaned then. Alison heard another voice in the room. It sounded female.

"Nurse Ratched has returned," Jonathon said. "And she's not happy."

The woman's voice, loud, clipped, said something else.

"Apparently, I'm not allowed to talk," Jonathon said. "Oh my God, she's going to snatch this phone from my weak and trembling hand."

"I'll go. I'll call soon. Good luck tomorrow," Alison said quickly.

"Call me after . . . Hey, I got Paris. You should visit."

A click. And he was gone.

Alison wished they had talked longer. There was no one else she could call. She realized, as she slipped into bed that night, that she had never felt so alone.

TWENTY-THREE

On the morning of the hearing, the sky was heavy with clouds, threatening rain. By the time Alison arrived at the municipal building where the meeting was to be held, the light was still dim and sullen, the wind cold.

She was early. It had been a night of tossed bedclothes and pillow punching. The images she had been unable to shake before bedtime had troubled her throughout the night: Matt and Sophie, laughing together, pressed together on the garden swing, Sophie on Matt's lap. It had all seemed so innocent then. Maybe it was. Alison badly wanted to believe that it was. But other scenes, long forgotten, now resurfaced: the woods on a summer evening; Matt and Sophie alone and whispering as she arrived, the first of the Savages to join them. She recalled the basement lit by candles, Matt and Sophie on the sofa, a movie playing on the TV screen creating distorted shadows on the walls.

Positioned on a corner of the building, able to see in all directions, she stepped back when she saw three people, deep in conversation, cross from the parking lot. Matt, in dark suit and tie, had his head down. He appeared to be listening to the woman in the center of the group: their solicitor, Alison guessed. Celine, on the other side, elegant as always in a tailored suit, waved her hands as if interrupting; she looked animated and excited.

Alison pressed back farther so that she was completely hidden by a pillar. She could not deal with conversation, not yet. When the solicitor disappeared inside the building, Matt and Celine remained outside, scanning the road for familiar cars. Left alone, both looked worried and pale and did not speak. They seemed relieved when Liz came into view. A few minutes later, Mrs. Stuart climbed out of a small white Honda and walked toward them. Alison hurried forward then, as if she had just arrived.

"Ah, you are here," Celine said, smiling. "Everyone is here."

Alison heard Matt say her name and tried to smile before looking away, unable to meet his eyes.

"Let's get inside," he said.

They followed him into the large, bright room. It felt like a classroom. Alison took a seat next to Liz in the front row and looked around at the people already seated opposite them.

Gary Lewis, arms folded across his chest, wore a dark business suit and looked solemn and determined; next to him sat an older man with graying hair and an air of mature authority: his solicitor, most likely. Gillian, in a neat dress, appeared nervous, her eyes darting around the room. Matt and Celine waited silently while their solicitor read her notes. Mrs. Stuart sat next to them, her hands clasped in her lap.

After a few tense minutes, a panel of arbitrators, the four decision-makers, entered the room and took their seats on a long table at the front. The woman seated at the center of the table seemed to be in charge. A heavyset woman in country tweeds, she had a brisk, business-like manner. She lifted the file in front of her, read the details, and gave a quick summing up: the hearing was for the custody of twin girls after the death of their mother, Sophie Victoria Lewis.

The chairwoman then asked the solicitors to identify themselves. The hearing had a simple informality, Alison thought, unlike a court of law. The solicitors were allowed to plead the case for their clients, and they spoke in turn, in a frank and friendly way, about the twin girls and how it was their needs that counted here. Both said similar things; both described their clients' potential for parenthood in glowing terms.

Then Gary was asked to come forward to answer questions. There was no dock, no swearing in. He stood at the end of the long table and responded in a firm voice, although as he looked at the panel members, his eyes flickered nervously from face to face. He had been with the same employer for the last five years, he said, and he had excellent prospects. He and Gillian were buying their own home with a mortgage, they were engaged to be married, they intended to marry next summer. When asked why he had not been in contact with his daughters, why he had abandoned their mother, he said that he had never abandoned them, that he tried to find them; he explained that his ex-wife was constantly moving, but still he tried to find them. He was not critical of Sophie at all. Alison thought that a clever move. He was careful to point out that he transferred money for the twins into Sophie's bank account.

"My solicitor has the statement," he said. "It shows the transfer. I tried to transfer more, but the account was closed."

The panel members smiled as he stepped down. Alison looked over at Matt and Celine. Matt's expression was calm, unchanged; Celine frowned, her mouth a hard line.

Gillian was questioned next. Clearly nervous, she stumbled over the girls' names, calling them Lillian and Rosemary until Gary corrected her quietly. Then she blushed and lifted her chin, ready to explain.

"I'm sorry. I'm just so nervous. I really, really want—" she said. The woman in the center of the panel said something soothing, and Gillian sat down again.

Then it was Matt's turn.

He smiled at the panel, seemed in control and assured. *If anyone wins on authority,* Alison thought, *then Matt has aced it.* He did not look at her, or at anyone in the small seats; he kept his eyes on the panel, looking from one to the other, answering questions in a calm, measured voice.

"We do live in France at the moment. We have a beautiful home with easy access to excellent educational facilities," he said. "But should it be necessary for us to move to the United Kingdom in order to gain custody of Rosie and Lily, then we are happy to do so."

Alison noted Gary's startled look at this, his glance at Gillian.

Celine was next and said, in essence, what each of the other three had said before her: she and Matt loved the girls; they wanted what was best for them. She sat down and shot a fast triumphant look at Gary and Gillian. *She thinks she has won,* Alison thought. *Maybe she has.*

References and reports were then produced and read by the panel. A dark-haired older woman, on the far side of the table, lifted her head and looked hard at Alison. The panel members conferred for a minute, their whispered voices not audible from the seats at the front.

They must be reading my statement, Alison thought, crossing her fingers. *They might decide on this evidence alone. I won't have to speak at all.*

But something else was shuffled between them. Another printed statement of some kind was passed from hand to hand. Then the chairwoman asked if Alison Eastlake would please stand.

Alison got to her feet, aware of a sudden weakness in her knees. She could feel her heart thumping now, loud and fast, as she walked to the side of the table and faced the panel. All three regarded her seriously. *Be careful,* she told herself. *Be very careful what you say.*

The chairwoman looked hard at her.

"You are a friend of the family, Mrs. Eastlake? You were a close friend of Sophie, the mother of these girls?"

"Yes."

"And yet you had little contact with Sophie in recent years. You live in California, in the United States. Is that correct?"

"Yes. But we always stayed in touch. We talked on the phone all the time. We e-mailed."

"You are recommending that Mr. Matt Stuart be given custody, along with his wife?"

"Yes, I am. I believe that's what Sophie would have wanted."

"And what is your relationship with Mr. Stuart?"

Alison, aware of Liz sitting up straighter in her chair, took a breath and tried to speak evenly.

"We're friends. We've been friends since we were seven years old."

"You have never had a physical relationship with Mr. Stuart. You have never slept together?"

Unable to look at Matt or Celine, her eyes skimming past Mrs. Stuart's white and frowning face, Alison settled her gaze on the chairwoman.

"Of course we have never slept together."

The panel members stared at her blank-faced. Alison had no idea if they believed her or not. She looked quickly at Liz. Her friend gave a small shrug. Another paper was passed to each of the panel members. Alison saw the chairwoman frown, glance at Gary and then back at Alison.

Alison did not look at Matt, nor dare she look at Liz. She kept her eyes fixed on the chairwoman's concerned face. The woman leaned back in her chair, then turned to the man at her side and requested another sheet of paper. She read it, looked again at Gary, and then whispered something to the panel.

Alison realized then, with a cold certainty, that they were reading Gary's latest statement. They intended to call him back to the stand to question him further. He would be explicit this time. He had threatened to be explicit. Alison felt a moment of trembling panic. *Let me step down,* she prayed. *Let me step down.* But the panel continued to whisper as they shuffled papers between them.

Alison risked a glance at Matt. His face stiff, his eyes searched the faces of the members of the committee. He had realized, Alison thought, just as she had, that they might bring Gary back to the stand. They might recall Matt, also. Matt looked at her directly then, and Alison saw something in his eyes she had never seen before: fear.

It was true, then. It was all true.

The chairwoman looked annoyed as she read again the statement in front of her.

"Mr. Lewis, there are some assertions here that need to be clarified. Would you and your solicitor join us in the side office?"

As the panel stood, the chairwoman addressed the people waiting in the warm and airless room.

"A few minutes only," the chairwoman snapped. "Please remain in your seats."

Gary and his solicitor stood, followed the members of the panel out. Alison, dizzy now, stood, too.

"I need some air," she said to Liz.

"What? She said we had to stay in—"

"I'll only be a minute."

Outside, Alison leaned back against the brick wall of the building, taking long, gulping breaths. The fear in Matt's eyes had betrayed him as clearly as if he had spoken aloud. Matt and Sophie? She shivered. She had to believe it now. She had to believe it. How could she get through this hearing? What else could they ask? About the camping trip? About Matt visiting her cottage? Exactly what had Gary written in that statement? They would question her again. Should she deny any knowledge? Would they believe her? Overriding her panic and all the buzzing questions, one fact continued to echo in her head: Matt and Sophie. It was true.

"Haven't missed it, have I? Is it finished?" The voice came from behind her.

Alison turned to see Deirdre from the shelter, barely recognizable in a neat blue coat and a scarf. She wore a smudge of dark-red lipstick.

"No. But it's almost over."

"Vivienne told me it was today. Wanted to see the little girls."

"The twins aren't here," Alison said. "No need for them to attend."

"Oh, bugger. That's a shame. Never mind. I can get a look at the brother and the Frog Princess.

"You didn't know that's what Sophie called her?" Deirdre asked, seeing Alison's frown. "She hated that woman. I wouldn't be too upset if the brother don't get 'em, if I was you. He let her down, you know. He let her down a lot."

"He was in France. It was difficult—"

"Not that. When he was here. He'd say he'd meet her and not turn up. Say he'd pick her up and then bail at the last minute. He was good to her in a way. But that Frenchwoman hated Sophie. She never did come with him."

It took Alison some moments to register this. She stared at Deirdre.

"Matt came to the shelter?" she asked slowly, carefully. "He met Sophie when she was staying there?"

"Oh no. Not to the shelter. He'd pick her up somewhere in the village in his car. Take her out." Deirdre lowered her voice. "Vivienne never knew. Nobody knew. Bloody hell, you won't tell her, will you? Promise me you won't! She'll have a real go at me if she finds out. I could lose my job."

"Of course I won't tell her. So he came to the village often?"

"Oh yeah," Deirdre said. "Used to cheer her up."

"I didn't realize—" Alison began, but Deirdre had turned away.

"Gonna sneak in, find a place at the back. See you, Alison."

Her mind spinning with this new knowledge, Alison watched Deirdre walk through the double doors. Matt had seen Sophie, then, met up with her as an adult. He had taken her out in his car. Alone, without his wife. Where? Hotel bars, maybe. Hotel rooms. She swallowed hard, her mouth dry. Matt had never mentioned his visits to his sister. He had looked around the village as if he had never seen it before. He had said that Sophie avoided her family, that they met only once in recent years,

221

at their father's funeral. He had lied. His relationship with Sophie had continued after all. Into adulthood. Until quite recently.

Dear God.

"Alison!" Liz was hissing from the doorway. "What the hell are you doing? Come on. They're back."

Alison turned to her friend.

"I can't," she said. "I can't go back in there. Tell them I'm ill."

"Are you barking mad? Come on."

"No. I can't. I just can't stand up there and—"

"What is the *matter* with you? They're waiting! Come on, Ali, for heaven's sake. Get it over with so we can go home."

Alison took one long, deep breath, then she followed Liz back into the hearing.

The panel members were settling into their seats. The chairwoman held a sheet of paper in her hand. Alison guessed that it was Gary's clarified statement. Gary returned to his seat, his head down. The chairwoman looked over at Alison, who stood, still uncertain, in the doorway.

"Ah, Mrs. Eastlake. Could we ask you a few more questions?"

Alison moved toward the long table. Her breath felt trapped in her chest. The panel conferred in whispers.

As she waited, Alison noted Mrs. Stuart leaning forward, murmuring something to Matt, and then to their counsel, and remembered what Liz had said: there was always the possibility that the girls would have to stay where they were, with Mrs. Stuart. She thought of the twins, delicate, nervous, still missing Sophie and all the warmth and spontaneity she gave to them, and she tried to imagine them living in that cold house with a woman who rarely smiled or laughed, or hugged her children, but instead caused bruising and pain. A woman who did not believe in birthday parties or sentimental souvenirs. A woman who found it impossible to forgive.

She imagined Celine with the twins. Little blonde girls she would want to dress in designer clothes; two tiny individuals she would treat like identical dolls. And Matt? A man with secrets. A man who lied so convincingly that even his closest friends were fooled. Then she looked again at Gary and Gillian, waiting anxiously, holding hands.

A few seconds of flickering fear and indecision and then, a sea change, a tide turning: she made up her mind and stepped forward.

"I'd like to change my statement," Alison said in a clear voice.

The room fell still and silent, the rustling stopped. The woman in the center of the long table looked up, surprised. The members of the panel regarded Alison and waited. Alison risked one fast look at Matt. His face had lost all color. His hands were clenched on his lap in tight fists. She looked away from him, back to the chairwoman.

"I did state that Matt and Celine Stuart would make excellent foster parents," Alison said. "And I have no reason to doubt that. But when I made my statement I had not met Gary and Gillian. I have met them now, and I think that they will love and care for the girls. I think their petition is based on a genuine concern for the welfare of the twins."

After a stunned silence, Gary breathed out a loud sigh, placing an arm around Gillian's shoulders. A moment later, Mrs. Stuart's whispered *How dare she* was audible to everyone in the room.

"What are you saying, Mrs. Eastlake?" the chairwoman asked, making no attempt to hide her annoyance. "That you want to change your recommendation?"

"Yes," Alison said. "Yes. I do."

Movement then, whispers. Matt leaned toward his solicitor and murmured something.

"I need a short break," the young solicitor said. "To consult with my client."

"Five minutes only, please," the chairwoman said. "This is taking up too much time. We have other cases to hear this morning."

Matt followed his solicitor to the small side room. Alison returned to her seat next to Liz. Her friend looked bewildered. "What on earth made you change your mind?" she whispered. "Why did you say that?"

"I decided to tell the truth," Alison said quietly.

"But when did you meet them, Gary and his fiancé?"

"They came to the cottage."

"What? And you never told me!"

"It was only yesterday," she said, looking away.

"Matt must be furious. And God, did you see Celine's face?"

"No," Alison said. "I didn't."

The two people in the side room returned only minutes later, and the solicitor took a sheet of paper to the chairwoman. She read it, passed it to the other panel members.

"Mr. and Mrs. Stuart, believing this to be in the best interest of the twin girls, have withdrawn their petition for custody. They have requested that both the grandmother and themselves be allowed visiting rights."

The chairwoman lifted her chin, her voice was now brisk and clear.

"Custody is awarded to Mr. Gary Lewis, visitation rights to be granted to the grandmother, Mrs. Thelma Stuart, and to Mr. and Mrs. Matt Stuart. Details of this must be worked out between the solicitors. Many thanks to everyone."

Celine stood and walked straight out of the room, her clicking heels a staccato sound on the wooden floor. Matt followed, moving fast, calling her name.

"Well, you certainly spiced that little hearing up," Liz said to Alison as they stood to leave. "Why didn't you tell me what you were going to say?"

Alison fumbled with her coat, avoiding her friend's eyes.

"Honest to God, I didn't know until I was standing up there," she said. "And—really, I just said what I believe to be true."

"Well, good for you," Liz said. "But keep your head down. Because if looks could kill—"

Mrs. Stuart, on her feet, looking like someone waiting in a pew for a coffin to pass by, was staring at Alison. The look was poisonous. Liz murmured hello, but the older woman did not respond, nor move her furious gaze from Alison's face.

"Face like a fist," Liz whispered. "Stay out of her way."

"Don't worry. I will."

Gary and Gillian waited at the doorway.

"Just wanted to say thank you," Gary said to Alison.

"Please take good care of them."

"We will. And we'll do it right. Let them take their time. They can get to know us over the next few weeks. We'll visit Mrs. Stuart. Make it easy for them."

"That's good," Liz said, listening on the periphery. "They need loving people around them. But make sure they know that home is where *you* are. You're their base. You know? They need stability now. And security."

Gillian nodded slowly.

"We will," she said. "You don't have to worry."

Gary turned to Alison, speaking quietly.

"Bit of a bloody ordeal, wasn't it? For everybody. He didn't have to go ahead with this, you know. He could have withdrawn his petition the first time I talked to him."

"You talked to Matt? When?"

"What? Oh, just before the funeral. Before we even got a solicitor."

"And he knew then—" Alison paused, unable to formulate the question with Liz standing so close. Gary understood immediately.

"That I knew about him and Sophie? And you could back up Sophie's camping trip story? Yeah. I told him. He just went right ahead anyway. Told me to get a lawyer."

Alison thought about this as she watched Gary and Gillian walk to the parking lot; they held hands as they headed toward their car. Beyond them, she could see Deirdre in her smart blue coat, hurrying to the station. Matt had known about Gary's threats before he invited her for drinks in the pub, before lunch in Shrewsbury. Long before their lovemaking in the cottage bedroom.

"Well, well," said Liz. "Simon's going to enjoy hearing about this little drama. You need a ride? I can drop you off if we're quick. I have to pick up Jamie."

"No. It's okay. I've got my train ticket. I can go straight back."

"You need a lift to the station, then?"

"No, thanks. I'll walk. I need to clear my head."

"I bet you do," Liz said. "I'll call you later. Think it's time we had a little chat. Don't you?"

Alison waited until Liz had driven away, and then she searched the area outside the building looking for Matt. She wanted, finally, the truth.

TWENTY-FOUR

Alison spotted Matt eventually at the far side of the parking lot, near the road, talking to his wife. Celine's face was white and angry, her hands moving like restless birds. A taxi waited at the curb.

Alison looked around for his Citroen. She would wait by his car.

"Alison McDonald!"

Her maiden name, said in a voice like an ax on wood. Mrs. Stuart, face gray, regarded Alison from ten yards away.

"You know, don't you, what damage you've done to my family?" she called.

Alison, aware of the curious looks from people heading into the building, walked toward Thelma Stuart.

"I really don't want to talk about this with you, Mrs. Stuart."

"You thought if he lost the girls, he would want you, didn't you? Well, that's not going to happen, you can be sure of that."

"I didn't say those things for that reason," Alison said. "As I think you know."

There was the slightest change in the woman's expression, and then her face went blank again.

"You're talking nonsense." The voice so hard, so hectoring. The same voice that called down the basement stairs all those years ago, demanding, insistent, always critical. Alison felt irritation that fast turned into anger when Mrs. Stuart added, "You always did talk nonsense. Politics and fancy poetry."

"How do you know what I talked about? You never allowed me into your house, except to the basement."

"Why should I have you in my house?"

Alison remembered cold rain dripping down her neck as she waited on the outer porch for Matt or for Sophie. Although Mr. Stuart, if he opened the door, would allow her to wait in the hallway, Mrs. Stuart would close the door in her face, then call up the stairs, *Somebody at the door for you.* She never said who was waiting, she never used Alison's name. Such contempt in her voice.

"Normal people would let a kid wait in the kitchen. My mum would give Matt and Sophie a glass of milk or orange juice while they waited for me. Liz's mum would, too. And Jonathon's mum always gave us a chocolate biscuit. That's what normal people do."

Thelma Stuart's scowl deepened.

"How dare you!" she said.

Alison straightened her shoulders, looked into the furious face of the woman who had caused her to tremble with fear all those years ago.

"You should be grateful that I said what I did. You wouldn't want details of Matt and Sophie's teenage years to emerge."

Alison stopped speaking. Mrs. Stuart had taken a step backward, her expression wary. The woman's face was so white that for a terrifying moment Alison thought she might faint.

She knows, Alison thought. *Or she suspected. Maybe she's always known.*

"It would have been made public today if I hadn't spoken," Alison said. "Gary knew."

Thelma Stuart straightened, looked away toward the street. It was a long time before she spoke. When she turned to look directly at Alison her voice was low, cold with distrust.

"Gary Lewis was going to say things about Matt and Sophie?" she asked.

They were both skirting around the truth, Alison noted. Unable to use the words that would articulate what really happened between the siblings.

"He knew, and he wanted to bring it up publicly in hearing. That's one of the reasons I changed my recommendation."

"Nonsense."

"Also—I meant what I said. I do believe Gary and Gillian Lewis will make good parents. I think Gary loves the girls. And Gillian is a gentle person."

They were silent for long moments. A standoff. Thelma Stuart, eyes like knives, regarded her, then she turned away and began to walk toward her car.

"Mrs. Stuart," Alison called. Thelma Stuart paused but did not turn around.

"You could have tried to love Sophie," Alison shouted, her voice shaking. "She wasn't Joanna. It wasn't her fault. You could have tried to love her."

If Thelma Stuart heard this, she gave no sign. The words were lost in a sudden gust of wind. Alison watched as the older woman continued on her way. In the shadow of the building, she looked smaller, somehow diminished. She walked slowly.

~

Alison waited by Matt's car as the wind picked up, waited in a kind of suspended fear, leaning back against the Citroen for support, clutching her purse in tight hands, wanting to grip something, hold on to something. Her knees felt weak and unreliable, the ground unstable.

She saw Mrs. Stuart drive off, and she watched Matt and Celine, still clearly arguing until Celine climbed into the taxi, leaving Matt on the pavement. He stood, holding car keys, his face grim. Alison walked forward to meet him.

"We need to talk," she said. "Please drive me home."

"Sorry. No time."

He continued to stare at the road where the taxi carrying his wife was now in the far distance. When he looked at Alison, finally, his eyes were sparked with fury.

"I know you're angry," she said.

"Are you surprised? I don't understand why the fuck you would promise to say one thing and then say another."

"You know why. Gary would have been made everything public. All he knew about you and Sophie. I'm sorry you're so disappointed," she added. "But you lied—"

"Disappointed?" he interrupted, a bitter note she had never before heard in his voice. "Is that how you would describe it? You have no idea."

He turned, walked toward his car. Alison followed him, stood resolute by the passenger door.

"I told you, Alison. I don't have time for this right now."

"Yes, you do," Alison said. "You can drive me home."

"Sorry. Not possible."

"Maybe your mother could drive me? I could bring her up to speed a bit. Tell her who was meeting Sophie in hotel rooms."

His face changed then.

"What the hell are you talking about?"

"Or, wait. Wait. Maybe your wife could drive me? I could call her."

"Get in."

He drove onto the motorway, moving swiftly through traffic, driving too fast. The rain had started again, and as he switched on the wipers, the hypnotic back-and-forth movement made a strange shushing sound. The atmosphere in the car was thick with tension.

"What is it you want to say?" he snapped eventually.

"I don't want to say anything. I want to listen. It's all true, isn't it? What Gary Lewis knew about you and Sophie? What he warned you he was going to say when he met up with you before the funeral?"

She waited during a long silence while he changed lanes, moved into the fast lane.

"Does it matter now?"

"Yes."

More silence, as heavy as summer humidity. Alison felt as if she could not breathe properly.

"I knew it was true," she said. "When he told me. I think, deep down, I've always known—"

Known what? That there was something buried and strange between the siblings?

"You should have told me the truth," she said.

"Why?" he asked, his voice cold. "Would you have made a different recommendation if I had?"

She felt a pulse of fear then, in the certainty. A fact now. There was no hiding from it.

He drove the rest of the way at a reckless speed, overtaking other cars, his hands white-knuckled at the wheel. At a near miss with a Toyota as he changed lanes, she gasped, frightened.

"Slow down, Matt. Please."

"Don't be absurd," he said. Moments later he pressed the accelerator again, harder.

He said nothing else. He drove too fast through the village, pulled up outside the cottage, switched off the car engine, and sat quite still, staring straight ahead.

"Go ahead. Say what you have to say."

She hesitated, not sure how to shape the words.

"You used me, Matt. You used a lot of manipulative talk to get me on your side."

"No. I thought I could trust you. I thought you wouldn't let me down."

"You lied to me. From the very beginning. When Gary Lewis came to you before the funeral, you planned the whole thing. You *played* me. With your wife's approval."

"No. It wasn't like that," he said. "Not exactly."

Not exactly.

Alison swallowed hard.

"Gary said you had sex with Sophie when she was thirteen years old."

"That's not true!"

"So what is true?"

Matt stared out of the car window, at the darkening sky, the bending trees, and gloom. When he began speaking, he talked slowly. She guessed that he had never disclosed this to anyone. He didn't look at her.

"It's complicated. We were always—close. Even when we were small. Our parents were so distant. We looked out for each other. Then—well, it changed."

Alison waited through a long silence.

"How? When?" she asked finally.

"Sophie grew up. She was tall, and she developed early, and she seemed older. Older than I was."

Not sure now that she wanted to hear the rest, Alison began to shake her head, but he continued speaking in that strange monotone, as if it had all happened to someone else.

"Our rooms were at the top of the house, and mine was the big room, at the end of the landing. I had to pass her room to get to it. One night her door was open, and she was sobbing. She'd had a big fight with Mother. So I went in, and we talked for a while. It became a little ritual. If her door was open, I'd drop in for a few minutes to talk. One night her door was open, but she was undressing for bed when I came by. I stopped in the doorway. Just stood there, gawky, uncomfortable. She said, *You can come in, Matt. It's okay.*"

He stopped, leaned back in his seat.

"We never meant for it to happen," he said. "Never."

"But you didn't end it, did you? Your relationship continued. Even when you were adults? Even during your marriage?"

A fast, sideways glance at her, then the same stiff expression as he stared straight ahead. He seemed reluctant to answer.

"We tried to end it," he said. "We couldn't."

"And Celine?" she asked. "Does she know about you and Sophie?"

"Of course not. She knows we experimented a little when we were teens. That's all. Celine and I—well, we don't have a conventional marriage. Celine has no interest in a heterosexual relationship. She has her own . . . friendships."

"So why marry? You wanted your relationship to appear conventional? The adoption? The girls?"

"For lots of reasons, but mostly for her family's sake. Her father— ah, it doesn't matter, but, yes."

She looked at his face, so familiar, so dear. This was the boy, now a man, she had once followed heedlessly, breathlessly, through woods, onto rooftops, down steps to a basement, would have followed anywhere. He looked the same. And yet everything had changed.

And then the question that had been circling her mind, the one she knew she must ask. She might never have the opportunity again.

"Was Sophie waiting for you when she overdosed? You were supposed to meet her?"

He let out a long breath before he spoke.

"Yes," he said. "I got tied up in France. Celine had found a surrogate. A girl in a village in the Dordogne. She wanted me to meet her."

"A surrogate mother? You were planning to have a child?"

"Yes."

"You told Sophie this? While she waited for you in a hotel room?"

He didn't reply. But she knew the answer.

"Oh Christ."

He turned to look at her then.

"I'm sorry, Alison. I am so sorry. Look, you have to understand something. I never wanted to hurt you. If I were capable of loving anyone else, I would love you."

She shook her head, reached for the door handle.

"Good-bye, Matt."

She got out of the car, began to walk up the path. The wind had picked up again, the rain felt hard now, cold on her face. She reached the shelter of the canopy over the cottage front door and turned. Matt had stepped out of the car, but he did not move toward the house. He stood on the path, watching her. The wind blew his hair back, rain soaked his face. He seemed oblivious to both.

She had inserted the key into the door of the cottage when a thought occurred to her, so shocking in its implication that she leaned against the doorjamb, her head light. If Matt had continued to see Sophie on and off for years, what if the twins . . . ? No. No! Gary had seemed so certain that they were his children. But he had no reason to think otherwise. He believed that Sophie's relationship with her brother ended when they were teenagers.

She turned.

"Matt," she called. He straightened, looked hard at her.

"Are they yours?" she asked. "The twins. Are they yours?"

She could hear the howl of the wind, the sliding sound of rain on the window. She waited an interminable time for him to answer.

"I don't know," he said. His voice sounded hollow, echoing in the empty lane. His eyes were bleak. "I don't know. When I called her from the Dordogne, she asked why I needed more . . . she told me . . ." He shook his head. "I don't know."

He climbed back into the car, drove away fast. The vehicle's wheels made a squelching sound on the damp leaves.

Alison closed the cottage door, rested back against it, listening until the sound of the Citroen was a soft whir, barely disturbing the air, and then silence.

TWENTY-FIVE

When the phone rang later that afternoon, Alison ignored it. How could she talk to Liz, or to anyone else, when she could barely breathe?

Her chest felt weighted with something, a stone where her heart should be, her mouth felt full of ash. She could not imagine the future, but her view of the past had been forever altered. Those happy days in the woods and in the basement? The Savages had been bit players, dress extras, in a drama with only two central characters.

We were all a little bit in love with both of them, Jonathon had said. And they had loved only each other.

Constantly interrupting her thoughts, an image, a sepia snapshot of the two little girls as they looked for their mother in a room full of strangers. If the twins were indeed Matt's children—the thought made her shudder violently—medical issues were possible, gene threats could lie hidden. Gary, so happily unaware, would not know to look for them. Had she made a serious mistake at that hearing? Unless she alerted Gary. Oh God.

She remained on the sofa, head back, eyes closed, for a long time, allowing, finally, the reality of her own foolishness and the consequences of it to sink in. She had hurt Jake, hurt him badly, for something that was no more solid than a summer cloud, a schoolgirl fantasy based on nothing but teenage dreams and baseless hope. She had destroyed her marriage and her own life for a mirage.

When Liz called again an hour later, Alison, lost in her thoughts, answered the phone automatically, and noted that her hands were damp; tears had been falling steadily onto her clenched fists. Agnes, her Scottish grandmother, would have called this *greeting*. An odd word for tears. *Wheesht! No more of your greeting.* Liz's concerned voice released something, and Alison began to sob helplessly.

"Ali? What is it, what is it?" Liz sounded terrified.

"It's—sorry. Sorry."

She tried to take a breath. It was impossible to speak. Liz said her name, her voice rising.

"Ali, are you all right? Are you hurt? Are you ill? Ali!"

"No. It's not that. Oh, Liz."

"What *is* it?"

"I've been so stupid. And I can't stop crying," she said.

She heard Liz's sigh.

"Hang on, love," Liz said. "I'm on my way."

~

Liz arrived at the cottage with a box in her arms. It contained a bottle of wine, a package of chocolate biscuits, and a soft cotton quilt. She was equipped to visit an invalid. After one look at her friend's swollen eyes and blotchy face, Liz began to treat Alison exactly like one. She sighed and fussed until Alison, wrapped warmly, a glass of wine in her hand, was settled on the sofa. Then Liz made a cup of tea for herself and came to sit beside her.

"Okay," she said. "Tell me."

Alison looked at her friend's worried face.

"I've behaved like a complete fool," she said.

"Ah. No surprise there," Liz said gently.

"I've been stupid and cruel. I've broken Jake's heart for no good reason for something that wasn't even real. A ridiculous fantasy, a bloody mirage."

"Ali, you are not making sense. What did you do?"

"I had, well, it wasn't even an affair. Not really."

Liz straightened.

"Matt? So you did sleep with him!"

Alison nodded.

"Oh, Alison. You idiot."

"I know. But I believed him. I believed he would—" Alison said. "Oh God."

"And he behaved like a tosser," Liz stated. "Well, I won't say I told you so. He's gone back to France with his wife?"

"Yes."

"You thought if he lost at the hearing he wouldn't go back to her? Is that why you said what you did? I mean, it was a bit of a shock when you—"

"No. No! I told the truth at the hearing," Alison said. "I thought I was doing the right thing."

"But—Matt. Jesus, Ali. Couldn't you see how it would turn out?"

Alison could not reply at first. She sipped at her wine, took a breath.

"I know it sounds stupid, but there's always been this little dream of him, in my head, in my heart, whatever. I'd think that one day we would meet again and—"

"Hardly fair on Jake," Liz said.

"No. I know that now. But it wasn't real. It was a schoolgirl fantasy. And when I saw him again, I thought . . . Oh, it sounds ridiculous. I thought I could somehow get back to being the person I used to be. And change everything. I could rewrite it, you know. Reshape it. So instead of him breaking my heart and leaving me, he would love me. But. No. He used me."

"You can't change the past, Ali. Anyway, he always used people. He was always manipulative," Liz said.

"No. Not always."

"Yes, he was," Liz said grimly. "Why didn't you tell me the truth?"

"I knew you would disapprove. You never liked him."

"Ah, I did once," Liz said. "A long time ago."

Alison stared, surprised.

"You had a crush on him, too?"

"For about five minutes. Years ago. Listen, darling. Forget him. He would never have left the Ice Queen for you, I can promise you that. There's a lot of status and family wealth tied up in that little marriage package."

She sipped her tea, looked for a long moment at Alison.

"And so," she said. "What about Jake?"

The gentle affection in her voice caused Alison's eyes to fill again, and she bit at her lip, unable to speak.

"It's over with Jake, Liz," she said at last.

"What? For good?"

"Yes. I think so."

"Come on—he loves the bones of you."

"He did once. I don't know what he feels now."

"Of course he loves you. And you love him. This was just a bit of insanity. He doesn't have to know."

"He does know. He guessed. When we met in London he figured out there was someone else. He'll never forgive me for that. Never. He's too proud."

"Try him. People can forgive. Do it every day."

"But I've behaved so badly. I've been selfish. Self-absorbed. God, Liz—my life is all fragments, broken pieces. It's like Sophie's death shattered everything. Past and present."

"God, that woman," Liz said. "Still causing trouble. Even from the grave."

Alison smiled for the first time.

"That's the truth," she said.

She thought for a few moments.

"I keep wondering," she said, slowly. "Do you think she'd have wanted her babies to go to Matt and Celine? Maybe I've done the wrong . . ."

"No. Honest to God, no. Celine as a mother? Can you imagine it? I can't. And if everything Gary said at the hearing was true, about looking for her, sending her money. No, they should be with their proper dad."

"We don't know that Gary *is* their proper dad," Alison said, carefully. "Sophie had a lot of lovers."

"Oh, he is. Definitely. Sophie knew that after the DNA test."

Alison, stunned, repeated the words in her head before speaking. "DNA?"

"When she and Gary first split up, and he wanted access to the twins, Soph had a test done. She hoped they weren't his. Could have been anybody's, I suppose, the way she was sleeping around in those days. Anyway, turned out they were Gary's."

"Oh. I never knew that. I never knew about the test," Alison said, leaning back, weak with relief. "Oh, thank God. Does Gary know about it?"

"Don't think he ever questioned the fact that they were his kids. Never doubted it."

"Jesus."

Liz looked at her oddly.

"No surprise, surely?"

"No. No. Of course not."

~

When Liz left, an hour later, Alison moved to the window to watch her drive away. The rain still lashed at the glass, the trees were bent in the wind. After Liz's taillights had reached the end of the lane and then vanished, Alison sank onto the sofa, exhausted. What had Sophie said to Matt during that phone call? Why had she given him the impression that the twins might be his when she knew very well that they were not? To keep him close, Alison concluded. To bind him. Sophie's old Savages chant—*To bind us, hold us.*

And now—Matt's secret would remain buried. But it was Sophie's secret, too. Sophie would not want Liz or Jonathon or any of her old friends to know it. Alison would never tell them. *You should have told me,* she'd said to Matt, in the car after the hearing. But Matt's relationship with Sophie was doomed, impossible. How *could* he have told her? Or told anyone? Who would understand? A taboo so deep and dark, who could forgive it? He had never been able to extricate himself. He had tried. She remembered him on the swing all those years ago as he told her of his plans to run away. And Sophie with all her warmth and wild laughter—she had found a way out.

What had Sophie been thinking, that night in the hotel room? She had waited for her brother one last time. She had heard news about a surrogate mother that must have devastated her. Had it become unbearable then? Was it Matt's face she saw as finally, finally, the drugs and the alcohol took hold and she drifted away? Or did she recall again those summer evenings, the Savages gathered together in their old fort in the woods, their voices clear and young, calling out to each other as the filtered gold through the trees faded with the light.

Alison felt her anger at Matt drain away, leaving only a deep sadness. Matt must be carrying a huge burden of guilt if Sophie had indeed overdosed because he failed to meet her in that hotel room.

For the first time, Alison felt something she had never imagined she would feel for Matt Stuart: pity. The only woman Matt had ever loved was Sophie. And she had loved him back. An obsessive love, perhaps. A perverse one. But love, nevertheless. And over now.

TWENTY-SIX

On a crisp morning ten days later, a morning with a weak sun and a silvery sky, Alison carried her bags downstairs in the now neat and scrubbed cottage to wait for the taxi that would take her to the airport. Liz had promised to meet her there, to wave her off.

Alison had talked to her father that morning, and spoken briefly to Wendy, too, now settled happily into the Scottish community. Josh loved play school, Wendy said. He had a new best friend.

She had sent a text message to both Jonathon and Ronnie, asking them to please keep in touch, with her and with each other. She had heard nothing more from Matt.

She placed her bags near the front door and had just conducted a last check that all windows were locked, all appliances off, when the black cab pulled to the curb.

On the crest of the hill, she turned to look back at the village, the compact center, the cottages at the edge of the countryside, the dark spaces of pastures beyond, the slate gray of the church spire, edges blending into the sky. Soon this view would be far behind her, just a memory, a glimpse from a taxi window, lost as the road curved, a misty image, softened by time, of a place to hide.

~

In the arrivals area at LAX, Alison, aching with tiredness, scanned the faces of the people waiting at the barrier. She had left a message for Jake on his cell phone and also texted the information, just in case, giving her flight number and arrival time.

I will understand if you're not there, she had written. *I will understand if you don't want to see me. But I hope with all my heart that you will. I love you and I am so, so sorry.*

She had heard nothing back. She feared that he would not come: she could still see clearly the pain on his face in the dim London bar. Nevertheless, the hope that he would find a way to forgive her kept rising to the surface. *People do forgive,* Liz had said. *They do begin again.*

At the edge of the crowd, she saw him. Jake waited on the periphery, his face impassive. He did not step forward to greet her. Fighting a tidal wave of nerves, Alison took a breath and moved toward him. She knew that if they were to have any chance at all, she must tell him the truth. She must make him understand that she was coming back to him with clear vision and a whole heart, that the foolish dreams she had carried with her since childhood had evaporated and gone. She must tell him everything.

She would begin by describing a gang of children who called themselves the Savages . . .

ACKNOWLEDGMENTS

My heartfelt gratitude to Julia Kenny, my agent, for her invaluable help and guidance, and many thanks to the brilliant Carmen Johnson, Editor Extraordinaire, and to rest of the dedicated and hard-working Little A team.

I owe so much to writer friends at Zoetrope Virtual Studio who read parts of this novel in short story form and offered their incisive views and suggestions. Thank you! I am enormously grateful to my sister, Helen Chappell, who listened, advised, encouraged, and remained positive throughout; and to my dear friend, Bev Jackson, for her keen insights and her unfailing and solid support. A grateful hug, as always, to Nick, Jim, Linda, and Chris.

ABOUT THE AUTHOR

Mary McCluskey is the author of the novel *Intrusion* and a number of award-winning short stories. Her fiction and essays have been published on Salon.com and in the *Atlantic*, the *London Magazine*, *StoryQuarterly*, *Litro Magazine*, and other literary journals in the United States, the United Kingdom, Australia, and Hong Kong.